Penalty Stroke

Penalty Stroke

Susan Leigh Shallcross

Double M Publishing

WASHINGTON, DC

Published by Double M Publishing.

ISBN: 978-0-9849809-5-6 (regular edition)
ISBN: 978-0-9849809-6-3 (digital edition)

Printed in the U.S.A.
First Edition, December 2012

To my mother who loves mysteries and read this one first

ACKNOWLEDGMENTS

I would like to acknowledge several people who contributed their advice and support to this book. Invaluable to my efforts were the medical personnel I consulted to make certain the murders were medically "appropriate." They include Dr. Kenneth M. Brooks, MD, and Barbara Shallcross, RN, ADN. As always, I also want to thank my dear friend Deb Lewis for her advice and counsel, and Vanessa Richardson, a talented voice-over artist who brought the book alive – no mean feat for a murder mystery – with her interpretation of the audiobook version of *Penalty Stroke*.

DISCLAIMER

This is a work of fiction. Names, characters, businesses, places, events and incidents are either the products of the author's imagination or used in a fictitious manner. Any resemblance to actual persons, living or dead, or actual events is purely coincidental.

PROLOGUE

She never came to this part of the great house anymore. And she was unhappy to be back here now, with her sweaty palms and pounding heart and her blood coursing through her head with such force it made her left eyelid pulse to a distracting degree.

But she had looked everywhere else for it: in her own bedroom, her father's study and even the little memento box of his things her mother thought no one knew about. And she had turned up nothing. This was the only other place to look.

They kept this wing locked now, although it was cleaned just as regularly as the rest of the house. But no amount of cleaning could take away the smell of disuse that hung heavily in the air, like a scarf wrapped too tightly around one's face to keep out the wind and the cold but ends up being suffocating.

And the stillness was overpowering. It was not the silence of a calm and peaceful place, but was rather an ominous quiet hiding something or someone with evil intentions, lurking until the right moment to appear and claim a victim.

She shivered, trying to shake off the irrational thoughts she knew would break loose any moment now. She knew she should not have come alone, *but she was loathe to allow anyone to see her weakness and loss of control.*

She took a deep breath, distressed to see her hand shaking as she fumbled to put the large, old-fashioned brass key in the lock. After two unsuccessful tries, she inserted the key and turned the lock, cringing as the sound of the tumblers in the mechanism reverberated down the long hallway.

She swallowed hard, opened the heavy door and hesitantly stepped inside. This place had once been the center of her world, many years ago when she and her brother were younger. Their nursery had taken up the entire south wing of the third floor of Whiddenhurst Hall. The main room was vast, with high ceilings, graceful six foot-windows draped in elegant golden damask and a fireplace that glowed with roaring logs in nearly season. The suite also featured an adjoining dining room, full kitchen and bedrooms for her and her brother, as well as their dedicated staff. Their servants had, at different stages of their childhood, included a cook, a nanny, a nurse and a governess. The nursery wing even had its own library in which the children could study and do their homework, as well as enjoy their nightly cup of cocoa before bed.

The rooms were entirely self-sustaining.

Eventually, they had departed for boarding school, she at thirteen when she left for Marlborough College in Wiltshire and her brother two years earlier when he had entered Eton at the same age. It was then that her mother had transformed the childish living area into a relaxed, comfortable space, which became, essentially, their own personal flat. Even though they only lived in the "flat" on holidays, the Abbott offspring considered it a private oasis, a retreat from the stifling formality and impersonality of the massive manor house.

They had kept one another company in this place while their parents were otherwise occupied, as they almost always were. They had entertained their friends here. Together they had conspired to live different lives than the ones so carefully planned out for them by their parents, by history and by the expectations of their positions in society. She had also gotten her first kiss from her brother's best friend before the fireplace in the family room during a weekend shooting party. She suspected her brother had had more significant firsts in the safe familiarity of these rooms.

But that had all changed ten years ago.

The change was not due to the natural progression into adulthood and the normality of growing apart as they matured into the people and the lives they were destined for. This change resulted when their idyllic world had been violently ripped apart.

It was here in their sanctuary that it had happened.

It was here in the warm haven created especially for their comfort and safety that she had found her brother. As she walked into the family room, she again saw him as he had been on that long ago night, splayed on the floor before the same fireplace where she had been kissed. Her handsome brother, so young and vital, lay pitiably, one leg twisted awkwardly beneath him, one hand grasping his chest and the other fallen in supplication as though he had been reaching out towards someone in the doorway. His face had been turned towards her when she found him. His eyes were open, seemingly pleading even as they were at that moment and forever more unseeing.

A small dark pool spread slowly on the rug beneath him.

They had told her later that her screams were so loud and so hysterical that they had been heard three floors below in the kitchens, in the courtyard in front of the house and in the drawing room where her parents had been entertaining friends. At least thirty people had come running to her aid.

But it had all been too late to save him.

It may have been too late to save any of them.

CHAPTER 1

The first shot felt almost as if it was a physical blow, and it took Madison Abbott by surprise as she exited the cool peacefulness of the stable. She stumbled backwards, grabbed unsuccessfully for a handhold as she tripped over the leg of the wooden bench and almost fell into the hay-strewn dirt. Only by slamming into the side of the stable was she prevented from actually falling. The blinding lights disoriented her, paling even the brilliance of the sunshine, and she did not have time to regain her equilibrium before complete chaos enveloped her.

Flashbulbs popped and cameras clicked like rabid insects. Photographers shouted questions she could not decipher. They sounded to her only like a guttural moans of wounded animals poised to attack.

Madison raised her hands in self-defense, feeling cornered and momentarily confused as to which way to flee. She was on private property. There was round-the-clock security on the estate. How had the paparazzi gotten onto private property?

Oh, right, she remembered as she dropped her hands dispiritedly. *She had invited them.*

She turned away from the horde and was prepared to run back into the safety of the barn in full, spineless retreat. And then it was over. The pandemonium instantly diminished into disgruntled

mutters almost as quickly as it had started.
Cameras were lowered. Their owners backed away,
looking disappointed at best and disgusted at worst.
She apparently had been deemed unimportant and
promptly forgotten. The majority of the pack turned
to go, immediately back on the hunt.

Madison tried to smile as she blinked away the
spots still lighting up her vision and shrugged
sheepishly. "I guess you realized it's just me."

"Aye, but you look a little like her, ya know," said
a voice she recognized but whose owner she could
not see.

She rested her hand against the side of the barn
to steady herself until the blinking spots disappeared
and her vision cleared. If Madison had met the
speaker in a dark alley, she would have been
frightened by the multiple facial piercings—
particularly the one that looked like a small, silver
knife through his lower lip—and the violent-looking
tattoos, one of which appeared to be dripping red ink
as though it were blood, covering every inch of
exposed flesh on both large, if a little flabby, arms.
But she recognized the speaker as one of the more
reasonable members of a group she had
encountered before.

Inwardly pleased at his comment, she still cocked
her head and wrinkled her nose. "Do you think so?"

The photographer shrugged and grinned, rubbing
the stubble on his chin as he looked her up and
down. "A little. Yer're not as tall as she is, a

6

'course, and yer hair's a bit shorter—and a little lighter. And yer eyes are brown, and hers are green." Madison laughed. "And I think ya weigh a wee bit more."

"Enough—you're killing me!" Madison interrupted as she waved to stop him before her self-confidence was completely flattened.

He laughed. "But yer're definitely as pretty as she is."

She nodded good-naturedly. "You're kind. Hard to say any different, though, isn't it?" She gestured towards the stable block and the paddocks beyond. "They're not here, though. Really, have a look around."

"They will be, though, right?"

She smiled. "I think that's the plan, but honestly, I haven't spoken to them in awhile so I really don't know for sure."

He narrowed his gaze and stepped menacingly towards her. Towering over her, he said, "Ya wouldn't be lyin' to me, now would ya, Lady Madison?"

Madison fought the urge to step back, holding her ground as she calmly replied, "Have I ever lied to you before, Joe?"

"Aye, that I can't be sure of, lass." He smiled broadly. "But yer're one of the good ones, for sure." He leaned down and surprised her with a quick peck on the cheek. "You take good care now," he said as he turned and waved his camera before departing down the dirt path with the rest of the stragglers.

As she watched them go, Madison wrapped her arms around her stomach and leaned back against the side of the stable. She had only encountered the paparazzi on five prior occasions—she was keeping count—so she was not yet used to her own reaction to them, which was, at best, disconcerting. As she waited for her heartbeat to return to normal and her breathing to slow, she realized she would never get used to that kind of assault, expected or not.

She knew she should warn her friends before they endured the same treatment, and, sighing at the prospect, Madison had just straightened when she saw Duncan Rand round the bend in the path leading from the new, makeshift polo field. He smiled broadly when he spotted her and waved. His smile was the only imperfect thing about him—or about his physical appearance anyway—and as she watched him approach, she thought how very like the thoroughbreds in the stable behind her he was. He was the only man she knew who could combine a taut, powerfully athletic build with a graceful fluidity of movement that had not an ounce of the effeminate in it. He was dashing in his polo whites, his chestnut hair tousled by the wind, or perhaps a practice run for the charity polo match due to start within the hour. Madison remembered that look from the mornings he had awakened next to her and felt a little thrill go through her at the thought. The memories were now good ones after years of steeling herself against the longing they evoked. But she knew caution was still called for where Duncan Rand was concerned.

Madison felt her heart rate quicken once again as he neared, and she was slightly annoyed that, although they had not been a couple for almost seven years now, his presence could still affect her in that way. She tried to eliminate any situations in which she could possibly be vulnerable, so she determined to ignore her own response.

"I'm so glad you made it," she said lightly as he kissed both of her cheeks. "I was worried you'd be too late for the match."

"I've been here for an hour or so. I thought you'd be at the field, but when you didn't show up, I came looking for you," Duncan said as he looked over her shoulder at the last of the departing scrum. "Is that the paparazzi, on your estate? Who are they after?"

"Seriously?"

"Yes, they've never been here before. Have they?"

"They were looking for Kate Middleton. They thought I was her for about ten seconds."

"You do look a little like her," he said as he stepped back and eyed her up and down. "Except you're not as tall as she is. And your eyes are brown—."

"Stop right there," she said as she pointed at him and narrowed her eyes in an attempt at a stern expression that fell far from its mark.

Duncan laughed mischievously. "I thought you'd be flattered to look like—."

"The prince's *girlfriend*," Madison said as her eyes opened in mock disbelief and her head fell dramatically to one side. "As my mother still calls her?"

"Yeah, I have no idea what that's about. But speaking of the Duchess—," he said as he reached for Madison's hand. She slipped away from his grasp making believe she was reaching into the pocket of her blazer for something. Duncan frowned but he continued, "How in the world did you convince her to hold this tournament on the estate? It will ruin the field, you know. And she seems so—."

"Superior?" Madison asked raising one eyebrow and stifling a smile as she turned to look at him. "Condescending, perhaps?"

"I was going to say 'particular.'" Duncan shook his head, but he smiled, too. "That's seems innocuous enough, doesn't it?"

"Innocuous is not a word I believe I would use in regard to my mother, but I appreciate the effort."

"So how did you manage it?" He asked casually as he sat on the wooden bench and started to remove his riding boot. "I never thought I'd see the day when your mum gave permission for so many strangers to be on the grounds of Whiddenhurst Hall. I thought she prized her privacy." He smiled mischievously. "To say nothing of exclusivity."

"She does," Madison answered as she sat next to him and removed a small token from her pocket. "But this match is in support of one of her charities, the Bobby Van Trust. Camilla specifically asked her to do it, and she didn't feel like she could say 'no.' And Daddy is going to have that field plowed under anyway to make way for an organic garden with a large apple orchard, so she agreed. Reluctantly, I think."

Duncan inverted his leather boot and a walnut-sized stone and several small pebbles fell into the dirt below. "That explains it," he said as he tugged the boot back on. "I took a fall this morning, and it must have gotten lodged in there then."

"And yet," Madison noted as her eyes ran over his still immaculate outfit, "you managed to not get a speck of dirt or grass on you."

"I walk under a star, as my mother used to say." He smiled and as he stood, he held out his hand to her. "Shall we join the rest of our party?"

"Before we do, I—I have something for you," Madison said shyly, feeling foolish now that she had brought something so personal for him. She realized that he would likely not appreciate the sentiment behind it, but since she had mentioned it, it was too late to renege. So she handed him a bronze horseshoe, clearly too small to have ever shod an actual horse. "For luck," she said softly, "to ensure you always do walk under that star. It—it," she said, pausing as her voice caught with emotion. She looked down at the token remembering the harrowing trip to retrieve it and swallowed over the lump that had arisen in her throat. "Well, it belonged to Charles. I know lucky charms are ridiculous, but he thought it kept him safe—." Madison looked up into Duncan's face, horror at what she had said clearly written in her own. "On the polo field," she finished quietly.

Duncan took the horseshoe and covered her hand in both of his own. As he stroked it, his voice was soft when he said, "I will treasure this, Madison, and I will keep it with me every time I play. Thank you." He leaned down and tenderly kissed her cheek, lingering there for longer than was polite under the circumstances.

Madison just nodded, uncertain now whether she could trust her voice. She started to walk down the path leading to the low roar of the gathering they could now hear in the distance. Duncan followed and pulled her arm through his own, holding her hand against his arm as they walked in silence for several minutes, the peace of their surroundings a paradox to the shouts and laughter they were heading towards.

As they approached the newly christened polo field, the path from the stable block opened up to a wide vista. Madison was amazed at the sight before her. She had arrived late this morning and had not had time to see the renovations, as it were, to the estate. Just last week the field had been a quiet pasture where the thoroughbreds her father raised frolicked, and now it was a hive of activity and noise. Over three hundred yards in length and one hundred sixty yards in width had been sectioned off, cleared of all trees and bushes and mowed shorter than normal. Goal posts centered eight yards apart had been erected at each end of the new field. Horse trailers, Range Rovers and sports cars ringed the playing field, and several players warmed up themselves and their mounts at the far end.

There were more people standing about and mingling than Madison had ever seen at one time on the estate. Several groups sat on picnic blankets on the edge of the playing area picnicking and clearly enjoying an afternoon libation—or two. She knew her mother would be horrified and was relieved Jacqueline Abbott had chosen to spend this weekend at their home in London.

Duncan tapped her arm and pointed. She followed his gaze to a rather large white tent under which, when she squinted, she thought she could see two women arranging dishes on a table. "You had a tent erected?" he asked. "For a polo match?"

Madison sighed heavily. "I didn't," she said shaking her head slightly. "This is all Peyton's party."

"You let Peyton Taylor organize something this big at your home?"

"I didn't *let* her. I begged her. Peyton is one of London best event organizers, and I'm clueless about these kinds of things. I think she went all out, and everyone is supposed to drop by—William and Kate, Annabel and Chris, Jules, Gig. Sydney, of course," she said, nodding as she narrowed her eyes again in an effort to make out the identity of a dark-haired woman carefully arranging something around what looked at this distance suspiciously like a champagne fountain. "Wow, that's excessive," Madison said hoping she was wrong about the fountain.

Even after all these years in England, Peyton's American roots still sometimes got the better of her, and she overdid their get-togethers, particularly when it came to polo which she always seemed to view as something as formal as Ascot. Nothing Madison could say would convince Peyton that polo was an informal affair.

They were almost upon the tent when Madison saw that the dark haired woman was, indeed, her friend Sydney Atwood. Duncan interrupted her thoughts when, dropping his voice, he said, "Sydney looks good."

Madison turned and looked at him. "She does," she agreed, surprised and inexplicably annoyed by his observation. "What makes you say that, though? I think she has always been a beautiful woman. I always wanted to look like Sydney. She's so, I don't know," she said as she shrugged, "*dramatic.*"

"You say that as though it were a good thing," Duncan said as he brought her hand to his lips and kissed it. "You are a beautiful woman in your own right, and you know it. I just haven't seen much of Sydney since the accident, and she seems to have recovered well. I had heard—," he said, his voice trailing off as he kept his eyes on Sydney as they approached the group.

Madison stopped and put her hands on her hips. "You had heard what?"

"That she hadn't." Duncan did not stop walking, so Madison followed, hurrying a little to catch up.

"I think she still struggles a little," she said. "But she's moving on. She may even be involved with someone new again, too, although she never talks about him."

"That," Duncan said, lowering his voice as they neared the tent and several of their friends turned to greet them, "either means it's a very good thing she doesn't want to share with the world." He paused and looked sideways at Madison. "Or it's a very bad thing she is afraid to."

CHAPTER 2

Kyle Ward stood a few feet away from the large white tent, just on the outskirts of the gathering of his old university mates. He generally preferred to observe people's interactions rather than to be part of them, even those groups in which he felt like he truly belonged. But he had never fully gotten over feeling like an outsider in this particular group. Raised in neither the aristocracy or with wealthy parents, Kyle had attended St. Andrews on scholarship, and he had never let himself forget that.

For a moment, Kyle overlooked his discomfort when he saw Madison Abbott, and he waved. She returned the greeting with an enthusiasm that made his chest ache as she made her way through the crowd over to him.

"Kyle," she said taking both of his hands in her own and smiling warmly. "I had no idea you would be here," she said as she shook her head in what looked like delighted disbelief that he was actually here. "It's been too long."

Before Kyle could reply, a familiar face in the person of Annabel Grisham practically floated by him and sidled up next to Madison. "You just missed Jeff Hawthorne," she said, laughing playfully as she kissed each of Madison's cheeks. "He asked about you." She nodded to Kyle and blew him a kiss.

"Oh, that *is* sad," Madison said wrinkling her nose. "Maybe next time."

Kyle saw, but knew Madison did not, that Annabel's husband Chris had come up behind her.

"Hey," Chris said in mock indignation, "that's my business partner you're talking about here." He put his arm around Madison's waist and kissed her neck, reaching over simultaneously to shake Kyle's hand. Chris grasped her waist a little too tightly as he swayed a little on his feet, but she laughed as he released her. "He's okay," Chris continued as he shrugged. "I thought we could make some key contacts with the people here today. Jeff is actually really good at that."

"Oh, please, no, Chris," said his wife Annabel, clearly exasperated. "These people are our friends." Please don't let's embarrass ourselves in front of them."

Chris' face immediately turned a disturbing shade of crimson, barely contained fury clouding his features as he glared at his wife.

Trying to break the tension, Kyle winked at Annabel. "What a spread you've laid out," he said, taking in the sumptuous buffet table in the tent, the champagne fountain and several directors' chairs over which had been draped tartan throws. "Thanks for doing this. The team will be well-fortified to win."

Madison joined in the distraction as she grasped Annabel's hand and also made a big show of looking appreciatively at the layout of freshly shucked oysters, sausage rolls, pasta and mozzarella salad, steak sandwiches, Cornish pastries, and Victoria sponge cake. "I think," she said, winking at Kyle, "that we have Peyton to thank for this feast. Here, here, Pey," she said as a lithe, beautifully tanned, very tall, blond woman joined them. "How many people are we expecting?"

"We've already had several people in and out this morning," Peyton replied, glancing at Kyle but not acknowledging him. "Gig was here for a bit but he went to warm up his mount." She looked at Duncan who by now had also joined the group and said, "He said he'd catch you later, after the match, and you'd know what he was talking about."

Duncan nodded and extended his hand to Kyle. "Good to see you. I didn't realize you'd be here today."

Kyle's reply was interrupted by Chris, his anger apparently forgotten as quickly as it had arisen as he looked around the tent with bleary eyes and smiled. "For some reason, this reminds me of that unbearably hot day when we all biked on the Coast Walk from Oban back to St. Andrews when we were at university."

"Same menu," Annabel said, not bothering to look up at her husband as she pulled champagne bottles out of the cooler and placed them in a large, silver bowl filled with ice next to the already flowing fountain.

"Same Scotch," Julian Marlborough said as he joined the group and plopped down in a folding chair as he reached for the bottle of Oban. Kyle saw the chair teeter and wondered if it could hold up under the six-foot-four Julian. "You have to drink a toast to the city that birthed this," Jules said as he poured three fingers worth of Scotch into a tumbler and drank it in one gulp. "Anyone else?" he asked gesturing with the bottle.

"Should you drink before you play?" Madison asked warily. "Won't that make you sick?"

"Real men don't get sick on Scotch," Julian replied smiling mischievously at her.

Kyle grinned at the inaccuracy of that statement and reached for a glass to join Julian. Eleven in the morning was early to start drinking, but Kyle always felt the pressure inherent in the masculinity of this group, like young bucks in the country engaging in subtle one-upmanship at every turn. He watched in dismay as Jules filled the highball glass to the top, but he smiled at the challenge in Jules' eyes as he topped off the glass.

"Champagne, anyone?" Sydney Atwood asked as she popped the corks on two bottles of chilled Krug and laughed as one of them bubbled out and over her hand. She started to bring the overflowing bottle to her mouth, caught Madison's wide-eyed look, seemingly thought better of the idea and instead filled the nearest glass.

"Real men don't drink champagne before a match either," Julian said, smiling as Chris nodded to Sydney and visibly flinched at his statement. "Sorry, mate," Jules said as he looked at Chris and shrugged. "But you're not riding with us today, so you're cleared for take off with the ladies."

"Yes, well, I'd rather *not* be the polo player," Chris said under his breath.

Madison snickered before she immediately put her hand in front of her face. Jules just looked at Chris with a confused expression. "As for us," he continued, "I think we'd better be off. There's William coming to fetch us. It looks like they're about to start play."

Prince William joined them at that moment and in the ensuing excitement that seemed to accompany the prince everywhere in the days leading up to his wedding, Kyle felt certain he was the only one who noticed as Julian leaned over, reached for Annabel's hand and kissed it. Kyle felt a slight jolt at the look that passed briefly between them. Annabel seemed to sense his gaze and she looked at him, shrugged and smiled a guilty little smile, which Kyle returned before quickly looking away.

As the players departed, Sydney poured champagne into four elegant crystal flutes. "Kyle Ward," she said trying to hand him a glass, which he declined with a wave of his hand. "Where *have* you been keeping yourself?" She continued as she glanced at Peyton, who made an exaggerated point of looking away. "You are looking good, Kyle," Sydney continued, shivering in mock excitement. "All masculine and scruffy in that leather jacket, classically worn out jeans and tousled hair. Kind of like you've been riding the range in the American West. Polo whites just would not do for you."

Kyle smiled but it did not reach his eyes. He watched as Sydney sipped her champagne, looking at him over her the rim of glass with her vivid violet eyes. Sydney Atwood was very definitely a beautiful woman. At least five foot nine and very slim with shiny raven hair now cut in a chic bob that cradled her lovely face. Kyle barely registered the four-inch scar snaking up her right cheek and another over her right eye. He had always found her captivating but somehow dangerous and was thus on alert for the attack he knew was imminent. Whether it would be a full frontal onslaught or a covert hit-and-run, he couldn't yet tell.

Kyle watched as Sydney evidently quickly lost interest in taunting her prey and turned to Annabel. "Are you expecting a lot of people?" she asked. "There's food here for fifty."

"Madison is essentially the hostess of this event," Peyton answered, "so we thought we should be fully stocked. Kate might stop by," she said, picking up, looking critically at and then rejecting a miniature steak sandwich. "Although I'm not sure she actually eats anymore. She's *so* thin."

"It's the wedding," Sydney said, as she started to fill a plate with oysters.

"It's the paparazzi," Madison countered. "Not only will they cause you enough stress to completely lose your appetite, but you also don't want to look heavy in any of the thousands of photos they take." She reached to accept the flute Sydney held out to her. "They caught me by the stables when I stopped by to check on our own horses, and it was like being physically accosted—really, really awful."

"You look like her," Kyle said as he pulled his buzzing Blackberry out of the holster on his jeans. He looked at the device and not at Madison as he continued, "Except—."

"No, seriously," Madison said, her tone uncharacteristically stern as she put down a chocolate truffle and held up her hand. "I have heard this enough to know it by heart."

Kyle looked up from his Blackberry, completely confused by the slight annoyance in Madison's voice. He had be going to tell her that her eyes were a deep brown instead of Kate's green and that there was always a touch of sadness in them, even when she was laughing or at play. Not knowing what he had stepped in, however, he just kept his mouth shut and went back to scrolling through the messages that kept relentlessly downloading to his Blackberry.

Chris took the champagne Sydney offered but shook his head at the artfully arranged plate of oysters. "Can't eat them, thanks," he said before he downed the entire glass of bubbly in one gulp, grimacing after he did so. "Kate knows what she's getting into."

Annabel's head popped up from slicing Cornish pastries. "Do you think? Do you think anyone really knows what they're getting into until they're actually in it?"

Chris' face twisted into a nasty little smirk when he turned to look at his wife. "They should, Annabel. We're not children anymore." Annabel visibly recoiled from the derisive tone in his voice.

Kyle continued to pretend he was completely transfixed by his email. He and Chris had been best mates in university and being well aware of the historical tensions between Annabel and Chris, he had no desire to be drawn into their war on such a beautiful afternoon. They generally maintained a dignity befitting their station as the Earl and Countess of Grisham when in public, and had, in fact, had several articles in the tabloids written about their great love story. It made for great copy—first love, meeting at St. Andrews, acceding to their titles at a young age, undertaking charity work together, et cetera—but everyone in their group of friends from university knew that there was trouble in the Grisham marriage. They had all long ago grown tired of the endless snipping and petty humiliations they inflicted on one another in private gatherings.

Rather than step in between the combatant couple now, Kyle held up his Blackberry and said, "It's the Yard calling. I have to take this. If you'll excuse me a minute." He stepped outside the tent and walked several yards away, breathing in the crispness of the brilliant spring day. He did have a message from the "Yard," but it was one of many routine, automated calls sent by the Chief Inspector at Scotland Yard.

There was a currently a shortage of five thousand detectives across England and Wales, and the Metropolitan Police Service was on a recruitment drive to up the numbers to counteract the worrying trend. The Yard's leadership had started an aggressive lobbying campaign aimed at Kyle to make him the face of the New Scotland Yard in an effort to appeal to young men and women coming out of university. He was one of the youngest detectives on the force and, according to his chief, he epitomized the kind of candidate they were looking for. He had read Psychology at St. Andrews and had taken a joint degree in Computer Science and Psychology before he entered service. Kyle had served only the minimum two years in uniform before he was made detective.

But he found it frustrating that, as detectives themselves, the Yard's leadership did not seem to appreciate the need for him to keep some semblance of anonymity. And plastering his face on recruiting posters, which they had, embarrassingly, actually resorted to was, in Kyle's view, a time wasting and useless exercise in vanity.

Kyle sighed as his fingers flew over the tiny Blackberry keys to let his chief know that he would be at the next recruiting meeting. He knew it was perverse to wish for a murder case that would get him out of it, but he could not help himself in doing so. It had been over three months since he had caught a case, and he felt his mental acuity slipped a little more each day.

Julian's Scotch probably hadn't helped.

CHAPTER 3

Madison watched her old friends begin the ritual she had seen them undertake so often. Chris and Annabel were almost like two prizefighters warily circling one another in the ring as they calculated the other's weaknesses and strategized where they should aim the fatal blow. Madison searched her mind in vain for something to say to diffuse the tension that was clearly still roiling between Annabel and Chris today before it devolved into an outright yelling match and ruined the day for all of them.

She had given up hope of manipulating the conversation into a more positive direction when she noticed the throng of paparazzi that had previously converged on her approaching in a huddle around someone she could not see. They moved as one in what she thought must be an unspoken agreement to not let their captive escape. She assumed that captive was poor Kate Middleton, and Madison felt a sort of desperation she herself had not known in a long time for her friend. When she had begun seeing her beautiful, accomplished friend as "poor," she could not remember, and Madison snorted. Much of the world seemed to envy Kate Middleton these days as she stood on the precipice of a finely crafted and long-awaited fairy story culminating in marriage to her prince, and yet Madison pitied her.

Perhaps, Madison thought, *the concept of a happy ending was so foreign a concept to her now that it was she who needed sympathy.*

Shaking off the thought of throwing her own pity party on such a beautiful day as disgusting self-indulgence and seeing an escape from her own situation as referee to the Grishams, Madison started to go to Kate's aid to help her navigate the gauntlet. But Sydney and Annabel were already headed towards her and were closer to the objective. Madison almost laughed outright when she saw Sydney lean over to whisper something to Annabel and then fall to the ground as though she had twisted her ankle. The photographers, or at least the males, immediately came to her side while Annabel and Kate made their getaway.

Madison sighed and decided to remain in the tent. Spying an empty chair next to Chris, she nodded towards it. "May I?"

"Be my guest," he said as he reached for a bottle of champagne and gestured with it towards Madison. "Would you care for another glass?"

She shook her head. "No, thank you. I need to take care in the sun. It can be brutal and makes me a little swoopy."

"You need to build up your tolerance," he said, pouring a glass and downing it without pausing for a breath. "Sickening sweet this stuff is," he said looking at the label and blinking his eyes as if in an effort to focus. He still refilled the flute and hung onto the bottle, holding it against his chest as if it were a child. "I think my wife is the only person in the world who likes peach champagne," he said as he swayed a little in his chair. "It really is an affront to good taste and—," he said pointing his glass at Madison, "good breeding."

"Why are you drinking it then?" Madison asked, her voice a little tighter than she had intended. She could not help but be annoyed with Chris and the none too subtle jab he had just directed towards his wife.

"Good question. Except that by the time you are on your second bottle, the taste is dulled and is more—," he hiccupped, "palatable. I beg your pardon."

Madison looked hard at him as she felt her brow furrow, which it always did when she was concentrating on something. She rubbed her forehead as she tried to relax in an effort to appear less severe and more understanding. "Is there something troubling you that you'd like to discuss, Chris? You seem a little, ah, agitated."

"So asks the psychologist in the group," he said as he raised his glass to her, nodded, and then downed its contents. He hiccupped again. "Are you too young to be called the Great Psychologist? Don't you have to cure serial killers or something like that to be called great?"

Madison bit the inside of her lip, thinking for a moment how best to respond. "Are you angry with me for some reason? Does it make you uncomfortable for any reason that I'm a psychologist? We've been friends for so long, I thought that no one really ever considered it anymore—."

"Ah," he said, pouring yet another glass of champagne, "you just pinpointed the only problem I have with it. You're asking questions like I'm your patient. Next you'll be asking me how I feel about it." He emptied his glass.

Madison glanced over at the throng around Sydney, Kate and Annabel, who had come back into view, and wished fervently that they would migrate over to the tent, even if it meant bringing the photographers with them. "So how *do* you feel about it, Chris?" she asked quietly. "Or about anything else? I really am interested, on a purely personal level."

"I feel," he said, slightly slurring his words now even as his voice got louder, "unmanned—and emasculated. I live and work among the most accomplished, most glamorous," Chris said, nodding towards the paparazzi, "people in the country." He poured another glass of champagne and Madison thought that must have finished the bottle. "Julian— *Looorrrd* Marlborough—is the brilliant surgeon who saves lives by his mere presence. And," he said, pointing drunkenly at Madison, "gets all the women. Viscount Stockton, whom for some reason we call 'Gig'—and who in hell made up that ridiculous name? And what *does* it mean?—owns the chicest club in London. And actually makes money from it. Because—," he hiccupped again, "his father isn't wealthy enough for him already." Chris glanced again towards the group of photographers and poured himself another glass of champagne. "And who also gets all the girls, by the way. Duncan," he said, gesturing towards the polo field with his glass and sloshing champagne over the side, "whom you still love—no, seriously, don't deny it—and who, *in addition to* being a lawyer, is widely considered the most successful young investment banker in London."

"Chris—," Madison said, putting her hand on the arm that held his glass.

"I'm not your patient, Madison," he snapped as he pulled his arm away, spilling even more champagne. "Don't lecture me." He only sipped his champagne now as he continued, "And let's don't forget the women in our little university group—all of you beautiful, accomplished and desired by, seemingly, the entire world." He downed the rest of his glass. "I won't even go into the fact that the bloody future King of England is part of the pack." He exhaled loudly and hung his head so his chin actually came to a rest on his chest, after it bounced twice on the way down.

Madison looked at the glass in his hand. "You might want to slow down a little. And really, what is wrong? What happened?"

He looked up at her and swayed a little as he blinked rapidly. "I can't feel my hands, Madison. And I think I'm going to be sick."

She stood immediately and, keeping one hand on Chris' arm, reached for a blanket. "You've had a lot to drink—very quickly," Madison said, making certain her tone did not betray how worried she really was. "Lie down for a minute, and you'll feel better," she said as she spread the blanket on the ground just before Chris rolled forward out of his chair, turning just in time to avoid crashing face first into the ground before collapsing onto the tartan that Madison noticed, curiously, was in Julian's family colors. "I'll get you some cold water. That might help."

"I want my wife, Abanell, um Ana—, Ana-something," he said blinking and obviously laboring for breath as he clutched Madison's hand, which he did not have the strength to hold onto.

"Chris," she said, gently slapping his cheeks. "Chris, have you taken anything today? Have you been ill?"

"Oh my God!" Annabel shrieked somewhere behind her, and Madison saw her start to run towards them. Sydney, Kate and the paparazzi were no longer in sight, and Madison was grateful at that moment at least for that.

She had just started to vigorously rub Chris' hands and arms when she sensed someone was standing directly over her and heard, "What can I do to help Madison?"

She looked up and saw that Kyle had returned and his concern was evident in the furrow of his brow. "Go get Jules," Madison said as calmly as she could. "Have them stop play if you have to and tell him it's urgent. Tell him to bring his medical bag." Kyle was gone before she realized that as a Scotland Yard detective he might have CPR skills she did not. She was not a medical doctor and, although she had taken one three-hour class back at university, she had never had an opportunity to use CPR and did not think she was capable of doing it correctly now.

"I don't understand," Annabel said with tears forming in the corners of her eyes as she dropped to her knees beside her husband. "He hasn't been sick. What happened?"

"He had a lot to drink," Madison answered tensely. "But I don't think that's all of it. It can't be."

Annabel laid a cool, wet cloth on Chris' forehead while Madison continued massaging his hands, periodically checking for a pulse. She knew enough to be concerned by his deep wheezing. He lips had a bluish tint, and he clearly was not getting enough air. His face was now a pasty grey, and his eyes were closed. She wasn't sure he was even conscious anymore.

Madison looked up when she heard the thundering of a horse's hooves and relief flooded through her as she watched as Jules galloped right up to the edge of the tent. He dismounted effortlessly as he unhooked the chin-strap on his helmet and threw it aside. He dropped to his knees and checked Chris' neck for a pulse.

"What happened?" he asked.

"I don't know," Madison said, shaking her head. "He was fine. You saw him. He drank about five, maybe six glasses, and more before, I'm afraid, of champagne really quickly but he didn't get sick. I mean he didn't vomit. He said he thought he was going to, but he really just sort of—faded out. His breathing has been ragged for the past ten minutes."

Jules leaned down and put his head against Chris' chest. He sat up and began CPR, rhythmically pumping his chest and alternating breathing into his mouth.

"Oh my God!" Annabel moaned. "Is he gone?"

"I know CPR, Jules. I can do the breathing," Kyle said as he returned and placed a large leather medical bag next to Jules.

Jules nodded and Kyle moved into place at Chris' head and leaned down to blow air into his lungs at timed intervals.

"I've called 999," Madison said. "What can I do?"

"Look in the bag," Jules said, not taking his eyes off his patient and continuing to do chest compressions as he nodded towards his medical bag. "There should be a defibrillator in there. It's yellow and black with EKG pads attached. Give that to me. There should also be a small brown bottle of Lidocaine and a sterile syringe. Can you fill the syringe?

"I—well—I," Madison sputtered as she searched frantically through the medical bag. She tossed aside two stethoscopes, a package of gauze and several bottles of prescription medications she did not recognize until she found the small bottle of Lidocaine, as well as several individually wrapped syringes.

"Fast, Madison," Jules said tersely. "We need to move fast."

Madison tore open the sterile packaging for the syringe with her teeth as she unscrewed the bottle of Lidocaine. She removed the plastic cap covering the needle before inverting the bottle onto it, glancing at Jules to make sure she was doing this correctly. Madison slowly withdrew the plunger on the syringe and watched as the bottle emptied. She had seen many injections given to patients over the years to sedate them, but she had never given a shot herself, or even prepared one, and she was pleased that she seemed to know what to do. Removing the empty bottle, she flicked the needle to eliminate any potentially lethal air bubbles and handed it to Jules.

Jules stopped compressions long enough to administer the Lidocaine to Chris

"What is that?" Annabel asked her voice barely audible.

"Lidocaine is an anesthetic," Madison answered in the preternaturally calm voice she always reverted to in emergency situations. "It will ensure that he—," she stopped as she looked into Annabel's tortured eyes. "It will ensure that he doesn't feel any pain. It's okay," she said confidently, without any real sense of whether Chris would be okay or not.

Jules ripped open Chris' button down shirt, ignoring Annabel's gasp as he did so. Madison watched, almost mesmerized by his self-assurance, as Jules flipped on the defibrillator and attached two flat pads. He watched the reading on the display and set another dial on the machine. He looked at Kyle as he rubbed the two paddles together.

"Clear," he said and Kyle sat back as Jules placed the pads on Chris and pushed a button. His patient's chest seized, rose for a moment and fell. Julian placed his stethoscope on Chris' now quivering chest, listening for a rhythm. "Clear," he said again as he shocked his patient once more. Madison heard the beep, beep, beep of Chris Grisham's heartbeat on the little machine she could only think at that moment looked like a bumble bee with its yellow and black casing.

The EMTs arrived and Madison and Kyle stepped away from the patient while the paramedics dropped to the ground and checked Chris' pulse.

"That was fast," Kyle noted.

Eyeing the medical bag and equipment, the first paramedic, whom Madison thought did not look old enough even to drive much less save a man in cardiac arrest, replied, "We were on site. We're with the detail that accompanies the prince when he plays." He turned to Jules, recognition dawning on his face only to be quickly replaced by something close to awe. "Lord Marlborough, sir," he said extending his hand. "It's an honor."

"Doctor," Jules replied reaching out to shake the tech's hand while keeping his eyes on his patient.

"Doctor Marlborough, this man was lucky you were close by. What happened here?" the young technician said as he inserted an IV into Chris' arm.

"Cardiac arrest in a thirty-year-old male. No medications, no previously known heart conditions. No exertion." He shook his head as he ran his fingers through his hair. "I don't know what caused this. I performed CPR and shocked him back into a stable rhythm. He seems to be stabilized for the moment, but he needs to go to hospital, STAT. I suggest you get on the line with your ER attending physician to confirm giving him bicarbonate of sodium to compensate for the acidosis that is likely now occurring with the arrest. I'll meet you at hospital."

The paramedic checked Chris' vital signs again and placed the IV bag on the patient's stomach while his colleague and Jules lifted him onto a gurney and then into the back of the ambulance. The lead tech looked around and asked, "Are any of you related to this man?"

Annabel just stared at Chris with a vacant expression on her face and her hands clasped in front of her mouth. Madison looked at her, hesitated a moment, then stepped forward and said, "Yes, this is Annabel Grisham, the wife of your patient, Chris Grisham. Can she ride in the ambulance with you?"

"Yes, ma'am, but we need to go now. We'll take him to Gloucestershire Royal Hospital if you want to follow."

Madison turned to Annabel and put her arm around her waist. She said, "You need to go with him. Jules will be there. I'll take care of things here and meet you there." She looked at Annabel directly and fought the urge to shake her. "Okay, Annabel?"

"We have to go *now*," Jules said climbing out of the back of the ambulance as Annabel still hesitated. "Now, Madison. We're leaving her if she can't make it."

With one more anxious glance towards Madison, Annabel reluctantly climbed in the back of the rig as Jules was shutting the back doors. The driver turned on the siren, and they were off.

Jules turned to Madison and said, "I'll meet you at hospital. Discourage Kate and William from coming if you see them. It will be a madhouse if they're there. That won't be good for anyone." He threw the contents of his medical bag back into it with seemingly no regard for order nor care, grabbed a sandwich off the buffet table and took off at a run.

Madison watched him go, marveling for a moment at the agility of such a powerfully built man as he maneuvered his way at pace through the by now interested crowd. She turned to Kyle, feeling momentarily lost and looking devastated. He put his arm around her shoulder as he said, "He'll be okay. I know it. He's too young for this to be anything serious."

Madison swallowed hard and nodded, unconvinced, as they stood there for a minute and watched silently as the game thundered on around them.

CHAPTER 4

Kyle turned when he heard Sydney cry out. Running up to them, she tried to speak, but her words were soundless as she attempted to catch her breath. She bent over, heaving, and clasped her arms around her stomach. Kyle thought for a moment that she would actually be sick. When Sydney finally stood, she had tears in her eyes but whether it was from emotion or gagging, Kyle could not tell.

Her voice was raspy when Sydney said, "Oh my God, I just heard. I can't believe it. Is Annabel okay?"

"Annabel went in the ambulance with Chris," Madison answered. "I think she's upset and clearly rattled, but she was fairly composed—sort of."

"Oh, I—," Sydney said blinking. "I should go be with her to see how I can help."

"That would be good, Syd," Madison said. "I need to find Peyton and Duncan—."

"And William," Kyle said. "We should at least give them a heads-up."

Madison nodded. "Or Kate, to let them know what's happened, and then I'll meet you at hospital. They're taking Chris to Gloucestershire Royal," she said, but Sydney was already running towards the car park before she finished her sentence.

As she watched her go, Madison pulled out her iPhone and sent identical texts to Peyton, Duncan, Gig and Kate: *Chris had heart attack. Looks serious. On our way to hospital. Will keep you posted.*

Kyle watched her send the texts and noted that her hands were shaking. "He'll be okay, Madison," he said again, fully believing it as he did. Young, healthy men did not just collapse and die, barring any sort of violence.

She looked up, something close to hostility in her eyes. "What makes you say that? People die unexpectedly all the time." Her lip started to quiver before she bit it.

Kyle just nodded. "I just think he will be, that's all." He jerked his thumb towards the far field. "My car is here, and yours is probably back at the house. I'll drive. Okay?"

Madison nodded, and as they turned to depart, Kyle waved to two men. Their appearance was curious because, like Kyle, they were the only people wearing leather jackets, jeans and aviator sunglasses. He shook each of their hands as they approached and turned his head away as he quietly said, "Can you secure the scene? Be discrete, but don't let anyone back in the tent, okay? I'll call you as soon as I can and let you know the plan."

Kyle turned back to Madison and, with his hand on the small of her back, guided her towards the makeshift car park on her father's previously unspoiled field.

Madison walked as if in a daze, so he asked lightly, "Are you sure you want to be seen in my car? It might sully your image."

"If you think that then you're the snob here, Kyle, not me," she said wearily as she glanced back towards the tent. "Who are those men?"

"They're with Scotland Yard."

"And they just happened to be at a charity polo match this far from London?"

"Not exactly."

"You're being cagey."

"Not intentionally," Kyle said as he took Madison's hand and skillfully navigated through the crowd. "I'd just like them to look after the scene until we see where this is going."

"The scene?" Madison gasped. "As in crime scene?"

"Please lower your voice," Kyle said, dropping his own even further. "I wouldn't call it a crime scene at this point. I'm just being cautious."

He studiously ignored Madison's questioning look as he opened the passenger door of his old green Range Rover and helped her climb in. His vehicle had not been new when he had gotten it while they were in university, and, except for Jules, they had all graduated seven years ago. He looked around at the cracked cream leather and breathed in deeply, the smell of it, combined with pipe tobacco and a slight undercurrent of his Labrador, resulted in a combined scent he found comfortingly familiar but worried would appall Lady Madison Abbott. They had been such close friends when they were at St. Andrew's. But they had drifted apart in the intervening years while Madison had gone on to read psychology at graduate school in Oxford and Kyle had moved to London and joined the Yard.

His concern was allayed when, after pulling out of his improvised parking space, she said, "I'm glad you're here, Kyle. We haven't seen a lot of you lately."

He smiled briefly but kept his eyes on the road. "I don't get the impression that I'm welcome in this group anymore," he said as he drove slowly and steered his way carefully through the milling pedestrians and haphazardly parked vehicles. "I guess I'm not sure I was ever welcome."

Madison sighed heavily, and she sounded exasperated when she said, "I keep telling you that that's you, not us."

Kyle was silent for a moment, unsure of whether she had a valid point. He glanced at Madison who was now looking at him expectantly. "How is Peyton?" he asked.

"Speak of the devil. She's good," Madison answered as she glanced back at the polo match before they turned onto and drove down the long, winding road through the estate that led out through the great iron gates marking the entrance. "You should call her and ask her yourself."

"She doesn't want to talk to me, Madison. You know that." He gestured back towards the field. "I wasn't actually invited to your little party here. I crashed it. What did Sydney always used to say about me—NOTD?"

Madison smiled. "Sydney can be a royal bitch, Kyle. We all know that. And 'not being our type' was never the issue and you know that, too. You were very much Peyton's type. But you slept with her, repeatedly, for what, a month, and then just disappeared and avoided her calls for the next six months."

Kyle stared straight ahead. "That was at university and almost ten years ago now. She's over that by now, don't you think? Isn't there some kind of statute of limitations on that?"

"On being a cad?" Madison shook her head. "No, it's like murder," she said and shivered. "You're always held accountable for both forever."

Kyle sighed but did not look at her. He wasn't proud of the way he had treated Peyton Taylor when they were in school, but he had no idea how to make amends to her after all this time. He realized it was a child's answer to say that he hadn't intended to be so thoughtless, but it was true. Kyle had gotten himself into an undesirable position, and he had panicked. He learned in the years since that when people had no idea as to how to extricate themselves from a situation, they almost never did the right thing.   Kyle Ward was no exception.

"I think," Madison continued in a gentler tone, "that you resent us so much it clouds your view of what's really going on." Kyle grimaced but still said nothing. "What do you think about that? Is it even possible I have a point?"

"Do you do this with everyone now that you're a trained therapist? Because if you do, I have to tell you, it's more than a little annoying."

Madison snorted and, crossing her arms, she sat back against the seat, she said, "Apparently, I do. You are the second person today to say this to me."

He turned to look at her and smiled a little. "Who was the first?"

"Chris," she said, searching through her handbag before holding up her iPhone. "Do you think it's too soon to get a status report on him? The ambulance just left."

"They actually left thirty minutes ago. And they drive a helluva lot faster than we do. I think you can call." She started to dial. He glanced over at her phone. "I'd call Jules. If he can't pick up, you can try Sydney. But I wouldn't bother Annabel."

She disconnected the call and dialed Jules' mobile as she drummed her fingers on the center console while the phone rang. "Jules, it's Madison. Any news?" There was a moment of silence, and Kyle saw Madison's face fall. "Jules?" she whispered with a stark plea in her voice just before the phone slipped out of her hand.

Kyle quickly reached over the center console and picked up the phone. "Jules, it's Kyle."

"He's gone," Jules said, almost brusquely. "He went into full cardiac arrest in the ambulance, and they couldn't revive him again. He was pronounced on arrival."

Kyle immediately pulled over on the side of the road and glanced over at Madison whose face had drained of all color. She stared straight ahead as her hands twisted and untwisted the strap on her handbag. Kyle himself felt a slight wave of nausea wash over him, but his voice was steady when he said, "He was fine an hour ago. And now he's dead? How is that even possible?"

Jules said, "It happens sometimes. It's not common, but it does happen. They'll do an autopsy, of course—."

"How is Annabel?" Kyle asked, interrupting before he got the details on doing the autopsy.

"Devastated, still in shock. I'll stay with her, of course. I'd also prefer that she not drive back to London tonight."

"We can figure that out when we get there. We'll see you in about ten minutes," Kyle said curtly before he hung up. He dealt with life and death every day in his job, but Chris had been his best mate at university and he was dismayed by the cold, business-like tone in Jules' voice and wanted to get away from it as quickly as possible.

"I don't want to go to hospital, Kyle," Madison said softly as she covered her face with her hand as she stifled a sob. "I know it's a character failing in a doctor to have an aversion to hospitals, but I do." She shivered. "Every since my brother was kil—died. Every since Charles died, I just—I just hate them."

Kyle's face softened, and he nodded. "I get that. I'm sure it must be unbelievably hard." He kept his eyes on the rearview mirror as he felt around in the back seat and then searched the center console and then the glove compartment for tissues. He found a small package and, grateful they were unused, handed it to Madison. His instinct was to put his arms around her and hold her as she cried, but he was worried she might take that the wrong way in the intimate confines of his vehicle. So he sat awkwardly tapping the steering wheel has he waited for her to speak first.

Madison dabbed at her eyes but did not take her gaze from the road. Her voice was dull when she asked, "Why did you secure the scene, Kyle?"

Kyle sat back and rested his head against the headrest. He sighed heavily as he passed his hand over his eyes, which he kept closed. "It was just a precaution, Madison. Standard procedure in cases of unexpected death."

She shifted in her seat as she turned to look at him, and he reluctantly met her gaze. "But you didn't know he was going to die."

"No," he said quietly. "I was just covering any scenario. I sort of go on auto-pilot in these kinds of situations, and my gut instinct told me to take that precaution. I was trained for that."

"I don't believe you," she said softly as she turned away from him and stared out the window at the brilliant spring day.

CHAPTER 5

"I think jumping to the conclusion that this is a suspicious death is a little over reactive, don't you?" Kyle asked as he drove the Range Rover back onto the two-lane road, which was still choked with traffic headed towards the second polo match of the day. "I'm a detective. We're trained to be cautious and keep all avenues of investigation open until we don't need them anymore. That's all it is, really."

Madison chewed her lip and continued to stare out the side window. Her hands were sweating profusely now, and she ran them up and down her jeans. With a great effort, she had stopped actively crying but her eyes were still full and threatened to spill over again at the slightest provocation.

Kyle watched her and his face softened. "Look, I'm sorry. I know how hard this must be for you. But it's really important to not jump to conclusions here. Not everyone who dies young is murdered."

She nodded without looking at him. Kyle sighed and waved to the parking attendant as they entered the car park at the hospital. "Is everything okay, Kyle?" the attendant asked.

"Everything's okay with me, Tom, thanks. We're here to visit a—er, a friend."

"This one is on me," the attendant said, pushing a button that raised the mechanical arm.

"That was kind," Madison said, trying to distract her attention from the awful news as they drove through the gate. "How do you know him?"

"You mean a lowly parking attendant?" Madison groaned but did not respond. "He's my father's neighbor," Kyle continued. "Remember Dad still lives in Tetbury, and the owner of the bakery knows everyone in town. He even knows your dad, who apparently comes in for a squidgy chocolate roll every couple of weeks."

"I had no idea Dad ever shopped for himself," she said as she unbuckled her seatbelt and opened the door.

"I wouldn't call it shopping exactly," Kyle replied as he killed the engine and jumped out to run around the vehicle so he could help her out. She had already slid to the ground by the time he got there. He locked the doors and as they started to walk into the building, he continued, "But apparently your mother has him on some kind of strict diet, so he sneaks off on a pretty regular basis to indulge."

Kyle nodded to a nurse coming out of the emergency room doors, and Madison was surprised at the overtly appreciative look the nurse threw him as her eyes passed over Kyle and she leaned towards him and smiled brilliantly. He seemed completely unaware of her feelings.

"He stays awhile and drinks coffee with my dad when he's there," Kyle went on as he stood aside and let Madison precede him into the hospital. "They're friends, of a sort."

"I didn't know."

"Do you disapprove?"

"Of course not. Why would I disapprove? I'm just surprised, that's all."

"That a baker and a duke could be friends?"

Madison rolled her eyes as she stopped and turned to Kyle. "Don't be absurd. I'm just surprised that Dad sneaks off without telling my mother. He's very devoted to her, and I didn't think he kept any secrets from her, that's all."

"Everybody has secrets, Madison."

They walked into an emergency room that, despite the fact that she had grown up in Gloucestershire, Madison had never entered. The antiseptic smell hit her, and she shivered. Being in the medical profession herself, she knew she should associate that smell with life and life-saving, but Madison could only think of death. She shook her head in a futile effort to shake off a descent into dark thoughts. As she stood before the receiving desk, momentarily unsure where she should go, she was relieved to see Jules speaking to someone in a white coat whom she assumed to be another physician. He nodded to her, and held up one finger before he pointed to the waiting room where Sydney Atwood was sitting alone staring blankly at the television set. Kyle silently tapped Madison's arm and pointed in the other direction before he headed down a corridor as she nodded to Jules and walked over to the waiting room.

"How are you?" Madison asked, sitting next to Sydney.

"I'm numb," she replied without taking her gaze from the television.

"I think we all are. I'm so dreadfully sorry this happened," she said as she looked around the empty waiting room. "Where is Annabel?" Sydney did not respond, so Madison gently put her hand on her arm. "Sydney," she said quietly. "Do you know where Annabel is?"

Sydney turned to Madison, blinking in what looked like surprise to recognize someone she knew. "Oh, it's you. I—I'm not sure where Annabel is now. She was apparently very overwrought, and I think I heard Jules say something about her needing to be sedated." She exhaled heavily as she leaned her head back against the industrial-looking light green of the cement wall and closed her eyes. "I'd kill for a cigarette."

Madison winced. "When did you start smoking again?"

"After the accident. My looks were gone anyway, so I figured it couldn't hurt now."

"Why do you talk like that, Sydney? You know it's not true."

"I was a weekend TV news presenter, Madison," she said, her voice heavy with weary resignation. "Of course, it's true. People want their news from a beautiful woman, not one who looks like bad news herself. I was gone for two months recovering, and they took the opportunity to remove me from that position. And any future on camera. Look, I get it. I probably would have made the same call myself." She sat up and reached for her handbag. "But let's don't kid ourselves by saying that I'm still beautiful, okay? I have heard that far too much." She pulled out a pack of cigarettes. "I guess I can't smoke inside, can I?"

"Not in a hospital, no. Would you like me to come outside with you?"

"No," Sydney said shortly as she stood. "I'm afraid we'd devolve into maudlin reminiscences of the dearly departed Earl of Grisham, and I just cannot take that at the moment. If you'll excuse me."

Madison nodded and watched Sydney go, thinking how wrong she was in believing that she was no longer beautiful but agreeing that she did not want to dissolve into an emotional wreck in a public place. Her long experience with her had also taught Madison that Sydney bit when she felt cornered, and she had vowed long ago to never put her friend in that position.

Madison turned, startled as Jules walked up and sat in the chair Sydney had just vacated. Still clad in his polo whites, he seemed out of place in the bleak atmosphere of the ER.

"How is Annabel?" she asked.

"Not good. She was rambling on about Chris being the love of her life and bordering on hysteria." Jules exhaled audibly, shutting his eyes tightly and pinching the bridge of his nose. "I asked that she be sedated for a couple of hours, and she's resting now in one of the private rooms upstairs. I know it was a shock for her—for all of us really—but I thought that marriage was on the rocks. The depth of her grief surprises me a little actually."

"It might be worse for her *because* the relationship was so unstable. They were sniping at each other just this morning. Can you imagine what that must be like? To fight with your husband and have him die an hour later, leaving you with no chance to make it better?"

Jules seemed to contemplate her question for so long Madison thought he had lost the thread of the conversation when he replied, "I can't actually. Marriage isn't really my thing, for any other reason than to produce an heir anyway. So it's hard for me to understand *any* of it." His shrug seemed overly nonchalant to Madison, but she remained silent and he went on, "I thought they were on the brink of divorce in fact, so in a way, however tragic, I thought this might be a relief to her."

"My God, Jules," Madison said gasping, "do you know what you're saying?"

"Yes, I do. And I'm sure I'm not reacting appropriately. You're a shrink. Do people ever respond well to the sudden death of a friend?"

"Sociopaths generally do. Well, no, actually that's not true. They fake an appropriate respon—."

Jules rolled his head slowly to one side and looked up at her. "Seriously, love, if you go any further, I'm going to ask that one of *us* be sedated, too." He picked up her hand and kissed it before he stood.

Chastened, Madison tried to smile when she asked, "Will Annabel spend the night here, too?"

"I don't think she should. If you don't mind, I think she'd do better at your house. She needs to be around people she knows, and hospitals can be so—," he paused as he gestured around the room.

"Spooky."

"I was going to say impersonal. Either way, you have a lovely home, and she can be properly looked after there."

"Of course. You are welcome to stay as well," Madison said before she just sat there for a minute considering what else to say. She was reluctant to go into the details of Chris' final moments until the acuteness of it wore off a little, but she was eager to know how something like this had happened to a young, seemingly healthy man.

Jules solved her dilemma for her when he said, "I've asked them to expedite an autopsy. It's standard procedure anyway in cases like this, and I'd like to know what went wrong here. I mean—," he said, hesitating as Madison saw his composure slip when his expression dissolved into distress.

"Jesus, I was there. If I somehow screwed up and caused his death—."

Madison wanted to comfort him, to tell him there was no way something like that had happened and she was sure he had done everything he could. But she knew the truth was that as the most senior medical personnel at the scene Jules could, indeed, have somehow contributed to Chris' death. Either way, Madison knew the likelihood was strong that he would be held responsible. She silently patted his arm.

"He was stable on the field, and I thought we had him," Jules said. "I was on the phone with the ambulance. We were almost here, and he arrested less than a minute out." He shook his head. "I couldn't get him back. That never happens to me. I don't have people die on my table—ever. I don't get it."

Jules looked up as another physician approached. "Doctor Marlborough, a moment if you will." the new arrival said.

Madison watched as Jules stood and followed the physician without another word to her. He and Kyle passed one another in the corridor by the reception desk, nodded to each another but did not speak.

"Okay, I admit I'm having a little crisis of confidence being back with the group," Kyle said self-consciously. "To say nothing of the fact that

Chris just died unexpectedly. Chris and I were really close mates at university."

She nodded, reached out to him and squeezed his hand. "I know. I'm sorry, Kyle. I really am."

He nodded towards the glass doors and they watched Sydney as she inhaled deeply on her cigarette before dropping it on the concrete and crushing it with her the toe of her high-heeled boot. "How is Ms. Atwood holding up?"

"I think it's impossible to tell at this point how anyone is holding up."

Sydney sailed back through the emergency room doors at that point, and Madison observed that several orderlies watched her go by, momentarily distracted from their duties. Sydney's face registered something close to a self-satisfied smirk before she saw Madison and Kyle watching her and immediately rearranged her expression into one of sadness.

"How're you doing, Sydney?" Kyle asked as he stood.

"I am devastated. How do you think I'm doing?" she snapped, her tone clearly defensive. Her eyes widened and she reached out to brush her fingers over Kyle's arm. "Oh, I'm sorry. I really am. I'm just all over the board. I must still be in shock."

Madison stood. "That's a natural reaction. You are welcome to spend the night at Whiddenhurst if you would like. A trip back to London this afternoon might not be a great idea."

"Why?" Sydney asked, looking around before she spied a coffee machine and glided over.

Kyle and Madison exchanged glances. "Sydney," Madison said walking over to talk to her as Sydney punched the buttons on the coffee machine. "I think you are more upset than you're allowing yourself to feel at the moment. It wouldn't be a good idea if the reality of that hits you while you're driving."

Sydney smiled as she shook her head. "Madison, Madison. You're so cute." She blew on her coffee before taking a sip. "Kyle, is there any reason I can't return to London tonight?"

He shrugged. "Not that I know of. I have no jurisdiction here—and no reason to think I need it."

"That's what I thought." She kissed Madison's cheek and brushed Kyle's arm again. "Please tell Annabel I'm thinking of her, and I'll be in touch tomorrow regarding plans for the funeral."

Madison and Kyle watched Sydney stride through the automatic doors and pause as an attractive young man in a white coat stopped to talk to her. She smiled and even laughed at one point during the brief conversation. Kyle seemed transfixed, and Madison's jaw dropped when Sydney and the man she assumed to be a doctor exchanged business cards.

"Wow," Kyle said under his breath.

"I don't know what to say," Madison said, "except that shock affects people differently."

"Yeah. I'm sure that's it," he said shaking his head. "Do you think you could get a ride back to Whiddenhurst with Jules after Annabel wakes up?"

"Probably. But why?"

"I'd like to go back to the polo field and take a look around."

"I'm coming with you," Madison said as she reached for her purse.

CHAPTER 6

By the time Kyle and Madison arrived at the polo field, the last match was over. There were several stragglers still sitting around talking, and drinking, but they were generally quiet and well behaved. Kyle looked around at the detritus of the match. The field was not only chopped up from the horses' hooves, but was also covered in trash and, bizarrely, discarded clothing.

"I don't think your mum is going to be happy when she returns," Kyle said.

"Well, the truth is," Madison said as she gingerly stepped around a pile of horse droppings, "Mummy is seldom happy about anything she cannot control. The plan is to have the field cleared before she returns tomorrow."

"We may need to preserve the cr—, the scene a little longer than that," Kyle said noting with relief the flashes of light within the darkened tent. The police photographer he had called for when he had arrived at hospital was already on site working to shoot all aspects of the scene before he lost the light.

Kyle saw the two off-duty police officers he had asked to stand guard, and he waved to them as he entered the tent. They were rapidly losing the late afternoon light, and it took a minute for Kyle's eyes to adjust to the growing darkness. He stood out of the way as the photographer snapped several more photos.

"Henry," Kyle said reaching to shake the photographer's hand. "Anything?"

The older officer shook his head. "Nothing as far as I can tell. It looks like a garden party everyone left early. What are your suspicions here?"

"Don't know that I have any," Kyle said, shrugging. "But when a healthy thirty-year-old male with no previously known heart conditions drops dead, I'd like to know why. And if does turn out to be suspicious, I don't want to find out later that I have questions that can't be answered because I neglected to preserve the scene."

"Makes sense to me," Henry said as he started to pack up his equipment. "By the way, did you know there's a beautiful woman lurking outside?" He smiled lasciviously.

"You've been married too long," Kyle said as he glanced back at Madison. "She's with me. Well, not with me. She's a friend, but I didn't want the crime scene to be contaminated."

"Sure, Kyle. Whatever you say," Henry said as he saluted and left the tent.

"Kyle," Madison called after the photographer departed. "May I speak with you a minute?"

He took one look around and stepped outside the tent.

"Is it standard procedure to bag the food and drink in this kind of situation?" she asked.

"I'm not sure it's standard procedure, but we can do it. I thought you said Chris hadn't eaten anything."

"I don't think he did, but I wasn't watching him the whole time. But I know for certain he was *drinking*. A lot. He put away at least one full bottle of champagne," she said shaking her head, "in less than fifteen minutes. And I think he had, er, pre-flighted before I saw him. I actually thought he was just drunk when he first went down."

Kyle turned back, leaned down and squinted as he looked into the tent. "Why was he drinking from a bottle when there was a champagne fountain?" He stood and looked quizzically at Madison. "At a polo match. There was a champagne fountain at a polo match?"

"I don't know. I didn't think it was odd at the time. But that was then. Now I think it may have been odd. Or maybe it was just disorganized. Peyton and Sydney, and maybe Annabel, were pouring champagne into the fountain and passing bottles at the same time. I think." She exhaled and shook her head as she rubbed her temple. "I don't really remember. There were a lot of people in and out of the tent, and I just wasn't paying that much attention. But I think it's worth checking out. Although maybe we should wait for the autopsy results," she said, her voice trailing off.

"No," Kyle said, waving to two officers talking to Henry the photographer. "Evidence degrades pretty quickly." He turned to the officers. "Guys, can you go ahead and bag and label the food and drink?" He stepped back into the tent, furrowing his brow as he rubbed the day's growth on his chin. "Take special care with the champagne. And the Scotch."

"You *all* drank the Scotch," Madison said as she remained just outside the tent. "Please tell me you don't think it was that!"

"Madison," Kyle said calmly as stepped outside again, took her shoulders and turned her to face him. "I haven't actually said there was anything amiss here. And you're right, we all did drink the Scotch and we are fine. As far as I know. I'm just trying to cover all our bases in case it turns out we need this information. In all probability, we won't need it." Madison looked as though she were on the verge of tears again. Kyle quickly said, "Remaining calm is key here."

She nodded and brushed a tear from her eye. "Right. I will." She watched as the police officers started carrying in coolers for the food. "I promise."

Kyle checked his Blackberry. "They'll wrap up the scene by eight tonight. Everything should be okay for your mum's return tomorrow." He scrolled down further on the device. "And Jules says Annabel should be ready to leave hospital in about an hour."

"I can pick her up," Madison said.

"Or I can. But if you pick her up, I'll be able to go to the local station and follow up on what they've collected here."

"I can do it. But—," she said, her voice getting softer as she looked at something in the distance.

"But?" Kyle said, looking up from his Blackberry.

Madison swallowed. "Our family mausoleum is on the grounds not far from here. I'd like to go by first if you think there's time."

An ache rose at the base of Kyle's throat when he saw the vulnerability in Madison's face. The day's events had clearly stripped away the defenses she put up against the world, and she appeared younger than she had the day they'd met as freshers at St. Andrews. "I'll come with you," he said.

"No, no," she said putting up her hands. "I appreciate the thought, but I just want to go by and pay my respects if you think there's time. It's been ten years this month, and I—."

"I'll come with you," he repeated softly. "Lead the way."

Madison and Kyle were silent as they walked more than half a mile over the breath-taking grounds of Whiddenhurst. The late afternoon sun bathed the rolling hills in a dusky rose glow that softened the vibrant colors of a blooming spring and made the entire landscape seem surreal to Kyle, like being inside a watercolor painting.

He had not known Charles Abbott well, but they had met on several occasions when he had come up to St. Andrews to visit Madison. He remembered Charles as a genial guy just two years out of Cambridge himself but still poised to take his place in his father's empire. His murder had made headlines all over the world. It had been shocking and brutal and unimaginable to most people. It had happened on a well-guarded, magnificent estate in the peaceful English countryside belonging to one of the wealthiest families in England. Nothing like that had ever happened in Gloucestershire before, and it changed forever the degree to which people felt safe and secure in their abilities to protect their families.

The shock waves rippled so far in part because the murder remained unsolved. The police had no motive and no suspects, just as they had not over a decade ago. The victim's father, the Duke of Abbott, had put substantial resources into the search to find his only son's killer, but nothing concrete was ever found. The murder of Viscount Charles Abbott was legend in the cold case files in Scotland Yard, and Kyle had been through that file many times. He wanted more than anything to solve this crime because he felt, on a very fundamental level, that Madison could never fully heal until she knew the truth of why it had happened even more than who had taken her brother's life. Kyle knew that the "why" did not always come with a satisfying answer.

But the who usually did and he wanted that answer for her.

They crested a hill, and the setting sun illuminated a white marble mausoleum as it came into view. It was an immense, imposing structure with Corinthian columns on all four sides. ABBOTT was etched in bold letters across the front with the family crest beneath it. The building sat amidst beautifully sculpted shrubs and flowers that were changed every season to ensure that this particular area never suffered the desolate bleakness of winter. The paradox of the vibrancy of the flowering trees and plants and the somber house of the dead was not lost on Kyle, and he slowed his pace in deference.

"I miss him every day," Madison said quietly as she stood before the tomb looking up at the inscription etched under the crest: *Strength is born in the deep silence of long-suffering hearts, not amid joy.* "Our parents were gone a lot, even when they were home. So Charles and I were on our own. He was my protector in that great big house—and the great big world." A single tear slid down her cheek, and she quickly brushed it away. And then she smiled. "And he was fun. There was always talk around him about his hereditary entitlements, but he never took it seriously. I mean he took his responsibilities seriously. But he wasn't full of himself."

Kyle nodded anyway, knowing she didn't see him as she kept her eyes on what he knew she thought of as merely Charles' grave.

"And he was kind, and respectful of women, always a gentleman." She laughed a small, sad laugh. "He got that from our father, who would have tolerated nothing less."

Kyle desperately wanted to put his arms around her, but he knew he was only a spectator here and not a participant, so he simply waited silently for her to go on.

Madison continued, her voice barely audible. "When he went, he took a piece of all of us with him. He was my father's only son, his heir—and the hope for our family's future. He was the only person I think my mother ever truly loved." She turned to Kyle. "And he was my best friend. I miss him every day," she repeated.

"Even after all these years."

Madison nodded. "Even after all these years."

She walked over and sat on the bottom of the marble steps leading to the massive wooden door of the crypt. Kyle sat beside her. Even on a day as sunny as today had been, the marble was cold and unyielding.

"Did you know that when Charles died, after the shock wore off, my father petitioned to have the patent for his dukedom amended by Parliament to allow the title to pass to me?"

"That must be unprecedented. I had no idea that was even possible."

"It isn't unprecedented. There have been a couple of other instances like it. It's rare, but it is possible. All of this," she said, sweeping her arms out towards the extensive grounds surrounding them, "will be mine when my father passes away." She inhaled deeply and caught her breath for a moment. "But all I ever wanted was to see my brother again. I would trade it all for that. Even for just one hour."

Kyle scooted over to sit closer to her, and he put his arm around her shoulders. He closed his eyes and silently exhaled when, for a fleeting moment, she rested her head on his shoulder.

"When did we stop being friends, Kyle?" she asked in a sad, soft voice.

He sighed. "After university, I think. When you returned to a dukedom, and I joined the police force."

CHAPTER 7

Less than an hour later, Madison returned to the hospital alone. She checked Annabel out and waited in front while the valet retrieved her car. A withdrawn Annabel sat just inside the sliding doors with a blank, almost catatonic stare on her face. Madison watched her nervously, more tired, both mentally and physically, than she remembered being since her brother died. She had just started to sit on a bench to wait when the tattooed photographer from the encounter at Whiddenhurst's stables stepped out from behind one of the entryway columns. Madison was so startled and so on edge that she cried out.

"It's just me, Lady Madison," the photographer said urgently. "I did't mean to scare ya. I'm sorry."

"Oh, I—," she gasped, feeling foolish but still struggling to catch her breath. "I didn't see you—."

"Joe Ward," he said extending his hand. "We've not met, official and all."

She nodded and glanced behind her as surreptitiously as she could, hoping that Annabel was still out of view.

"I was the only one what saw the ambulance go, and I've been waiting here all this time." He shook his head. "It warn't carryin' the prince or his missus, that much I know."

Madison sighed with the resignation that on such a trying day, she would now have to deal with the media, too. "No," she said, nodding. "It's not the prince or Kate Middleton. A friend of ours became sick at the match."

"Will ya share with me who it was?"

She didn't believe it was her place to *share with him* the news of Chris' death, but nor did she want to put either Annabel or the Palace through the media circus questions could set off, so she decided to level with him. "Lord Christopher Grisham suffered a heart attack, Joe." She glanced inside again. "He—he didn't make it."

Joe followed her gaze inside and jerked his head towards Annabel. "Is that his widow?"

She looked him directly in the eye. "It is. And I understand you have a job to do, but if you could just give her a little time to adjust to this, I would be personally grateful." Madison made a snap decision, pulled her wallet from her handbag, removed a business card, and said, "I don't think there's anything else to tell, but if you can just give her some privacy and time to deal with the shock, you can call me later for more information."

Joe leaned over and peered through the sliding glass doors at Annabel, whom Madison feared would actually slip out of her chair as she swayed. He nodded and took the offered card. "I'll do that," he said looking intently at her card. "No one in your group has ever handed me their card before. I'm always treated like an enemy."

"Not entirely without reason," Madison noted. "But I'm willing to call a détente if you are."

"I can't tell if that's somethin' I ought to be callin' or not, to be honest."

She smiled. "It is. It's an easing of a strained relationship and a dawning of a new era of respect."

The photographer just shook his head, but he was smiling as he pointed at her. "We have a day-tant then," he said as he looked once more at Annabel, slung his camera strap around his neck and departed.

Madison breathed a sigh of relief as the valet pulled her Cygnet in front of the entrance. She turned to take over from the nurse guiding Annabel out of the hospital. Thinking she would have more room to stretch out, Madison helped her into the backseat of the car.

"Is Jules coming with us?" Annabel, clearly still groggy, asked as stared out at the hospital building.

Madison shook her head and said, "No, I couldn't find him. He has his own car, so I assume he'll show up at some point." Annabel swallowed hard, looking somehow disappointed. "I could go look again—," Madison said, gesturing towards the building.

"No, I'm fine," Annabel mumbled as she pulled her feet up on the seat and curled herself around her knees. Madison leaned in and buckled the seatbelt awkwardly around her, took off her own jacket and wrapped it around Annabel.

As they pulled out of the hospital courtyard and onto the road on their way back to Whiddenhurst Hall, Madison couldn't help herself as she glanced repeatedly at Annabel in the rearview mirror.

"I'm still here," Annabel said as she too watched Madison in the mirror.

"I just want to make sure you're okay."

"I'm not okay," Annabel said, leaning her head against the window and staring morosely out at the beauty of the passing landscape. "Except that, of course, I am," she went on in a disturbing monotone. "I hate it when people say they can't handle something. What choice is there? You just go on, whether you feel like doing so or not."

Madison searched for comforting words, found all choices inadequate and simply nodded, relieved that the match traffic had dissipated and they were making good time. She was eager to be out of the confines of the vehicle and its atmosphere of suffocating sadness.

"Is there anyone I can call for you?" Madison asked as she again glanced in the rearview mirror.

"Jules called Mummy and Chris' mother and sister. I assume someone will let the rest of the group know. I'm certain Chris' mother will take over the funeral arrangements."

"You don't have to think about that now, Annabel," Madison said quietly as they turned onto a country lane and drove through the elaborate wrought iron gates of her family's ancestral estate.

Whiddenhurst Hall graced the top of a hill, and the first glimpse of it before it disappeared around the bend in the long drive, always stirred Madison. The entire estate was particularly spectacular in the spring when the leaves were filled in and the flowers were in full bloom as they shook off the dull bleakness of winter in the English countryside.

As she drove down the mile long gravel drive leading to the house, Madison let her mind drift from the current situation and was reminded why her home had often been described as the most beautiful house in England. In 1927, the British magazine *English Country Life* had published a set of three articles on the house in which the author described Whiddenhurst Hall as "the most incomparable house in Britain, the one which created the greatest impression and summarizes so exquisitely English country life qualities."

Set on over twenty-five hundred acres, Whiddenhurst Hall was an imposing, Grade II listed manor house. Built in the sixteenth century, the great north front of the house was Palladian in character and dominated by a massive, six-columned Corinthian portico. The roof of the mansion was meant for walking on and there was a breath-taking circular view above the tree line of the rolling hills of the estate, which included the new stables and several thoroughbred racehorses grazing in the pastures. From the rooftop, one could see in the distance the elegant architecture and beautiful gardens of Highgrove, the country home of the Prince of Wales.

Madison breathed a sigh of relief as she pulled into the circular courtyard in front of the house and parked. She turned around to look at Annabel and said, "I hope you are going to spend the night." She gestured towards the house. "I know it would make me feel better seeing that you are properly taken care of. I'm sure we can find some clothes that will fit you, and we have a lot of rooms."

"Something like thirty bedrooms, not to mention the servants' quarters, if the press is to be believed," Annabel said dully as she stared out at the house.

"I make it a general practice to seldom believe the press. Whiddenhurst is just my home," Madison said softly as Parker, the Abbott family butler, came out to open the car doors for her and Annabel.

Madison stepped out of the car and caught her breath when saw Duncan Rand coming out the front door. He had changed out of his polo clothes and was so effortlessly elegant she was almost dismayed to see him, even more so when she saw her little Scottish Terrier, Morgan, trotting after him as though they were lifelong mates. "I hadn't realized you were here," she said, mustering a smile.

"I wanted to check on you both," he said as he put his arm around Annabel's waist. "Are you okay?

What can I do to help?" he asked softly as he directed his questions to her.

Annabel shook her head with a demeanor that implied that any further conversation was too grueling for her. Duncan nodded, and Parker ushered her inside. Duncan waited for Madison as she came around the car. He put his arms around her and held her tightly.

"I am so sorry," he whispered. "This is just dreadful."

Madison returned his hug and tried not to struggle against the comfort of his embrace. "Me, too. I am so very, very sorry for everyone." After what seemed like an eternity, she finally broke the hold. "Are you staying for dinner?" she asked bending down to pick up Morgan before they turned to walk inside.

"That would be great, but it seems dangerously close to inviting myself since I was lurking here when you arrived home. I just wanted to see how you and Annabel were. Wills thought we should finish the match to minimize the disruption and by the time it was over, well—." He shook his head.

"It was *all* over."

"Yes," he said sadly, shaking his head again. ""It never occurred to any of us that this was anything more than some kind of anomaly, like an anxiety attack or something. How is Annabel really?"

"Not great."

"I simply cannot believe it. Do they know what happened?"

"Other than that he had a heart attack?" she asked as they walked into the richly decorated drawing room and she headed towards the drinks cart. "No." She held up a decanter of Scotch in question to Duncan as Parker hurried towards her. "It's okay, I've got it," she said smiling at him. "I assume Annabel has been taken care of?"

"She's upstairs in the west gallery, ma'am. Mrs. Wilkes is seeing to her personal needs, including having a tray in her room for dinner. She said she'd prefer to not join you if that is okay with you."

"Of course it is. Thank you, Parker." As the butler discretely retreated, Madison resumed her discussion with Duncan. "Anyway, they'll do an autopsy, of course. I just can't believe it," she said sitting next to Duncan on the sofa as she handed him a tumbler of Scotch. She was grateful for the blazing fire that was among many that were always stoked at Whiddenhurst, no matter what the season. It was always cold in the massive house, although Madison's chill today had nothing to do with the temperature.

Duncan drained half his glass before he asked, "And how are *you* doing?"

Her eyes immediately welled with tears. "I'm struggling a little. Not only is this awful in its own right. But this also brings up some very hard memories for me."

He leaned closer to her so his shoulder was now touching hers as he dipped his head towards her. His voice was gentle as he said, "Except that Chris' case was different. His was just a heart attack, not something more—sinister."

Madison pulled back from him and looked directly in his eyes as she tried to gauge what he knew. He did not flinch from her gaze. She turned back to stare at the fire. "Of course, you're right. It's just hard."

Duncan stood abruptly, startling Madison as he began to pace back and forth in front of her. He finally stopped and asked casually, "How much did you know about Chris' business?"

"Not much, I guess. Truthfully, I know everyone's titles, but I don't really know what's behind that or what anyone does on a day-to-day basis. Like you—I know you're a solicitor who never practiced law and are now an investment banker. But what you actually do is a mystery to me. I know that Chris owned his own firm, and I think they did something with property."

Duncan smiled very quickly and then it was gone. He closed his eyes and started aggressively rubbing his forehead with his thumb.

"Okay," she said slightly concerned now, "what business *was* Chris in?"

Duncan sighed heavily before draining the rest of his drink. "Chris was a developer." He looked at her and she just nodded. He walked over to the drinks cart to refill his glass as he continued, "He and his partner—Jeff Hawthorne, whom I heard was at the match today—developed commercial property. And that means, essentially, that they raised funds from people willing to provide the financial backing as investments for their developments, which they designed and then had built."

"I thought I remember hearing, or reading somewhere, that he was doing something down on the waterfront last year."

"He was. Or rather, he conceptualized it last year and it was off to a good start really. It was to be a mixed-use property next to Battersea Park, alongside Wandsworth Bridge—high-end retail, restaurants, and luxury condos. He always had great vision in that regard."

Madison tried to remember what Chris had done just out of university to see if she could figure out whether it was remotely possible that a killer had come out of his past to exact a long-held need for revenge, or retribution, but she could not recall. She had a vague recollection that he had done something with property then, too, but she couldn't remember exactly what, or with whom. And then she thought she was being paranoid and letting Kyle's innocuous precautions provoke her imagination, which tended to go to dark places in distressing situations. The descent into paranoia was never pretty, and she always tried to recognize the signs and avoid any repetition of the black weeks after her brother's murder.

She shook her arms in an effort to shake off the suspicions nibbling destructively at her fragile psyche and tried for a positive tone when she said, "That sounds as though that could have been his big break. I think he struggled a little after university."

"Yes, and in the intervening years, too. So I, too, thought this latest development plan was brilliant and could be the break he's really always needed," Duncan said as he grimaced and then sighed heavily.

"But?"

"But Chris was still struggling, and he needed new investors to be able to have any hope of saving the project and recouping some of the money they'd already lost. Grisham Investments was hemorrhaging money."

"Uh-oh. I'm afraid of where this is heading."

Duncan nodded tightly. "You got it. He came to me to bail him out."

"And did you?" she said, trying to keep the alarm out of her voice.

"Yep," he answered before finishing his Scotch. "I didn't feel like I could say 'no'."

"Do I want to know how much?"

He shook his head as he turned when Parker re-entered the room. "It would shock you."

The butler paused, looking uncharacteristically unsure of himself before he said, "Dinner is served, ma'am, sir."

CHAPTER 8

Kyle followed the unmarked van more closely than was safe as they drove without stopping the hundred miles from Tetbury to South London. When they arrived at their destination, the van stopped briefly at the guardhouse in front of the fenced enclosure and the driver spoke momentarily to the guard who waved both vehicles through. Kyle nodded and waved as he followed the van as it pulled up to the loading dock of a grim, concrete bunker. There were no identifying marks on the buildings in the secure compound, and it looked to the outside world like a fairly downtrodden, industrial warehouse complex.

He parked the Range Rover and got out to supervise the unloading of the evidence from the Abbott hospitality tent at the day's charity match. Still reluctant to even mentally regard the tent as a crime scene, he watched the policemen carry five white coolers of food and drink into the laboratory of the Forensic Science Service. Upon receipt, he knew the items would be recorded on the central computer's filing system where an inventory was kept of who has handled what, where and when. Because of the unique, perishable nature of the potential evidence, what had been intended as party food would then be transferred directly to an on-site lab to be examined. Kyle had phoned a technician to call in a very large favor and he hoped he was already prepped and in his lab awaiting delivery.

Kyle signed in and was buzzed through the security door of the nondescript building. He walked slowly down a sterile hallway bathed in a slightly florescent glow and tried to remember which research room belonged to Jim DiCarla. He and Jim had met doing Jagermeister shots in a run-down pub in Chelsea the day Kyle had solved his first murder case.   They talked of forensics and new crime scene investigation techniques until the wee hours of the morning and had ended up horrifying several other patrons in the pub with their talk of blood spatter, near decapitation and exsanguination. But they had remained good mates ever since.

A door at the farthest end of the hall opened, and Kyle was relieved to see Jim walk through. The forensic analyst leaned against the doorframe and crossed his arms. "So you got me in here on a Saturday night—via blackmail I might add—and you send me a picnic? What's up with that?"

"For the record," Kyle said as he reached out to shake the tech's hand, "it's extortion, not blackmail. I don't think this will take a lot of time, but I need to have some of the food checked for poisons."

"Who got killed?" Jim asked as he turned and walked back into his lab.

"I'm not sure he *was* killed. That's what I want to know, and it's kind of circular. If there's poison here, then we can look for it in the autopsy. And vice versa with the autopsy."

"That's an ass-backwards way to go about it, mate. But this is your party."

Technicians in white lab coats were already bringing the coolers into Jim's lab and setting them on the stainless steel worktable in the middle of the room. Kyle watched as they meticulously unpacked each one, labeling each item as they did so.

"They move fast," Kyle said as he looked over the contents and realized there really was not as much food as he had originally thought. He identified about two dozen shucked oysters, several sausage rolls, some kind of pasta and mozzarella salad, steak sandwiches, Cornish pastries, and two Victoria sponge cakes, most of which looked untouched. One cooler held only three plates of largely uneaten food sealed in plastic wrap and another held the Scotch and champagne bottles and flutes.

"Yeah, well, it's Saturday night and the quicker we get this done, the quicker we can have a life," Jim said. "So set the table here for me." He smiled. "So to speak."

"I was at a charity polo match this afternoon in Gloucestershire. This," Kyle said as he gestured to the now extremely unappetizing layout, "was what I would call a tailgate party and others would call a hospitality tent for some friends of mine from university." Kyle felt his chest tighten and he took a deep breath before he continued. "One of them died this afternoon. Thirty-year old male. Cardiac arrest." His hand cleaved the air. "Total surprise to everybody, including his wife. I'd like to find out what happened."

Jim put his hands on his hips and exhaled as he looked at the neatly wrapped food. "I'm sorry to hear that, mate. But food isn't generally a cause of cardiac arrest."

"Poison can be."

"Yeah, but at a party, where a lot of people are coming and going and eating the same food?" Jim shook his head. "That's risky if you're only trying to whack one guy."

"I'll grant you that. For all I know, he had something congenital and that's what got him," Kyle said, vigorously rubbing the back of his neck. "But I just don't think so. Call it intuition or a gut feeling."

Jim pulled up a metal stool and sat down. "Okay, let's break this down. You eat any of this?"

Kyle shook his head. "I did have some Scotch, though."

Jim glanced at him out of the corner of his eye. "Got a jump start on the day, eh?"

"Something like that. So I think the Scotch is okay. But," he said, snapping his fingers, "Chris wasn't drinking Scotch. He was drinking champagne—a lot of it as I heard it."

"Okay, we'll test the champagne—fountain? Is that what that is? A champagne fountain? *You* were at a party with a champagne fountain?"

"No kidding. But if we have to prioritize, I think he was drinking from the bottle. Not directly, of course."

Jim stood and walked over to the fountain around which stood four open bottles of champagne. He pulled on a pair of latex gloves before he lifted each one by one. "Most of these are full. But depending on the poison, a little dab could do you, so that makes sense." He lifted a bottle and smelled it, wrinkled his nose and pulled back.

"What?"

"This bottle, the only one that's almost empty has an overwhelming smell of something familiar," Jim said his brow furrowed in concentration. "Like the beach. Ah, I know – salt. I really don't know pricey champagne, but as far as I do know, none of it has a salty taste." He smelled the other three bottles. "These don't."

Kyle scrutinized the labels. "I'm more of a beer man myself, but I'd have to agree. This is odd," he said pointing to the suspicious bottle.

"Watch your hands, mate," Jim said as he tossed a pair of gloves to Kyle. "Wearing a glove is critical here, as in so many other key areas of life."

"Check out the labels. The empty bottle is different." He flinched. "It's peach flavored. You wouldn't mix two different kinds of champagne in a fountain, would you?"

"No idea. But we'll test that one first and then the others. Talk to me about nourishment. What were people eating?" Jim picked up two plates with partially eaten meals. "'Cause by the looks of it, it wasn't much."

"Yeah, I don't know. I didn't have anything to eat, and neither did the players, or least the polo players, that is. Other than Chris, the deceased, the only other people there were women. And in my experience, they seldom eat at these things." Kyle walked slowly around the table, carefully taking note of each item. "Why oysters?" he said under his breath.

"Huh?" Jim said distractedly as he took the cover of his microscope off and turned it on. He then pulled a box of tongue depressors from the shelf and removed one.

"Oysters aren't a natural picnic food to me," Kyle said. "They're difficult to transport safely and hard to eat. They can go bad easily. They're not a morning food. Why oysters?"

"We can test them for spoilage if you'd like. But if they were bad, it likely would have caused vomiting, not cardiac arrest."

"I know. I'm just thinking."

Kyle turned to watch as Jim tipped the peach champagne bottle and inserted the tongue depressor just far enough in to wet half of it. He then held the depressor under a hand dryer mounted on the wall as he reached over to pick up a miniature blow torch like the kind used for browning the sugar on top of crème brulee. "Watch this," Jim said as he lit the torch and held the dry depressor in the flame. The flame changed immediately from blue to an intense yellow. "Just as I thought," he said turning off the torch.

"What is it?"

"Sodium, in the champagne. Sodium is not an ingredient in champagne, and it shouldn't be there. Not at this level anyway."

"Salt is something we all need and get everyday. That wouldn't cause a heart attack. Would it?" Kyle asked.

"Not under normal circumstances. But some underlying pathologies could cause someone to be more susceptible to sodium at this level. Did your friend have any chronic conditions?"

"Not that I know of." Kyle shrugged. "But I don't know that he would have discussed it with me. You know that men don't talk about that kind of crap." He sat on the stool and spun around to look at the table of food again, focusing specifically on the uneaten food on the three plates. "Okay. How long would it take to test for poison in the oysters, the pasta salad and the steak sandwiches?"

"Just poison or spoiled food, too?"

"No one else got sick, so for now just poison."

"Well, considering the fact that there are about a million compounds that could kill you, it could take a long time."

"No, let's be real here. Most of those compounds are not available to the average Joe. I'm looking for the easy ones," Kyle said, ticking the names off on his fingers, "arsenic, cyanide, formaldehyde, strychnine. But only those that would kill in a one dose situation."

"I can test for the ones you just mentioned tonight, and maybe a couple of others as well. An American company actually makes handy little color-based detector kits that show results immediately. They sent me loads of them to try."

Three hours later, Kyle was on his way back to Tetbury with Gloucestershire Royal Hospital as his destination when his mobile rang.

"You bailed too early, mate. I got a hit," Jim said.

"Oysters?"

"Yeah, how'd you know?

"Lucky guess. Are we talking bad seafood or was it with intent?"

"With intent. These guys were soaked in formaldehyde, but only the ones on one of the individual plates, not those on the serving dish. The ones in the 'general population' were okay. I guess the perp figured the cocktail sauce could hide the taste initially, and then it'd be too late. Breathing it is bad but ingesting it, even in small amounts, causes an immediate reaction. And it ain't a good one. It causes tearing and severe abdominal pain, followed by collapse, loss of consciousness, shutdown of the liver and circulatory failure. Sound like what you saw?"

"Maybe, at least some of it. What about prints?"

"I haven't gotten to that yet. I'll stay tonight, er, this morning and see what I can find."

"I'll let you know what the autopsy turns up. I owe you, Jim, thanks."

"You bet you do, mate. And I'm keeping track."

CHAPTER 9

Madison knocked shyly on the heavy oak door to the library. Hearing no answer, she walked cautiously into her favorite room in Whiddenhurst. The "double library" had its heyday during the late Victorian period, when Whiddenhurst had undergone the extensive renovations that resulted in its current layout, so the manor contained one of the finest in England. At the time, the library had been used by the 4th Duke of Abbott as a "withdrawing" room, where the duke, who was an active Tory in Parliament and a member of Disraeli's Cabinet in the 1860s and 1870s, could discuss politics with friends or retire in peace.

This room epitomized masculinity to Madison, as she saw her father in every detail: the two-tiered, forty- by sixty-foot library containing over ten thousand books housed in mahogany-paneled bookcases, a fireplace surrounded by a carved, black-marble mantle, the imposing burgundy leather sofas tufted with brass buttons, and the massive desk made by Jacob Frères of Paris and rumored to have come from Napoleon's rooms at the Palace of Fontainebleau. It all reminded her of the statesman-like presence of her beloved father.

On the second floor of the library, there was even a secret door that her father could use to come down directly from his bedroom to locate or return a book, a feature that had fascinated both her and Charles as children when they had concocted all manner of clandestine plots involving secret agents ultimately responsible for helping the Allies win the war.

She brushed her fingers over each of the silver-framed photos on the table behind the sofa. The majority of them were of her mother, always beautiful but imperious, regardless of the setting or activity. There were several of Madison and many more of Charles, eternally young, handsome and full of life. A lump formed in her throat as she picked up the photo taken just the day before he died. He was astride Khartoum, his prized stallion, laughing at something she would never know.

It had been two hours since Madison had dined quietly with Duncan, and she had expected to find him where she had left him, working at her father's desk. The lamp was on and papers and files were strewn about, but he was not in the room. She put her hand on the coffee cup next to his reading glasses. It was still warm.

She glanced back at the door and stood still as she listened for anyone approaching. Hearing nothing, Madison sat in the big leather chair behind the massive desk from which she had seen her father run his estates and investments since she was a child. She ran her hand along the inlaid leather, looking there for tactile evidence of the comforting presence of her father.

Her eyes were drawn to the small crown in the midnight blue logo of Grisham Investments prominently displayed on several documents spread haphazardly across the desk. A small stab of nostalgia nicked her heart, as memories of Chris flooded in. His privileged background could not make up for the insecurities born of a childhood in a fractured family, and Chris had not yet come into his own before his life was prematurely cut short.

Madison's attention traveled from the logo to the memorandum below. It was addressed to Duncan Rand from Chris Grisham regarding "Company Structure." She looked up, listening again to see if Duncan were approaching. Madison heard nothing. Thinking the document could give her additional insight into the issues to which Duncan had alluded before dinner, Madison picked up the memo and read, a feeling of unease growing with every line.

She heard a noise in the hall outside the library and jumped, nearly knocking over Duncan's coffee cup in the process. At night, especially when Madison was alone, the vast size of the house unnerved her. The manor was never completely silent, and its marble hallways and cavernous rooms echoed with sounds from throughout the great house, making it impossible to ever be certain exactly where people were or from where the noises of the household originated.

Charles had been killed at Whiddenhurst Hall when the entire family and a full complement of servants had been in residence. And no one had heard a thing.

But Morgan was still curled peacefully at her feet, and Madison knew the little terrier would have stirred immediately if anyone had been in the vicinity.

She quickly scribbled key points from the memo on a notepad before she replaced it in its exact previous position. She tore the top sheet off the pad, folded it and put it in the top drawer of her father's desk.

Morgan raised his head, his ears straight up and alert now. Madison glanced towards the door and down again at a file folder labeled Grisham Investments. Her heart was pounding. She opened it anyway. Madison caught her breath when she saw the copy of a check for ten million pounds from Titan Investments to Christopher R. Grisham.

Titan was Duncan's firm. And it was powerful. Often in the financial press, Titan was a privately held property corporation with offices in eighteen cities. It had four regional investment and development businesses in Britain and Ireland, the Americas, Australia and Asia Pacific; an international fund management business, which operated across these markets and in continental Europe; and a portfolio of indirect investments.

Even so, ten million pounds was not an insignificant investment.

Madison cocked her head at the check in her hand. Property development and investment banking were clearly not her forte. But she thought it odd that the check was made out to Chris personally rather than to Grisham Investments. She wished she could make a photocopy of the check but her father was adamant about not having machines that looked "out of place" in his library unless they could be hidden in a cabinet. Alas, a copier could not be concealed.

She immediately replaced the copy, closed the file and stood when Morgan started to growl. Madison walked quickly across the room and to the fireplace, and she was standing before it warming her hands when Duncan entered the library. She turned and smiled at him, arranging her face in a demeanor she hoped hid her pounding heart. Duncan glanced towards the desk and then back at her before returning her smile with a brilliant one of his own.

"I was looking for you," he said. "My eyes were starting to glaze over, and I was hoping I could entice you into something more interesting."

Madison's heart skipped a beat. "I—I'm sorry? What?"

Duncan laughed, and she remembered how thrilling it was to be in his company.

"I'm not inviting you to bed, Madison." His smile was mischievous now, and his eyes twinkled with amusement. "Unless, of course, you'd like me to."

She instinctively stepped back from him, caught her shoe on the rug and stumbled before catching herself by grabbing the fireplace mantle. He laughed again, adding annoyance to the other confusing emotions coursing through her.

"I'm sorry," he said throwing his hands out. "I didn't mean to make you nervous. I swear I will not repay your hospitality by making a pass at you."

"I'm not nervous," she said, struggling for a composure she did not feel and angry with herself for indeed being unnerved at the suggestion of being intimate with Duncan again after so many years apart. Madison was always physically attracted to him, and his nearness now was unsettling. She cleared her throat and tried for a serious tone. "It's a fairly well known dynamic that people often seek comfort sex in an effort to deal with their grief. It's something that can fill the emptiness you feel after a loss," she said, her voice trailing off.

"Show me," Duncan said, his voice husky as stepped towards her, took her face in his hands and kissed her softly.

Madison was momentarily lost in the warmth of his body, his intoxicatingly familiar scent, and the electric impulses firing up and down her own body as his kisses became more intense. He had always been the most exquisite lover—sensuous, deliberate and insistent, yet gentle and unhurried.

She reluctantly pulled away from him and took a deep breath. "I don't think that is a good idea."

Duncan softly kissed her neck. "If this isn't a good idea," he murmured, "I can't wait to see what your idea of a good one is."

"I—I thought we put 'us' away so long ago," she stammered as he continued to kiss her and started to gently caress her arms.

"Take off your professional hat and don't think so hard about this, sweetheart," he whispered. "Better yet, take off everything."

There was a knock on the door, and Madison jumped. Duncan looked at her with a curious look on his face. "This is your house," he said. "If you are uncomfortable being here with me, I can get a room in the village. Or perhaps even stay with Wills. Highgrove isn't far from here."

"Don't be silly," she said, touching his arm lightly as she slipped past him on her way to the door. "I'm just a little jumpy because of Charles—I mean Chris. I'll be okay." She opened the door slowly, willing herself to not peak around the corner like a small child caught with her hand in the cookie jar.

Parker stood before her with a silver serving tray on which sat an empty bottle of 1982 Chateau Latour, a crystal decanter into which the wine had been poured, two wine glasses and a small dish of dark chocolate truffles.

"You are a wonder, Parker, thank you," she said stepping back to allow him to enter.

"It's been a stressful day, and I thought you might want to relax a little before turning in," he said as he placed the tray on the low table before the sofa. "Shall I pour for you?"

"No, thank you, I'll take care of it," Duncan answered. "You're a good man, Parker."

"Yes, sir. Will there be anything else for either of you this evening?"

"No, that will be all," Madison replied. "Thank you again. And goodnight." She closed the door behind the butler and leaned against it, watching as Duncan waved the decanter beneath his nose, inhaling it as one would a bouquet of flowers.

"What are you thinking?" he asked as he poured two glasses of wine.

She was thinking that this was going faster than she was prepared for, and she wasn't in the right emotional state to have her willpower tested this evening. The look on Duncan's face two minutes ago, an incongruous combination of unbearable sadness and powerful desire, was still with her. She said, "I was thinking how glad I am that he didn't bring champagne." Madison shivered. "And marveling how the staff in this house always knows what's going on—and almost always before I do."

He handed her a glass of wine. They clinked glasses, and he said, "To Chris."

"To Chris," she said solemnly as she sat on the sofa. She put the glass on the table and wrapped her arms around her. "It's always cold in this house, no matter what the temperature outside."

"It's big," he said as he moved closer to her and put his arm around her shoulders. "I'll keep you warm. And I'll protect you from any ghosts lurking about."

"I don't believe in ghosts," she said emphatically while looking directly at him before she turned back to the fireplace. Madison stared into the fire for a moment. "Only the boogeyman."

Duncan pulled her into a full embrace. She pulled back to look at him. "What's this about Duncan? It's been so long. Why now?" She took a bracing sip of her wine. "Why me?"

He immediately let go of her. She didn't let her disappointment show. Duncan pushed himself further from her but turned to face her as he did so, never losing eye contact.

His voice was husky when he said, "I have missed you a great deal since you left —."

"*You* left."

"Since we broke up. And as we approach thirty, it's been more acute. And then Chris' death drove it even further home. But unwanted seduction isn't my thing, Madison. If this isn't what you want, I respect that. I did a lot of stupid things when we were together—and even more afterward. I certainly don't want to open old wounds."

She saw a naked sincerity in his eyes she didn't remember him capable of. It pulled her in. But she knew that Duncan was a consummate manipulator, both professionally and personally, and Madison had learned long ago to be cautious of that aspect of his character. He was successful because he knew what he wanted and was singularly focused as he then set about manipulating people and situations to get it.

Her training and innate people skills enabled Madison to be, in her father's words, "good at people"—at understanding their motives, agendas, and the real truth behind what they said. But she had a blind spot where Duncan was concerned. She could not see through to his motives because her own desires and needs got in the way and clouded the picture.

That dynamic both frightened and excited her.

Madison suddenly stood, prepared to say goodnight. Duncan looked momentarily surprised but quickly nodded his head and stood as well. He cupped her face in his hands and kissed her lightly on each cheek. Without really thinking and just reacting to the nearness of him, she turned her head into his kiss and rested against his warm lips, closing her eyes and breathing in the scent of him. She had always had a visceral reaction to the smell of Duncan; it may only have been his cologne, a heady, sophisticated scent, but to her, embodied in that smell was power and leather and Scotch and cigars – and masculine men. It made her feel safe. As she breathed him in, her breath came faster and deeper.

Madison and Duncan stood silently for a moment before they slowly turned towards each other. His arm went around her waist and pulled her close to him. She put her hands against his chest to stop herself from leaning into him but they crept around his neck, and he kissed her gently, slowly. She had not kissed Duncan in a very long time and was surprised by the intensity of her physical reaction to him, and his to her.

Madison felt lightheaded, and she swayed a little. Duncan moved quickly then to enfold her in his arms, and he kissed her deeply and more passionately. She struggled with a sudden inability to take a full breath. She felt disoriented, practically floating—but almost unbearably excited and hungry for this man she had given up on so long ago.

Duncan was highly accomplished in all areas of his life, including those ways in which a man who has studied and truly loves women usually is, which, of course, included being a superb lover. But Madison had sometimes found him merely an excellent technician and a skilled aficionado, giving her an incredible experience but somehow still holding himself a little apart. She knew him to take his own pleasure only after giving it and yet in doing so, becoming even more inaccessible to her.

But there was more here now, and she was lost in an emotion between them she could not identify. There was an urgency in Duncan that night she had never felt with him—and had not felt herself in a very long time. Their need for each other rose, and she inched backwards towards the sofa behind her; he moved with her, not releasing her from his reassuring embrace as she sat and lay back on the cool leather. She pulled him down with her, needing to have this man lie on top of her, to feel his weight cover her with his protection and warmth. Her fingers dug into his neck and his muscular arms, and her body instinctively arched to fit with his. She gasped with pleasure and excitement when she felt him get hard against her thigh and part her legs slightly as he lowered himself effortlessly between them. Still fully dressed, they moved instinctively against one another, finding their old rhythm with each other's bodies. It was too easy to fall back into this.

Still locked in his embrace, she felt she was in a cocoon of safety and comfort as he kissed her mouth with a hunger she returned, juxtaposing that hard passion with soft kisses on her eyelids and a gentleness that took her breath away again. Duncan kissed her jaw line down to her neck, causing her heart to lurch into the base of her throat before he buried his face in the crook between her shoulder and neck and paused there, breathing her in. He stayed there for several minutes, neither moving nor speaking.

Duncan eventually picked his head up slightly and whispered into her ear very softly, in the most seductive of tones, "I have wanted you again for a very long time, my darling, before even—." He stopped with a slight intake of breath. "Well, for a long time. I want you now more than I've ever wanted any woman."

Madison had not allowed herself to feel wanted in such a long time, and her entire body reacted to his words. She may even have whimpered a little as she reached for him, wrapping her legs around him and pulling him even closer.

So it took her a full minute to cognitively process that he had pulled himself away from her ear and was up on his elbows with both hands cupping her head, his thumbs caressing her eyebrows. His face was only inches from hers and in his eyes she saw, for the first time since she met him, a look she did not recognize on his handsome face. She was confused and, difficult as she believed it was for both of them, they held each other's gaze. Her brow furrowed as she looked at this most competent of men, a true Master of the Universe, always in control, always guarded and almost unknowable, and saw vulnerability.

"But," he started, his voice huskier than before, the smoothness of seduction gone and replaced by raw emotion. Re-entry into reality came swiftly for Madison. *But?* "But," he continued, "I agree with you that this probably isn't a good idea. I am sorry to have been so carried away."

"I—I—," Madison stammered, struggling to figure out why she was in this position and what exactly they were doing. She could not form a coherent enough thought to continue, and she shook her head slightly in an effort to clear it enough to be able to comprehend what he was saying.

He smiled sweetly. She had never seen Duncan smile sweetly before and that killed her desire more than his words when he said, "I *do* want you, Madison. But not like this. Not here. Not now. This isn't really what you need." And then with a wicked little twinkle in his eye and a rakish smile, her familiar Duncan was back. "Okay, that's not entirely true; I think this is absolutely, positively what you need right now—over and over. I need it, too, and I want it. But this isn't going to get us where we need to be, sweetheart. And I have spent a lot of time thinking about where we need to be with one another. And this will sink us both. I realize you're not really reacting to me right now. You are just reacting, period. To being sad, scared, lonely, even angry. We can throw a lot of words at the situation here, but love—God help me, do you actually believe you hear this coming out of my mouth?— love is not what's bringing us together now. If we ever take this step again, that is what needs to bring you to me."

Her fingers still grasped his arms, but she slowly brought her legs down. Madison knew he was right, but her body ached with the unfulfilled promise of two minutes ago and abject frustration. "You're—," she said before she stopped and cleared her throat. "You're right, of course."

He pulled himself up off her entirely, scooped her knees under his arm and swung them around so she was sitting on the sofa facing the fire. He sat beside her and put his hand on her knee as he leaned his head against hers and said, "I'm sorry. I'm sorry about Chris, and what happened before between us." He shook his head. "I wish I could change it all."

Her eyes filled with tears, and she swallowed hard. "I don't know what to do here. I don't know how to be in this situation. I've been here before with my brother Charles, and I know that nothing I know how to do works in terms of making this better." One tear escaped and slid down her cheek.

"I know. I thought being close would help, too. Hell," he said, raking his hand through his tousled hair, "I think this was my idea. But I know that making passionate love to you will not make anything else going on any easier. It would be only a momentary escape, but everything is still what it is." He smiled weakly.

She blinked away the rest of her unshed tears, and, frustrated now, said, "You don't have to keep saying that, you know. I got it, really. *Really.*"

He smiled and said, "Yes, I know you do. But I have to say it to myself a couple more times to actually be convinced that I really just threw away an experience I've been thinking about for so many years now—and would have enjoyed immensely. I'm struggling with that a little and am, frankly, mystified by it. I'm not generally a self-sacrificing kind of man." He grinned again, looked at her sideways and said, "It's one of the things you love about me, you know."

CHAPTER 10

Kyle stood before the massive oak doors of Whiddenhurst and lifted the heavy brass knocker. He figured that the mansion was at least twenty times the size of the small house in which he had grown up, and he had no idea how anyone standing anywhere other than the great hall could hear someone knocking on the front door.

He pulled out his mobile and was about to dial Madison's number when Parker opened the heavy door. "Good morning, Mister Ward," he said standing back to let him pass into the great hall.

Although he had been invited to weekend house parties many times over the years, Kyle had never been inside Madison's country home before, and he tried to disguise the fact that he was a little daunted by its grandeur. It was clear that no expense had been spared in the creation of Whiddenhurst Hall. Its opulent staterooms had been built and decorated to impress. And they succeeded in doing so.

He had once read an article that claimed that Whiddenhurst boasted one of only two silver staircases in the world. At the time, he envisioned something like stadium bleachers, and he was eager now to see the real thing. Kyle waited until Parker had departed to fetch Madison before he walked over to examine the staircase. He smiled as he recalled being perplexed as to why anyone would aspire to build a staircase made entirely of silver, how it fit into the architectural design of the house and by what means it would support itself, much less a person's weight.

Kyle was inexplicably relieved to see that Whiddenhurst's staircase was really made of white marble rising imposingly from a black and white parquet floor. The banister alone was made of silver and crafted into an elegant filigree design topped by the Abbott family crest.

Feeling out of place and somehow clumsy in such grand surroundings, Kyle was about to scribble a quick note to Madison saying that he had to leave and would call her later when he looked up to see her descending the magnificent staircase.

"Kyle?" Madison said, sounding surprised but clearly pleased. "I thought you were still in London."

"I drove back this morning. I have some news," he said, conspicuously checking his watch, "but I realize how rude it is to just drop in so I'll call you later."

"Don't be silly," she said as she tried to hide a yawn behind her hand. "Have you eaten?"

"Not yet. Just as the cobbler's children go without shoes, so the baker's son goes without breakfast."

Madison laughed and motioned for him to follow her. "Come on. We'll feed you here, and you can fill me in. I have some news myself."

He felt his stomach lurch as he started to walk after her. "Uh-oh," he said. "Please don't tell me you and Duncan have reunited."

She froze before she slowly turned back to look at him. Her tone was overly casual when she asked, "What makes you say that?"

"I'm a good detective."

"And a funny one. I can't imagine why you would think that was even a possibility," she said as she turned again and headed into yet another imposing room. "I am famished this morning for some reason."

"I bet," Kyle muttered under his breath.

He followed her through several rooms into the dining room, which was elaborately set with china place settings for eight and a massive sideboard that held a half dozen steaming silver chaffing dishes, bowls of fresh berries next to pitchers of cream, milk and orange juice and a large basket with an impressive array of breakfast breads.

"Good morning, ma'am," a young footman greeted her. "May I pour you coffee this morning?"

"Yes, please," she said. "Is anyone else coming down for breakfast?"

"Mr. Rand departed for London already this morning," the footman said, looking warily at Kyle, who noticed a flush rise in Madison's cheeks. While he felt his jaw clench, he was pretty certain he kept his expression impassive.

"Lady Annabel is taking a tray in her room," the footman continued, "but she said she would be down later. I believe Lord Marlborough is still sleeping."

"He's here?" Madison asked.

"Yes, ma'am. He arrived late last night. He said you had invited him."

"Yes, of course, I did. Thank you for taking care of everything," Madison said.

She picked up *The Citizen*, the local Gloucestershire paper, and the *Financial Times* before she sat and thumbed through the news. Kyle filled his plate before he joined her. He looked around the elegant room, warm and inviting with the bright sunshine streaming in through the floor-to-ceilings windows and thought how at odds it seemed with the tragic events of the previous day.

"What news of Chris?" he asked.

"Not a lot, fortunately. The local news has the story of the charity match but nothing about Chris. There is nothing in the *Financial Times* either, but I don't expect they would cover what is really just an obituary at this point."

"I've got it from here, thanks," Kyle said sheepishly as the footman returned and laid a napkin in his lap while he filled his coffee. "That just makes me uncomfortable," he whispered as he watched the young man depart.

"It's his job. He's not an indentured servant. He has chosen this profession, and he takes great pride in it. Much more, in fact, than most other people I know." Madison took a sip of coffee and seemingly reconsidered breakfast as she looked over at the sideboard. She rose, walked over to the buffet and picked up a croissant.

"So what is your news?" he asked as tucked into his meal.

"You first. I'm not sure what mine means, if anything at all."

"I got a call late last night with the results of Chris' autopsy."

"And they called you?" she asked as she returned to the table.

"I'm a detective with Scotland Yard. That's impressive in the countryside."

"That was fast," she said as she sat and laid the uneaten croissant on her bread plate.

Kyle shrugged. "We're not in London. They don't have many suspicious deaths here, and the ME is going out of town for a week so he wanted to get it done."

"And?" she asked, her anxiety causing her to lean forward as he spoke.

"And he had a heart attack."

"Oh," she said, sitting back in her chair.

"Are you disappointed?"

"Of course not. But did they say what caused it?"

"Well," Kyle said as he buttered a scone, "that's the thing. He couldn't find anything that would cause a heart attack. Apart from some signs of the early stages of kidney disease, Chris was, ironically, in excellent physical shape—no high cholesterol, diabetes, or hypertension. He was slim and had no plaque in his arteries and no congenital heart defects. He didn't smoke, wasn't a heavy drinker." He caught himself and looked up at her. "Except, you know, that last day."

"Did they do a toxicology screen?"

"They did, and the lab is working on that. It takes a bit longer out here." Kyle paused when Parker entered with several additional newspapers and focused on his breakfast until the butler departed.

"So we wait for the toxicology report to come back. Do you think now that murder is a distinct possibility?" she asked.

"It is always a possibility. But who had a motive to kill Chris?"

"I'm working on that." She paused, not sure now that she wanted to share what she found last night.

"This is about Duncan, isn't it?" he asked.

"Aaaggh," she exhaled, clearly exasperated with him on the subject of Duncan. "What makes you say that?"

"I keep telling you. I'm a good detective."

She glared at him. "Okay," she said. "It *is* about Duncan. But it may be nothing."

"Madison."

"Duncan backed Chris in his latest development deal, and I think he was in pretty deep. He wouldn't tell me how much, but he said I would be shocked."

She paused. "He was right. I, um, found a copy of a check from Duncan to Chris for ten million pounds."

"You found it?"

"I don't think that's the relevant part. Anyway, Duncan said Chris' company was losing a lot of money. He didn't actually say he'd lost money personally, but I think it's worth looking into."

"And just like that," Kyle said as he snapped his fingers, "we have a possible motive."

"I knew you would say that. You're grasping at anything negative when it comes to Duncan."

"I think we both know I don't have to grasp for something negative when it comes to Duncan." He narrowed his eyes at her. "And don't forget that you're the one who thought the whole deal was questionable enough to bring it to my attention. Can I assume that you did not bring this up with Duncan during—whatever took place last night?"

"Nothing took place last night, so assume away," she said as she started to tear her croissant into small pieces without eating. "So can you look into this without arousing Duncan's antennae? I know from experience that it's easier to get to the bottom of something if he doesn't know that you're trying to do so."

Kyle put his cup down and dropped his head to one side. "So you know that from personal experience, and yet you are still willing to let him back into your life." He shook his head. "Seriously, Madison, what are you thinking?"

"I am thinking this is none of your business. What are the next steps in terms of following up on the deal? I am an excellent researcher, but since neither Duncan's nor Chris' company is public, I think it will be impossible to find anything in the public record about this."

Kyle looked intently at her for a moment but knew he needed to tread lightly on the Duncan issue if he was going to get anywhere. He decided to drop the personal aspect and said, "I saw Jeff Hawthorne yesterday at the match. I can follow up with him."

Madison pulled a face.

"What?" he asked.

"I might have better luck with Mr. Hawthorne. He's always been a little, um, overly friendly towards me. He might try to impress me and let something slip."

"That's too much to ask," Kyle said as he repressed a smile.

Madison stood and took a folded piece of paper from the pocket of her khakis. "There's something else," she said not meeting his eyes as she slowly unfolded the note. "I ran across a memo to Duncan from Chris."

"Ran across?"

She looked up and blinked innocently. "It was on the desk. . .my *father*'s desk. . . out in the open. Listen," she said as she looked down again and tried to decipher her handwriting. "In the event of Chris Grisham's death or disability preventing him from carrying out his responsibilities in regard to the development at Battersea Park, Duncan Rand will assume majority interest and control of Grisham Investments, and in doing so, consider himself reimbursed in full for his investment."

Kyle whistled softly. "That's not good."

Madison sighed dejectedly and sat back down. "No, I thought not."

"It means," Kyle said, "that if Chris dies, Duncan takes over his company."

Kyle had not noticed Annabel Grisham entering the room, and he almost dropped his coffee cup when he saw her standing there, her eyes wide as she looked directly at him. Annabel looked especially pale, and there were dark smudges under her eyes. With her light blond hair and slight build, she had always been an ethereal beauty, but Kyle thought she looked particularly vulnerable this morning.

"Annabel," he said rising too quickly and grimacing as he banged his leg into the table, making the china rattle. "We didn't hear you come in. Come sit down, and I'll pour you a cup of coffee." Annabel walked slowly over to Kyle, and he leaned over and kissed her cheek. "How are you this morning?"

She smiled wanly. "I am still here. I hope I'm not intruding."

"Of course not," Madison said reaching over to squeeze her hand reassuringly as Kyle pulled out the chair next to her. Annabel slid into the chair, and Kyle feared for a moment she would continue the slide all the way to the floor.

Parker was instantly at her side and she nodded when he gestured with the coffee carafe. Annabel weakly brought the cup to her lips and took a small sip of coffee before she put the cup down as though it were too heavy to hold under the weight of her grief. She looked at Madison, her eyes clear and direct. "So where does that leave me?"

Madison blinked and leaned closer to Annabel as she said, "Pardon me?"

"If Duncan now owns my husband's company, where does that leave me?"

Madison exchanged a quick, wary glance with Kyle. "Oh, Annabel, please don't take what I said as a given. I saw a memorandum I probably should not have. I have no idea if it is in force or not. It wasn't a contract, so it actually may be nothing at all."

"I take it you were unaware of this?" Kyle asked softly.

Annabel sighed. "I was unaware of a great deal where my husband was concerned."

An awkward silence fell, and Kyle was relieved when it was broken by Jules' arrival a minute later. He came into the room looking more like a university student in an old St. Andrew's hoodie and jeans than a surgeon of growing renown. Jules leaned down and kissed Madison's cheek.

"Good morning, love. Thanks for letting me bunk here last night," he said yawning. He turned and looked down at Annabel. Kyle felt a jolt at the look on Jules' face as he lightly brushed her cheek and said, "How are you this morning, Annabel?"

"I know everyone means well, but I need you all to stop asking how I am. Please. I feel like hell. I hurt all over, and I want to go back to bed and wake up in five years when this pain has dulled," she said looking up at Jules as her eyes welled with tears. "Please," she whispered.

"Of course," Madison said quickly.

"Done," Kyle agreed.

"I'm sorry," Jules said. "We can't help but care, though," he mumbled as he turned away from her and started filling a plate. Kyle thought he looked embarrassed and tried to remember another instance when he had ever seen Jules self-conscious.

"I need intravenous caffeine this morning," Jules said. "I didn't get here until 3:00am."

"Where were you?" Kyle asked.

"That sounds awfully like a detective asking," Jules said as took the seat opposite Annabel.

"Not meant to. Just curious what you were up to. There's not as much to do at that hour in the country as there is in London," Kyle said as he saw Annabel's lip quiver.

"I was at the hospital," Jules said, looking cautiously now at Annabel. "There was an emergency quadruple bypass. They asked if I would do it."

Annabel stared at him across the table. Her voice was cold and steady when she asked, "Did he live?"

"She, but yes, she did," Jules said, seemingly unable to meet her gaze as he studiously cut his eggs.

"So you managed to save a stranger's life, but you let my husband die?"

"Annabel," Madison gasped.

"No," Jules said, putting his hand up as if to stop her from admonishing Annabel. "Let her speak. If she feels that way, she should be free to say so." He swallowed hard but did not break eye contact with Annabel. "I've thought of nothing else myself since—well, yesterday. But I didn't let him die. I don't know why he did die, but I'm going to get to the bottom of it if I can."

Annabel's eyes remained fixed on Jules' as though she were searching them for the truth. "I'm sorry," she said dully. "That was out of line." She stood and turned to Madison. "I think I'd like to return to my room and rest for awhile. If you'll excuse me."

Jules and Kyle stood quickly as Annabel left the room, clearly trying to stifle her sobs. Kyle saw the look on Jules' face as he watched Annabel go, and it was clear to him that he was suffering right along with her.

Madison reached over to put her hand on Jules' shoulder. "She's in shock. You know she doesn't mean what she's saying."

"I don't know that actually. It seems to me like she has real doubts." He exhaled and pushed back from the table. "I did have an emergency last night, but what I didn't mention was that I also observed Chris' autopsy."

Madison pulled her hand back from Jules and blanched. Kyle winced.

"I know," Jules said. "It's gruesome, but I wanted to find out what went wrong. The autopsy cleared nothing up and, frankly, just added more questions. Chris was a healthy, thirty-year-old male with no underlying pathologies that would have predisposed him to non-trauma related cardiac arrest."

"I thought the autopsy turned up the beginning stages of kidney disease," Kyle said casually.

Jules looked up in weary surprise. "How do you know that?"

Kyle shrugged. "I also heard the results."

Jules sneered. "And were you just waiting to catch me out? Jesus, Ward, what kind of game are you playing?"

"No games—just asking." He got up and walked to the sideboard where he poured another cup of coffee. His back was to Jules when he asked, "Could the hepatitis have played any role?"

Jules choked on the coffee he was sipping. "What . . .are you . . .talking about?" he said between coughs.

"Chris had hepatitis. Surely the autopsy found that," Kyle said as he turned and watched Jules' expression change from confusion to alarm.

"Jesus, I had no idea," Jules said, still coughing a little. "How did that happen?"

"Bad shellfish in St. Bart's last year, I think. It's been awhile, so maybe it's gone now. Anyway, could that have given him a heart attack?"

Jules shook his head. "No—at least not directly. We'll have to wait for the tox report. But I just don't get it."

"This wasn't your fault, mate," Kyle said.

Jules turned to him, an almost defiant look on his face. "Are you sure about that?"

"I'm sure about it, Madison said.

"I appreciate the vote of confidence, Maddy. But quite apart from not really knowing anything about the physiology involved, there are other circumstances of which you are unaware."

Madison flinched as though she took Jules' words with the force of a physical blow. The heat of humiliation flushed her face.

"Come on, that was out of line," Kyle said. "We're all upset, but there's no need to be insulting. The woman has a PhD in Clinical Psychology and a

Master of Science in Neuroscience, for God's sake—both from Oxford. I think she knows a little about physiology."

"I'm sorry," Jules said as he reached over to take Madison's hand. He brought it to his lips and kissed it gently before he let go. "I really am tired, which is certainly not an excuse."

Madison said calmly, "What else aren't we aware of?"

"Nothing. Look, I really am sorry. I'm running on empty," Jules said as he pressed the heel of his palm hard into his forehead. "I've never dealt well with failure, and to be the one to preside over the death of a friend." He shook his head. "Christ, it's just surreal."

"Why don't you see if you can catch a few more hours of sleep—?" Madison said.

"No," Jules said, standing abruptly. He poured and downed an entire cup of coffee in what seemed like a single gulp. "I'm heading back to the hospital. I need to do something useful or I will go mad. Thanks again, Madison."

They watched him leave the room before Kyle casually remarked, "So he never answered. What else don't we know?"

CHAPTER 11

The insistent ringing of the phone the next morning got Madison out of the shower. She grabbed a towel and slipped on the marble floor as she reached for the phone, catching herself on the towel bar before she went down.

She didn't even have a chance to speak before she heard Kyle say, "Chris was murdered."

"What! Oh my God," she said, sitting down hard on the edge of the tub. "I know I wanted to see if this was a possibility, but to be honest, I didn't really think it was true."

"Well, it was. I'm standing outside your flat. Can I come in?"

"I—uh—yeah, just a minute." She disconnected the call.

She hurried down the stairs, dodging Morgan who always approached any accelerated activity as some kind of game. She wanted to answer the door before her neighbors noticed Kyle lurking outside and called in concern. More than one had expressed apprehension that she lived alone, and she knew they all kept an eye out for her.

Madison had returned to London the previous night and was glad to be back in her two-bedroom flat on Coleherne Court. It was a cozy, safe home located on a prestigious block of period mansions and lovely communal gardens. Her friendly neighbors watched out for her well-being while almost always still respecting her privacy.

Madison secured her towel and opened the door while standing behind it, shielding herself from any passersby on the quiet street. Kyle entered with two large cups of takeaway coffee and a bag of doughnuts. His eyes widened and he went slack-jawed when he saw her.

"Wow. I—I didn't realize I was interrupting—something."

She tightened her towel even more firmly around her. "All you interrupted was a shower," she said. "I hurried down because I thought my neighbors might call the police."

"I *am* the police."

"So you are in the position to tell me everything about Chris. Just let me get dressed first. I'll be back in two minutes. Have a doughnut," she said nodding towards his bag.

"I can come with you."

"I don't think so," she called down as she ran back up the stairs to her master bedroom. She quickly discarded the towel and threw on a pair of jeans and an Edinburgh University sweatshirt given to her as a joke.

"Why do you think Chris' death has not made the news yet?" Kyle asked when she returned downstairs as he was leafing through *The Times, The Telegraph,* the *Daily Mail* and the *Daily*

Telegraph lying on Madison's coffee table. "He was a pretty high-profile guy."

"Why do you say that?" Madison asked, peering into the bag to see if anything was worth blowing her diet over.

"He was an earl, a friend of the prince's—and a financial heavyweight."

"Not a heavyweight, I'm afraid. But *The Financial Times* is doing an obituary on him next week; they couldn't get it in time for the service tomorrow. But your news this morning puts the whole situation in an entirely new league, and *that* would make the news, especially in the tabloids. Can we keep it quiet?"

"Yeah, I think so. For now, anyway."

"Tell me what you learned," she said as she curled up on the end of her sofa.

"He died of cardiac arrest brought on by acute salt poisoning, exacerbated by the sodium bi-carbonate administered by the EMTs in the ambulance."

Madison's face fell. "That Jules asked be administered."

"That Jules asked what be administered?" Kyle said.

"The sodium bi-carbonate. He was calling the shots to the EMTs, remember?"

"Yeah. Well, no, I had actually forgotten that. That may have pushed Chris over the edge, as it were, but that wasn't enough to cause acute salt poisoning. In fact, the ME said it was pretty standard procedure when somebody has a heart attack. It was the champagne Chris was drinking that had twenty times the normal level of sodium in it. I don't know how he could have stood drinking it, but maybe the peach flavor and the sugar in the champagne covered it a little."

"He was already so hammered by that point he might not even have known," Madison said.

"Maybe. Combine that with fact that Chris suffered from the beginning stages of polycystic kidney disease and the residual hepatitis, thus compromising both his kidney and liver functions, and it produced a confluence of events that gave him a heart attack on the field, with the bi-carb resulting in cardiac arrest in the rig. Unbelievable really."

"Maybe it was an accident."

"That there was that much salt in the champagne?" Kyle said, smirking. "Be real. We'll check with the manufacturer, but sodium isn't an ingredient in champagne."

"Actually," Madison said, "sodium *is* an ingredient in champagne. There's a chemical called sodium metabisulfite that is used as a preservative in champagne."

Kyle shook his head and shoved his hands in his pockets. "How would you even know something like that?"

"I toured the wine country in the Loire Valley a couple of years ago, and we all had a little too much to drink one night at dinner with the winemaker at one of the vineyards. I don't remember which one. Anyway, apparently it's not uncommon for people to be allergic to it, so maybe it really was a manufacturing error of some kind," she said, knowing her tone a little too hopeful. Then she sighed. "So is this an official investigation now?"

"Yes, as of right now. I caught the case, since I was on the scene. The local constabulary is unequipped to deal with a murder investigation, so the Yard has taken over. And there's something else."

"Uh-oh."

"There was formaldehyde in the oysters."

Madison's eyes widened, her face momentarily contorted. "What?! I don't believe it. I mean there could have been a manufacturing error with the champagne—."

"I don't think so."

"But formaldehyde in the oysters? No way that could have been a way to preserve them in the heat—?"

"Oh, Madison," Kyle said as he shook his head.

She sighed. "Okay, okay. Do you have any suspects?"

He nodded. "A lot."

"I was afraid of that."

"So in all of your quasi-medical training have you run across the information I just told you of the clinical reason behind Chris' death?"

"I beg to differ on the characterization of 'quasi,' but I'll let that go because I'm not a medical doctor," she said. "And no, I haven't. For all I know, this may be first year medical school stuff, but it's new to me. And frankly, it sounds implausible."

"Wouldn't that work to someone's advantage?"

"You mean cause him to die of something that sounds implausible? So no one would be looking into it?" she said.

"That's exactly what I mean. I think only medically trained personnel could conceivably know something like this."

"Jules," Madison said, alarmed. "Are you really thinking it was Jules? Why would he possibly do that?"

"I don't know the why yet. And I didn't say it was Jules. You said that, which may be telling. Frankly, I think Duncan is the one I should be looking into," Kyle said and then waited for her reaction.

"Duncan couldn't have done anything like this. Don't be absurd."

"Which part of your anatomy is so distressed at that thought? 'Cause it sure doesn't seem to be your brain."

"And it doesn't seem to be yours either," Madison snapped. "I don't know what's going on between you and Duncan, but accusing him of murder is low even for you."

"Even for me, huh?" Kyle said, standing. "I find it interesting that you are not horrified to think that Jules—a man who has taken the Hippocratic Oath—could have knocked off a mutual friend but are adamant that Duncan could not. I think something is skewing your perspective here."

"I'm sorry," she said as she reached out to him. "I really am sorry. Please sit back down. I think either possibility is so shocking that we are not seeing, or reacting, clearly here."

He looked down at her, his eyes narrowing suspiciously.

"Really, I mean it. Let's talk about this a minute. Don't go."

He sat. "Okay, Madison. This is where your training actually does come in. You know that people do things that no one thought them capable of all the time. You know they act in ways contrary to their nature and almost always in their own best interests."

Madison leaned her head back against the sofa and closed her eyes. She put her hand over her eyes thinking it might help her concentrate. "Criminal justice wasn't my focus at university, but I did take several classes in criminal behavioral science," she said.

"I know you did. Because of Charles," Kyle said softly.

Madison swallowed hard but her voice was calm when she said, "We don't know what Charles' killer's motivation was because we don't know *who* he—or she—was." She exhaled. "But most of us generally dissociate ourselves from murderers by assuming that all killers are psychotic." She opened her eyes and looked directly at Kyle. "I'm sure you know that most are not. Psychiatrists don't know precisely how those who have killed are different from those who haven't, because nearly all of us have the same motivations at one time or another as those who have actually murdered."

"That's a charming thought," Kyle said.

She nodded. "Isn't it, though? Most murders are very personal matters. In your line of work, I'm sure you know that in three out of four cases, the murderer and victim know each other; in one out of four, they're related by blood or marriage. So that's where we need to start." Madison started chewing the inside of her lip. "So that means that someone close to Chris was, in all likelihood, his killer."

"That's not always the case. But it is a good place to start. Are you okay being this close to a murder investigation? It may be too much for you, all things considered with your brother and all."

Her voice was resigned when she said, "You sound like Duncan."

"No," he said emphatically. "I do not sound like Duncan. I care about how this affects you. I think Duncan was trying to throw you off the possibility that Chris had actually been murdered by making you feel irrationally emotional."

Madison was struck by how unpleasant a possibility that was, but she had to admit that it was not implausible. And then another worrying thought occurred to her. "Who else knows about the results?" she asked.

"Do you mean who else knows Chris was actually murdered? No one. You and I are the only ones at this point.." He shrugged a little sheepishly. "And, well, you know, the person who killed him."

"Yeah, right. That's good. Then I'm going to try to have a drink with Jeff Hawthorne," Madison said.

Kyle pulled a face. "I'm not sure I'm comfortable with that. He's a creepy guy and a possible murder suspect. You need to be careful."

"I'm a grown woman."

"Yeah, I know. And grown women never get attacked. And grown men are never murdered—in broad daylight in front of hundreds of people."

She stared at him. "Point taken. You can shadow me—if that is what they really call it—if you want."

"Maybe I will. Why drinks, though? I think I should just call him in for questioning."

"I think he's a suspicious guy. Being under-handed yourself tends to make you suspicious of others, and I was hoping that having a drink would seem less like an inquisition."

"And more like a come-on," Kyle said, his brow furrowed. "That's risky for you."

"I know. Moving on—you know about the personal killings, but there are 'business killings,' too. And not all of them are committed by the American mafia, or by the drug cartels."

He shook his head. "I don't think Hawthorne is sophisticated enough to have pulled this one off, but he's certainly worth talking to. Just be careful."

Madison nodded. She knew she was trying too hard to convince herself that Chris's murder must have been a "business killing" by someone who had been cheated or betrayed by his development deals, or by some kind of misunderstanding. It wouldn't make him any less dead and it wouldn't ease the pain. But it would absolve her friends. And then the realization hit and her hands were instantly clammy.

Duncan may have been a friend of Chris'. But if he were the murderer, it would have been business.

CHAPTER 12

Chris Grisham, The Right Honorable The Earl of Grisham, was laid to rest on a Tuesday. He was buried in the Grisham family crypt in the cemetery of St. Alban's Cathedral just north of Greater London in Hertfordshire.

Kyle and Madison had arranged to attend the service together, and he was waiting in front of his flat when a large, formidable looking vehicle pulled up to the curb directly in front of him. The windows of the car were darkened, and he did not recognize Madison behind the wheel until she put the window down.

"Would you like to drive?" she asked.

"No. I wouldn't want to risk it. What is this?" he asked as he swept his hand over the length of the car.

"It's a Bentley Mulsanne," she said, clearly ignoring his answer as she opened the door, got out, and walked around the car. "It's big and heavy, I'll admit, but it's an easy car to drive."

Frustrated, he watched her slide into the front passenger seat. Rather than argue on the street, however, he slid into the driver's seat. "Is this your new car?" he said as he took in the hand-stitched leather and rich wood paneled dashboard.

"No, of course not. This is my father's car. I thought it was more appropriate for the funeral than my little Cygnet. My parents wanted to come, but Dad was called out of town on an emergency."

"Is there a secret to driving this car I should know?" Kyle asked as he slipped it in gear, feeling the power of the engine beneath his hands.

"Don't hit anything."

"Good tip, thanks. I hadn't thought of that," he said as he pulled the massive vehicle into traffic. He had to admit that it felt as though it floated beneath them as he drove.

They were en route to the cathedral when Madison's mobile rang with the ringtone of *The Twilight Zone*. Kyle gripped the steering wheel harder when he heard the tenor of Madison's voice. The conversation was brief.

"Who was that?" he asked pretty sure he already knew the answer.

"That was Duncan," she said as she disconnected the call.

"And he has the ringtone from *The Twilight Zone*?" he asked, smiling in spite of the situation.

"Yes."

"And that is—."

"The height of passive aggressive."

Kyle snickered. "And how is Mr. Rand this morning?"

"He sounds okay. He said Annabel called this morning and asked if we could all ride to the funeral together. She has apparently had all she can bear of Chris' mother and sister and would like a little respite so she can prepare herself for the service."

"Where are we meeting them?"

"Chris and Annabel's." A cloud fell over Madison's face. "Or just Annabel's now, I guess."

Kyle turned the Bentley around and drove towards the Grisham townhouse. They arrived less than fifteen minutes later to find Duncan leaning against a very large, two-tone sedan and checking his mobile. Kyle smoothly pulled the Bentley to a stop less than a foot from Duncan, who did not flinch or even look up.

"Is he driving the hearse?" Kyle asked.

"Shush," Madison said although he thought he heard suppressed laughter in her voice. "That's one of his cars. It's a Rolls Royce Phantom and is not so very different from this one."

"Except," Kyle said as he opened the door, "that this one belongs to your father, who is in his sixties. Wait there, I'll come around." Before Kyle could get out and around the car to get Madison's door, Duncan had beaten him to it.

"Good morning, Madison," Duncan said as he took her hand and helped her out. "Kyle," he said with a curt nod.

They mounted the stairs to the townhouse with Madison in the neutral middle. Kyle was shocked at Annabel's appearance when she answered the door. It had been less than forty-eight hours since

132

he had last seen her, but she looked even thinner than usual, and the dark bluish smudges under her eyes had the disconcerting effect of making her look as though she had been beaten up. He could not help but think that in a way, she had.

Madison leaned forward and kissed Annabel's cheek. "How are you, darling?"

Annabel's lip twitched, and she put her hand up to cover her mouth. ""I can't spend any more time with Chris' mother and sister. Their grief is," Annabel said, wringing her hands, "overwhelming. I can't breathe here."

"I understand. I am so sorry," Madison said as she started to slip around Annabel. "I'd just like to pay my respects to his mother and then we can leave—."

"No," Annabel said with such vehemence they all stopped. She exhaled slowly and wrapped her arms around waist. "I'm sorry. But please, not now. There will be plenty of time later. I have got to get out of this house before I scream," she said through clenched teeth before she grabbed Kyle's arm. "Please," she said again. "*Please*."

"Yes, of course," he said glancing at Madison with an almost desperate plea for confirmation in his eyes. She nodded once so Kyle offered his arm to Annabel as she teetered down the stairs. He was uncertain whether her instability stemmed from her emotional state or her impossibly high shoes but he was prepared to catch her if she started to fall.

Annabel and Kyle reached the sidewalk first and stood before the two massive sedans. "Who is driving?" she asked.

Duncan and Kyle responded in perfect unison, "I am."

Kyle looked questioningly over his shoulder at Duncan. "I'm good either way," Duncan said, shrugging.

"Let's take this one," Annabel said, pointing to Duncan's Phantom. Kyle almost laughed out loud when she continued, "It looks more appropriate for a funeral procession."

Duncan moved swiftly to open the rear doors of his car, but Annabel walked slowly around the vehicle and stood resolutely before the front passenger seat. Kyle moved quickly to open that door while Duncan helped Madison into the backseat.

"I'm sorry we couldn't be of more help to you in making the arrangements yesterday," Madison said as they pulled away.

"I did nothing," Annabel said dully. "His mother and sister handled everything, with almost no input from me. I tried and was rebuffed. They always treated me like an interloper in my own marriage. They never liked me when he was alive, so there is really no further need to fake it now that he's dead. The funeral is at St. Alban's, which is the only detail I know."

Kyle had no idea how to handle this kind of conversation, and in his growing unease with the tone of it, he decided to remain silent and let the professional take care of it.

"Where are your parents?" Madison asked. "I thought they would be staying with you."

"No," Annabel said tightly. "They are not here. They are not coming."

Kyle glanced at Madison and saw her go pale. "I—I am so sorry," she said quietly. "I would have come sooner had I realized."

"There's nothing to be sorry about. My father is very ill, and Mummy didn't think she should leave him."

"I'm so—."

"And, of course," Annabel continued, "Mummy could never stand Chris. She thought I married beneath my potential. I am not sure she is anything other than relieved that he is gone."

Madison opened her mouth to respond, apparently thought better of it and closed it again. Kyle thought that there was really no appropriate follow up to that statement and Madison and Duncan must have agreed as they all lapsed into an uneasy silence for the remainder of the drive to the cathedral.

The car park was already full when they arrived. Annabel's voice sounded completely detached when she said, "Chris was popular. People really seemed to like him. I'm relieved to see that it's crowded."

She unbuckled her seatbelt and continued in an emotionless tone. "Or, I suppose, people might be expecting to see William and Kate. I'm not actually sure if they are coming, but that could be a draw."

Madison dropped the compact she was using to touch up her makeup and Kyle patted her hand. "She is in shock," he mouthed to her. She only nodded as she reached to retrieve her makeup from under the seat.

Duncan reached out to Annabel and patted her shoulder. "He was loved, Annabel. We all know that, because we loved him, too. I'll drop you, Madison and Kyle at the front of the church, and I will go park."

"No," Annabel said firmly. "I would rather walk with you."

"Annabel," Madison said softly and she leaned towards the front seat. "You are his widow. You cannot walk from the car park."

"I can," Annabel insisted. "And I will. I will wait in the car with you until the limo arrives, and we can all go in together so I won't be the center of attention. I just can't bear it, especially in light of— everything."

So the four of them sat there in the car in an awkward silence as they waited for the limo carrying Chris' mother and sister to arrive. Kyle knew any attempt at conversation would only exacerbate the unpleasantness of the situation so he did not attempt small talk.

He was seldom in a suit and tie and he pulled uncomfortably at his collar. The atmosphere within the car was tense to the point of being suffocating, and Kyle was glad that Duncan kept the engine running and the air conditioning on.

As they waited, William and Kate arrived with a single personal protection officer and walked discreetly into the church. Kyle thought he heard Annabel murmur Jules' name when he arrived with Gig Stockton, and he watched as Annabel's eyes followed them into the church. He was starting to feel so self-conscious with the four of them just sitting there that he began tapping his foot against the door until Madison threw him a look that made him stop mid-tap. He then watched Sydney Atwood and Peyton Taylor arrive shortly after and slunk down a little so they did not see him.

Madison nodded politely when Jeff Hawthorne waved a little too enthusiastically to her, but she looked horrified when it appeared he was going to come over to the car to speak with her. He apparently thought better of it, nodded and followed the other mourners into the church.

The limousine carrying the family finally arrived, and as Chris' mother and sister got out, so did Duncan, Annabel, Madison and Kyle. Annabel clung to Duncan's hand as they walked into the church right behind her in-laws. Kyle thought he saw the flash of a photographer's bulb and heard the whirl of a camera coming from behind the bushes off to his right, but he felt it would make a scene to even acknowledge that, much less try to stop it. If necessary, he would flash his badge but at this point everyone was so overwrought that he feared it would not take much for Jules and Duncan to go after the man, which would turn the event into an even bigger story. He wanted to leave his old friend what remaining dignity he had by not allowing his funeral to turn into a public spectacle.

Over seven hundred fifty mourners from the surrounding counties attended the young earl's funeral service, but even that number was dwarfed by the enormity of the cathedral. Despite her wishes, Annabel was, of course, still the center of attention as she walked the full length of the nave. She looked neither right nor left but kept her head held high, and her eyes straight forward as she slid into the front pew. Duncan, Madison and Kyle started to slip into the pew directly behind hers, but she did not let go of Duncan's arm, and they were all forced to sit beside her. Kyle felt certain he saw a look of disapproval flash across the imperious face of Chris' mother, and he nodded self-consciously.

The service was dignified and somber. It was not the celebration of Chris' life Kyle would have chosen for his old mate as it was almost completely devoid of Chris' humanity and what fun he had been in university and before the years of professional wandering had started to take its toll. But it was comforting in a familiar, formal sort of way. Jules gave the eulogy, and he did a beautiful, almost inspiring job. Kyle wondered if it gave him some small measure of comfort towards alleviating his crushing sense of guilt.

Annabel had somehow found the courage to defy the wishes of Chris' family by insisting on a private burial and a low-key reception at her home after the service. The burial service itself would be brief, and Madison seemed relieved that Annabel had at least consented to ride in the limo with Chris' family, and as she watched them depart she dialed a number on her mobile.

"Peyton, it's Madison," she said quietly. "I saw you leave early, and I just wanted to confirm you would be there to greet the limo at the house after the burial. We're stuck in traffic from the funeral, and there's a funky dynamic going on between Annabel and Chris' mum today. Great, thanks. See you soon."

"That dynamic has existed since they married," Kyle said as she hung up. "I suppose this will be the last time they have to deal with it." Madison gasped. "Oh, I didn't mean anything by it. It just is what it is."

"It's okay. I know what you meant," she said as she turned around in the front seat and looked at Kyle. "You were closer to Chris than the rest of us. Do you know what that's all about between Annabel and his mother?"

It took a minute for Kyle to answer as he watched Duncan skillfully navigate the traffic departing the cathedral. By now several police officers had shown up, and he watched as they blocked traffic so the Range Rover carrying William and Kate could pull out ahead of the crowd. William himself was at the wheel, and Kyle thought he looked rather sheepish as he nodded to the officer and drove away.

"I was close to Chris at university," Kyle said. "But that was a long time ago. He played things pretty close to his vest in the past few years."

"As most men do," Madison said.

Duncan smiled.

Kyle nodded and said, "As most men do. But I do vaguely remember that Chris once said something before they married about his parents— his father was still alive then—thinking he could 'do better.' I thought that was a little harsh, but I didn't get a straight answer when I asked him what he thought they meant by that."

"Interesting," Madison said.

"What?"

"Annabel said something similar about her parents' reaction to Chris. I'm still appalled that they weren't here." She shook her head. "That's poor form at best, and really offensive at worst."

"I don't know much about Annabel's parents, so I don't know what they were referring to either, or why they didn't come to the funeral. I think Chris' parents were referring to Annabel's lack of—er."

"Money?" Duncan said as he met Kyle's eyes in the rearview mirror.

"Yes," Kyle said. "I mean it's not like she was poor—like, you know, me. But she wasn't going to bring the kind of cash infusion the Grishams needed to save the estate in Somerset. I think that was very definitely what the Earl and Countess wanted for their son, or perhaps for themselves."

"They lost the estate two years ago, didn't they?" Duncan asked.

Kyle nodded. "Yes, and then Chris' father died. Chris always thought that the shock of losing Rutherford Manor caused his fatal heart attack. I think it definitely added additional stress to an already tense marriage."

Madison furrowed her brow as she asked, "Because he resented Annabel for not 'bailing him out?'"

"Oh, I don't think it was anything that overt, or even conscious on his part. I think, in a way, they both resented one another for not having the financial wherewithal to enable them to live the life of, well—."

"Some of his friends?" Madison said quietly.

"Something like that," Kyle replied as they finally pulled out of the car park.

"It didn't start out that way. They were so infatuated with one another at university," Madison said, a sad disappointment evident in her tone.

"It never does *start out* that way, Madison," Duncan said, gunning the heavy car's engine as the Rolls accelerated into the traffic on the parkway. "But when people bring secrets into a relationship, it is always a shock when they start to out."

Madison looked at him in surprise. "Did they have secrets in their marriage?"

"Everyone has secrets," Duncan said.

CHAPTER 13

Less than an hour later, Madison, Duncan and Kyle had arrived at the reception back at the Grisham's lovely little townhouse, just off Pelham Crescent in Kensington. Madison reached for the doorbell before she realized the door was slightly ajar. She knocked lightly before pushing the door open and entering the front hall with Duncan and Kyle following closely behind her.

There were already several people milling about, and Madison saw that Annabel was ensconced in a corner of the small living room seated between Chris' mother and sister looking absolutely miserable. Several mourners filed past them as though they were in some kind of ghastly receiving line, and Annabel nodded and smiled wanly. Her blank expression gave Madison the impression that she was going through the motions in a daze from which she would remember nothing. It was, she decided, probably for the best that she did not.

Madison started as someone touched the small of her back and she turned to see Peyton standing next to her. She was relieved to see her, and Madison kissed her cheek.

"I didn't realize she had asked you to coordinate this," Madison said.

"She didn't exactly ask. But she seems so lost, and I wanted to help." Peyton did not take her gaze from Annabel when she said, "Annabel always had a tendency to get rolled by the dowager countess—and the earl when he was still alive—and I didn't think that dynamic should permitted to happen this time. It is her house, after all—and Chris was her husband. So I was a bit pushy about it."

"Why is she so intimidated by them?" Madison asked, subconsciously dropping her voice to a whisper.

Peyton shrugged. "They're aristocratic. You Brits are far more impressed by that than us Yanks."

"Annabel is a member of the aristocracy now, too. It doesn't seem to have made any difference."

"Oh, ho," Peyton said, stifling a small chuckle. "Even I know that being to the manor born counts far more than who you—um, marry."

"Speaking of," Madison said, dropping her voice even further, "who did Chris' sister—."

"Caroline."

"Right. Who did Caroline marry?"

"I've never met him," Peyton said looking around. "But I think he's here. He's wealthy, some kind of bigwig in manufacturing something or other, but not a member of the aristocracy either. But Caroline and her mother are extremely close. She went to live with her daughter after their dad died, thereby sparing Annabel that trauma."

"So Annabel is the odd man out, now that Chris is gone."

"In more ways than one, from what I hear. Their father had a pretty elaborate trust of what family money there is left from what used to be a pretty substantial fortune—it's several million pounds, like five or so—and it says that if Chris predeceases Annabel at any point before his thirty-fifth birthday, she gets none of that inheritance. It all goes to—."

"Caroline."

"Yep. Uh-oh," Peyton said looking at Jeff Hawthorne as he made his way determinedly towards them. "This guy keeps showing up like a bad penny, and he gives me the creeps."

"I actually want to talk to him this time, though."

Peyton squeezed her arm as she said, "Don't let me horn in on that conversation then. Good luck," she whispered and she slipped away just as Jeff Hawthorne arrived.

"Madison," Hawthorne said as he leaned in to kiss her on both cheeks. "It seems inappropriate to tell you at a funeral that you look lovely—."

She smiled slightly, giving her best impression of her mother's perfected *I am acknowledging something for which you undoubtedly think I owe you a thank you while letting you know at the same time that the comment is, indeed, inappropriate* look.

Hawthorne stopped, looking momentarily confused. "But you do," he said in a smaller voice.

"Mr. Hawthorne," she said coolly as she nodded.

"Jeff, please."

She smiled briefly again, managing to interject zero warmth or encouragement into it. "Jeff, then. You have my deepest condolences. I'm sure this is very hard on you."

"It is always difficult to lose someone so young."

Madison found that an odd reaction to losing a supposedly dear friend and valued business partner, particularly in light of the fact that she guessed Hawthorne himself to be no more than thirty-five. He was staring directly at her, and Madison found the intensity of his gaze disconcerting, as though he were searching her face for a sign of something she could not even fathom.

"If you are a religious person, you could say this was 'God's will,'" he continued.

"I suppose one could say that. Without commenting on my own spiritual leanings, I still find it tragic to lose such a dear friend. And particularly one with such potential."

"Ah, potential. Indeed, there was a great loss of potential. Very sad."

"How are you holding up, under the circumstances?"

Hawthorne shrugged. "Fair to middling, I'd have to say."

Madison winced. She looked at his smoothly handsome face and dark blond hair clearly styled to casual perfection and wondered, not for the first time, what exactly it was about Jeff Hawthorne that made her skin crawl.

"You know," Hawthorne continued, "I was really always the business side of things while Chris was more the creative side. Or what it is all those MBAs and politician would have called him?" he asked before snapping his fingers and pointing directly at her. "A visionary. Chris was a visionary. Alas, he didn't always have the business acumen to figure out how to realize that vision. There were," he said, looking around covertly as if to ensure he was not overhead, yet seemingly making no attempt to lower his voice, "irregularities in his accounting practices."

"What does that mean, Mr.—er, Jeff?"

"We should talk. Can I meet you for a drink later today or this week?"

Madison glanced at Kyle who was rapidly approaching them with a determined look on his face. "Yes," she said quickly. "How about tomorrow? In the Vertigo bar in the financial district, at 8:00pm?"

"Perfect, see you then," Hawthorne said, lifting her hand to his lips and kissing it while looking up at her with heavily lidded eyes. Madison felt a slight wave of nausea flow over her, and she recoiled from his touch. Hawthorne looked at Kyle and departed hastily just as he walked up.

"Classy," Kyle said as he watched him walk away.

"How in God's name did Chris Grisham get mixed up with such a person?" Madison asked quietly.

"Not just Chris Grisham but Duncan Rand, too," Duncan said as he joined the two of them.

"Seriously," Madison said as she wiped the back of her hand with her napkin. "The ick factor with him is sky high. What happened there?"

Duncan glanced suspiciously at Kyle who looked at him innocently. "Can I get you a beer, Dunc?" Kyle asked.

"No. Thank you. And don't call me Dunc." He looked around the room. "Come into the study for a minute." He gave Kyle a once over. "Both of you. Please."

Madison and Kyle followed Duncan through the dining room and into a small study where Chris had tried so hard to find his way professionally. Madison knew he had struggled since university, and she found the tokens of his small successes—two plexiglass cubes marking small real estate deals, a T-shirt with the name of an investment company and a hat with the logo of another—heart-breaking as she looked around at the detritus of unfulfilled possibilities. The one impressive thing she saw in the office was a rather elaborate model of what she assumed was the proposed development of Battersea Park.

Kyle unceremoniously sat in the chair behind Chris' desk.

"Kyle!" she said, as she put her hands on her hips.

"What? He's not using it anymore, Madison."

She looked at him, exasperated. Instead of pursuing that issue, however, Madison turned to Duncan. "So—Jeff Hawthorne. What is up with that?"

Duncan exhaled. "My involvement with Grisham Investments was not about Jeff Hawthorne. It was strictly about Chris. But, admittedly, I didn't do any due diligence—or not enough, anyway. It was a bad investment, for a number of reasons, not the least of which is because Chris wasn't exactly— stable. He had had a revolving series of partners over the years. Apparently none stayed with him more than six months. I actually thought briefly in the beginning that Hawthorne was the first good move he had made in awhile."

Kyle nodded slowly and said, "Hawthorne had been considered something of a finance prodigy in his mid-twenties, but since then he has come under investigation by the Financial Services Authority for insider trading on more than one occasion. No charges have ever actually been filed against him, but he was sacked by the financial services giant UBS for improprieties in the sub-prime mortgage crisis, and he left under a heavy cloud of suspicion."

Madison looked at him with a surprise bordering on incredulity.

Kyle shrugged. "I *am* a detective."

"What, exactly, are you investigating?" Duncan asked tightly, his body clearly tense.

Kyle smiled. "I don't know yet. I'm just gathering information."

"On?"

"On everything. And everyone. It's what I do." Kyle's smile was a little cooler this time.

"I see," Duncan said. Madison saw realization dawn on his face, and his eyes widened. "Is this some kind of investigation into Chris' death?"

Neither Madison nor Kyle spoke.

"No way. Do you think there's anything suspicious about that? He died of a heart attack," Duncan said, his tone rising uncharacteristically.

Madison's voice was cool but gentle when she replied, "Don't you find that in and of itself a little suspicious? He was only thirty years old. And in really good shape."

Duncan's face relaxed, and his voice was softer when he said, "Not everyone who dies was murdered, sweetheart. I know the fact that Charles was murdered makes any shocking death kind of seem that way. But it's just not the case."

Kyle glared at Duncan.

Madison felt as though she had been punched in the stomach. It had been ten years, and she had yet to reach the point where any mention of her only brother's death did not reopen the shock and grief of that time. She briefly wondered if Duncan was right.

"I think you're out of line, mate," Kyle said in a clearly controlled tone. "This isn't an official meeting. And you're the one who wanted to tell us something in private. What was that?"

Duncan stared at him a minute, his eyes narrowing. Kyle leaned back in the chair, put his hands behind his head and stared back, his gaze intense and unblinking.

Duncan exhaled, clearly frustrated. "I pulled the latest financials from Grisham Investments last night."

"Did you see anything you hadn't seen before?" Madison asked.

Duncan sighed. "I think I saw it before, but it clearly wasn't as meaningful to me then. There was a lot of smoke and mirrors at the time, and I knew that. I guess I overlooked it and just viewed my participation as a bailout of an old friend rather than a sound financial investment. I haven't been carefully tracking the information he's been periodically sending me, but I see now that there are real inconsistencies in his numbers."

"What kind of inconsistencies?" Kyle asked.

"Embezzlement kind of inconsistencies. I've asked my firm's CFO to go over everything in detail, but even my quick examination shows a company hemorrhaging cash disproportionate to the expenses needed for operations, particularly when the projects weren't getting done."

"Which means in layman's terms that someone was stealing?" Madison said.

"That's what it means to me," Duncan said.

"Do you think it was Chris?" Kyle asked.

"I have no idea who it was, or what his—."

"Or her," Madison said.

"Or her motivation was. Chris and Jeff were the principals, but there were over twenty other people who worked there. I don't know who kept their books."

"Jeff Hawthorne," Madison said. "Well, let me restate that. He handled the 'business side,' in his words. He didn't say he actually kept the books. He's an interesting guy."

"Interesting in what way exactly?" Duncan asked a little too casually as he perched on the edge of the desk and fiddled with a paperweight.

"Perplexing," she said. "He ticks all the boxes on the surface of what looks good. But as Kyle mentioned, he's gotten himself into a lot of trouble over the years but has never really been caught. Being under investigation so many times isn't a positive. If he hasn't been caught, that means to me not that he's innocent but that he's just really good at being bad."

"It certainly seems possible he could be pleased that Chris is dead," Duncan said. "And he was at the polo match."

Madison blinked several times. Her voice was almost breathless when she asked, "Does that mean you think Chris was murdered?"

Kyle's eyes widened and his head fell to one side as he looked at her.

But Duncan only smiled. "I didn't say anything about murder."

CHAPTER 14

When he returned to the reception, Kyle spent several almost unbearable minutes speaking with the Dowager Countess of Grisham. Chris' mother was a formidable woman, but for some reason he never could figure out, she had always liked Kyle and she kept her gaze steadfastly on him, refusing even to acknowledge the other people standing behind him waiting to offer their condolences. No one was more surprised than he when her eyes teared up and she dabbed the corners with a delicately embroidered handkerchief. He stood there awkwardly, not knowing whether he should pretend not to see her tears or to put his arms around her. He was about to do the latter when Sydney approached them. The Dowager Countess' eyes darkened at her arrival.

Sydney's tone was exceedingly respectful when she said, "I beg your pardon, your ladyship, but there is an urgent call for Kyle. They said it could not wait."

Chris' mother sniffed softly, nodded her head to Kyle in quiet dismissal and turned to the next guest in line, all traces of emotion neatly back in the box.

Sydney took Kyle's hand and led him away. "You looked like you needed a drink," she said pushing her own into his hand and waving at the waiter.

"Let me take my call first, and then I'll join you."

She smiled at him, her eyes lit with a twinkle of mischief. "You are adorable, detective. I just thought you needed saving."

"No call?"

Sydney shook her head slowly. "No call. I am just your lady in shining armor sent to rescue you."

Kyle leaned back from Sydney's grasp, his headed tilted and his brow furrowed suspiciously. He scratched the back of his neck slowly. Having never been on the receiving end of one of Sydney's infamous flirtations, he could not help but be wary now at her behavior. She laughed, a deep-throated, sexy laugh that he felt reverberate through his lower body. He had always found Sydney gorgeous, but somehow dangerous. She had always had a short attention span when it came to the opposite sex, and she toyed with men for sport, spending considerable time and energy to hook them only to throw them back when her mission had been accomplished. Fortunately, she had always hunted outside their little group of friends—until now apparently.

"What's going on, Syd?" Kyle asked, trying to keep his tone light.

She took a highball glass of amber liquid off the waiter's tray. "Nothing's going on," she said stepping close enough to him so only he could hear.

He inhaled her perfume and lost his focus. Sydney continued, "It's a sad day and reminders of the brevity of life make me want to reach out and grab hold."

"Of?"

"Life," she said as smiled slyly before she downed a third of her drink.

Kyle smiled, too. "I assume that's not ginger ale you're putting away."

She sighed. "Don't be a stick in the mud, Kyle. You and I have never really gotten to know each other." Sydney leaned even closer so her chest brushed his arm as she whispered in his ear, "We really should change that."

"Ah, so, like, you want to hear my life story? Where I grew up? What my father does for a living? The name of my first dog? That kind of thing?"

"No," she said with a dismissive wave. "That kind of stuff has never interested me. I want to know who you are. And what you can do." She ran her fingers lightly up his arm.

Kyle was disappointed in his physical reaction to her, and he knew he should extricate himself from this situation. But he was intrigued on too many levels. He decided to play along.

"Hmmm," Kyle said. "What I can do, huh? I can take you out for a drink. Is that what you had in mind?"

She stepped back and looked up at him up through eyelashes framing those mesmerizing violet eyes. "It's a start."

"Let me say good-bye. I'll meet you outside. Do you have a car?"

"I do. I'll be idling out front, waiting for you."

Jesus, Kyle thought as he went to find Madison, *I am out of my depth here.* His palms were sweaty, and he wiped them on the cocktail napkin from his untouched drink. He quickly found Madison and she stepped away from the group she was speaking to when he approached.

"I'm heading out," he said. "I'll find my own way home."

She looked at him, her eyebrows drawn together and her voice low when she said, "With Sydney? Really? That's dangerous ground."

"I know Sydney. I'm just interested in what she's got to say."

"Oh, yeah. I'm sure she's interested in a good long talk. She specializes in that."

"I'm a big boy, Madison."

"I don't think you know her very well, Kyle," Madison said. "She was never all that nice, and she's a little like a wounded animal since the accident."

"What does that mean?"

"She bites."

"I'm up-to-date on my shots. I'm investigating here."

Madison nodded. "Is that what they're calling it now?"

"Look, she approached me. So she's either looking to impart information or fishing for it, which can be just as revealing. Either way, I'd like to know what her agenda is. If there's one thing I know for certain, Kyle Ward has never been on her agenda before."

"Don't sell yourself short. Just remember, she blows hot one minute and cold the next."

"I beg your pardon," he said, his eyes widening in mock horror.

"Oh come off it, Kyle. You know what I mean. Just be careful."

"Thanks, Mom. I promise I will be. I'll call you later." He kissed her cheek and left quickly before he could be waylaid by any of the other guests.

When Kyle stepped outside he saw a silver Jaguar XK convertible idling in front with Sydney behind the wheel. "Does anyone in this group drive a normal car?" he asked as he started to go around to the passenger side.

"Define normal," she said. She smiled and slid over the center console and into the bucket-like passenger seat in a way that made Kyle's stomach hurt. "You drive. I've had too much to drink."

"Where are we going?" he asked stepping into the car.

"Hmmm," she murmured. "How shall I answer that?"

"With something I can key into the nav system."

"Okay. You've never been to my place. Let's go there." She tapped a screen on the navigation system, and route guidance came up. "I live just off Cadogan Place, not far from Madison." She smiled. "I bet you've been to Madison's before."

Kyle let that go. He found it difficult to pay attention to the road as he saw Sydney cross and uncross her legs several times during the trip. Her dress had slipped up her thighs when she slid into the passenger seat and she had made no attempt to pull it back down. The lump in his throat told Kyle that he was in trouble.

Sydney's flat was sophisticated and modern, decorated almost exclusively in black, white and chrome. Kyle could envision it in *Architectural Digest* but could not imagine spending any time there himself.

She opened a bottle of Krug, poured a splash of pomegranate juice into two flutes and filled the rest with the champagne. "To Chris," she said as she handed a glass to Kyle.

"To Chris," he seconded and clinked her glass.

"Did you know," she said as she kicked off her heels and curled up on a chrome and leather chair, "that champagne was the last thing Chris drank before he died?"

Kyle swallowed hard. He touched the flute to his lips but did not drink. "I didn't realize you were there, at the end."

"I wasn't exactly there, but you know I was at the match. We were all drinking champagne." She shook her head before she downed her entire glass. "It's so sad, isn't it?"

"It definitely is. Were you and Chris close? I've been a little out of the loop these last few years, and dynamics change as we get older."

Sydney shrugged and poured herself another glass of champagne. "I don't know if I'd say we were close. I saw him, or them I should say, a couple of times a year." She wrinkled her nose. "But Annabel and I were never especially close. They seemed an odd pair, and it could be uncomfortable being around them."

"So I gathered. Did you think there was trouble in that marriage?"

She snorted. "Oh, Kyle, there's trouble in every marriage. It is," she said taking another sip, "an imperfect institution."

"And yet we all keep trying to get it right."

Sydney cocked her head. "Not all of us. Not very many in our little group have taken the plunge—including you and me."

Kyle laughed. "That's certainly true. Are you interested in ever getting married?"

"Is that a proposal?"

"As you said, we don't know each other very well."

"We could change that." She smiled so seductively that Kyle's heart seized a little.

"We *are* changing that. So tell me," Kyle said casually. "Are you interested in ever getting married? Is there anybody special now?"

She shrugged and looked past Kyle. "I don't know. My parents had a lousy marriage." She waved her hand dismissively and sipped her champagne. "Fighting, infidelity, divorce, remarriage, stepchildren—the works. It was dreadful growing up with that, and it didn't make marriage anything I really aspire to."

"I thought I met your parents at graduation."

She shook her head. "No, you met my father. And my stepmother, whom I loathe."

"That must have all been rough on a kid."

She stretched her beautiful legs and stood up. Kyle gulped, and she smiled. Sydney walked slowly over to the sofa on which he sat. For a second, he was afraid she was going to sit on his lap, but she dropped to the sofa right beside him and slithered closer as she draped one of her unbelievably long legs over his lap and snuggled under his arm.

"You could make it all better, you know," she said and then kissed him softly on the mouth, lingering there. "At least for a little while."

CHAPTER 15

Madison arrived at 25 Old Broad Street early the next evening. She paid the taxi driver as she got out and stood for a moment looking up at the second tallest building in the London Financial District. She vaguely recalled that the building had been seriously damaged in an IRA bombing in the early nineties, and she thought at least one person had been killed. This was not heartening given the building's height and the challenges that would present in trying to exit in an emergency.

Nevertheless, Tower 42, as it was also known, was a breathtaking structure, and it still boasted one of the highest rents in the city. Madison wondered how a struggling company such as Grisham Investments could afford the lease.

Hawthorne had sent her a note suggesting that she come up to his office rather than wait in Vertigo, Tower 42's bar, so after checking the lobby directory, she took what she amusingly thought of as a supersonic lift to the fortieth floor. Madison felt her ears pop as it came to a halt.

She stepped off the lift and saw the offices of Grisham Investments before her. A workman was already starting to remove the "Grisham," and Madison assumed that Hawthorne would replace it on the lobby door before the end of the day. *Unless,* she thought as she recalled the memo she had seen in her father's library, *it would read* Titan *instead*.

The offices of the late Earl of Grisham were luxurious, and Madison shook her head as her hand trailed over the marble statue in the lobby. She inadvertently shivered. Madison had read somewhere that in the game of high stakes real estate development, you had to look the part if you wanted to attract high-end investors so they believed you were already successful. It gave them confidence to give you their money. But to her, the Persian rugs and granite reception desk were examples of gratuitous pomposity that only put the company further and further in the hole financially.

Madison took a deep breath and introduced herself to a receptionist who looked more suited to the pages of a high fashion magazine than an office environment. She buzzed James Hawthorne. "He'll be right with you," she said, smiling. "May I get you something to drink?"

Madison was about to respond when Jeff Hawthorne bounded down the hall and stuck his hand out. His smile this evening was dazzling as he looked at her, grasping her hand between both of his, and said, "Lady Madison, it's so good to see you again."

Madison was momentarily confused considering the fact that she had seen this man only the day before. She wondered if this was an act of some kind, or if he was trying to impress her, or the beautiful young receptionist, to whom he turned and said, "Sandra, if you could please get us tea and biscuits, I'd appreciate it." He gestured to Madison, and said, "This way, please. My office is just down the hall."

"I thought," Madison said, pointing at the door behind her, "that we were going to grab a quick drink at Vertigo."

"Yes, we are, but I wanted you to see my office."

"I—," she started, but Hawthorne was already walking confidently down the hall as if he knew she would follow. Madison felt she had no choice other than to reluctantly fall into step behind him. As they walked she was able to more fully check out the offices fronting the corridor. There were at least six offices, all elaborately decorated in mahogany, leather, and oriental rugs. She felt as though she had stepped into the offices of one of the high-priced City law firms that also occupied the building.

They came at last to Jeff Hawthorne's corner office, which was just as richly decorated as the others and at least twice as large. The floor-to-ceiling windows offered stunning views of London. Hawthorne gestured to and Madison sat in a chair opposite the leather sofa on which he sat as Sandra rolled in an extravagant tea service. She poured tea for both of them and discreetly left, closing the door behind her.

Hawthorne hung his head and, in stark contrast to his exuberant greeting, said in an overly sorrowful tone, "I really am still so very sorry about Chris's passing." He glanced dramatically out the window, and Madison was afraid for a moment he was actually going to cry. He shook his head and put his hand to his heart. "I simply can't imagine what Sydney is going through."

She cocked her head. "Sydney?"

"What?" he asked bringing his gaze back to Madison.

"You said Sydney. That you couldn't imagine what Sydney was going through."

"I think you're mistaken. I said Annabel."

"No, I think not, Jeff. You said Sydney. I didn't realize you knew her."

"I don't. Except, of course, through Chris. He spoke of the St. Andrews group quite a bit, and I am sure you are all undoubtedly bereft at his passing. No doubt that's what I was thinking."

"No doubt," Madison said, nodding before she took a sip of tea and looked at Hawthorne over the rim of her cup.

"Anyway," he said as he stood. "I thought you might be interested in seeing the model of the development we're building at Battersea Park. Come," he said as he held out his hand to a horrified Madison.

She smiled weakly but stood without his assistance and followed him over to a table on which stood an exact replica of the model she had seen yesterday in Chris' office. It was a detailed miniature of the 28-acres of waterfront property Grishman Investments was developing. As she looked more closely than she had previously, she saw that the elaborate model was built to scale, with tree-lined streets on which tiny cars and pedestrians traveled to a sports center, three restaurants, over twenty high-end specialty stores, a luxury condominium building and a high-rise office complex.

"It's stunning, isn't it? This was to be our crowning glory. And now," Hawthorne said, sniffing, "well, Chris won't ever get to see it knocked into reality."

Madison had been raised in the English tradition where women seldom cried and never in public and men simply never did. She was unimpressed with the affect and suddenly extremely uncomfortable being alone with this man in a nearly deserted office building after hours.

"It is splendid," she said looking pointedly at her watch. "I wish you the best of luck with this endeavor, Jeff. But if you will pardon me, I would like to have that drink now if we can as I have another engagement in just under an hour."

Hawthorne looked disappointed, but he nodded. "Of course," he said, putting his hand on the small of her back and guiding her towards the door.

Madison stepped away from his hand but continued walking as he flipped off the lights and they headed back down the hall. "I think you'll like Vertigo if you've never been there. It's the finest champagne bar in London with amazing views of the city."

Madison blanched, certain she would never again drink another glass of champagne. But she nodded anyway and smiled politely as they entered the lift.

Ten minutes later they were seated in what was arguably one of the chicest bars in London, imbued with a super stylish ambience. The funky, colorful plush chairs sat before floor-to-ceiling windows six hundred feet above pavement level, and Madison was reminded of where the bar got its name. Mirrored walls reflected sophisticated patrons engaged in subdued conversation, and a waitress came over immediately and placed a small bowl of cashews on the beveled glass table between them.

"A bottle of Cuvée Winston Churchill," Hawthorne said, "and a selection of canapés, please."

The waitress nodded and departed before Madison had the opportunity to say anything. Annoyed that he had ordered for her, she said, "I would have preferred something else to drink."

"No, no," he replied waving dismissively. "There is a fun story behind this vintage. Our wartime prime minister was such a fan of his that champagne maker Pol Roger named his prestigious cuvée after him. He was actually granting a request of his wife's, whom Churchill had charmed at a dinner party one evening. Apparently, old Winston was quite a lady's man."

"Indeed. But I have recently given up champagne."

"Oh?" he said, clearly still unconcerned. "Why would anyone in their right mind do that?"

"Chris was drinking champagne right before he died."

"Don't be silly, Madison. Chris was not an embittered man, and he would want his friends to go on without him and live their lives to the fullest."

"You think so? I didn't realize you and Chris were that close, on a personal level. I was under the impression you had only been in business together for less than a year."

"No, no," Jeff said again, smiling as the waitress poured the champagne into beautifully crafted, modern flutes. "We've known each other since you all graduated from university. I tried to recruit him to work with me at UBS."

"I had no idea," Madison said as she reluctantly took the glass Hawthorne handed to her.

"To Chris," he said raising his glass.

"To Chris," she echoed, clinking his glass before she put her own back down on the table.

"Who is Kyle Ward?" Hawthorne asked, catching her a little off-guard.

"He's a friend of ours from university. Why do you ask?"

He shrugged. "Just curious. He seems rather taken with you."

"I think you're mistaken," she said coolly. "Kyle is a detective with Scotland Yard, and he tends to be interested in everyone."

Madison watched as a flicker of something indefinable—interest, concern, fear?— passed over Hawthorne's eyes and then was gone. "Is there anything suspicious about Chris' death?" he asked with a studied casualness.

"I don't know," Madison said. "Is there?"

"Well, that's what I wanted to talk to you about."

"I'm listening."

"I think," he said before he drained the rest of his glass and the waitress reappeared immediately to fill it again, "that Chris was embezzling money from Grisham Investments."

"What makes you think that?" Madison asked as she watched Jeff's attention wander from her to something, or someone, behind her.

"The company has been hemorrhaging money for the past year."

"I thought you were the 'business side' of things and kept the books. Wouldn't you be the one to keep track of that?" Jeff was still staring over her shoulder, so Madison swung her chair around casually and glanced in the direction of his gaze. She was surprised to see Sydney Atwood standing at the bar with a man she did not recognize. Madison started to wave to get her attention, but something in Jeff's manner as he watched her stayed her hand. "Do you know Sydney well?" she asked again as she swung her chair back to face him.

Jeff turned back to her. "Sydney? Atwood? No, I told you I don't know Sydney at all. I'm not even sure I'd recognize her in a crowd." He seemed to shake the darkness from his demeanor as he popped a small canapé into his mouth. "Although I seem to recall she read the news on television, didn't she?"

A small bud of anxiety took root in Madison's stomach. "Yes," she said calmly. "She did read the news, although I think she's taken a new assignment." She glanced at her watch. "I'm afraid I don't have much more time this evening. But I do want to follow up on why you think there were some, er, irregularities in Grisham Investment's books."

"There were too many entries made out to 'cash.' And too many contractors not getting paid on-time, resulting in too many project delays. And," he said dramatically, "too many really pissed off investors, to say nothing of the contractors themselves." He glanced towards the bar again, and when Madison turned back she saw that Sydney was no longer there.

"Duncan Rand was one of them. In fact," Jeff said as he poured another glass, "I'd say he was more pissed off than any of them."

CHAPTER 16

Kyle watched as Madison left Jeff Hawthorne in
Vertigo to finish his bottle of champagne alone. The
Financial District was not as active after hours, and
Kyle did not see anyone else in the building as she
exited. He hung back so she would not see him.
He was fairly certain she would be furious if she
knew he was following her, even if it was only to
ensure her safety. As she waited for a taxi, he
wondered why she had not brought her own car,
and then thought unpleasantly that perhaps she was
waiting for somebody specific and not a hired car.
They were in much shorter supply after hours, and
she would have known that.

After ten minutes of only seeing off-duty taxis,
Madison began to walk. Kyle surmised that she was
headed towards the nearby Liverpool Street
underground tube station which could take her close
to her flat. She had walked only two blocks when
she started to look around nervously, as though she
were worried she was being followed.

Kyle was too far behind her to get her attention
when he saw a person slip out from an alley. At
this distance, he was unable to tell whether it was a
man or a woman. What was clear to him was that
the hooded figure was walking rapidly towards
Madison. Clearly sensing someone, she pulled her

handbag closer to her and walked more quickly, as did Kyle. When the person got close enough to grab her, Kyle withdrew his gun and shouted, "Police. Stand down."

The probable assailant turned, saw Kyle and took off running, as, despite her high heels, did Madison in the opposite direction. Momentarily uncertain whom to follow, Kyle decided to give chase to the hoodie and sprinted after him, his firearm still drawn. He chased the person for three blocks at a full-out run before he turned a corner, and was immediately brought to the ground by a well-directed blow to the head. He did not even see his assailant as he slumped to the ground.

Not knowing what he had been hit with and whether he was in further danger, Kyle struggled to maintain consciousness so he could get back to Madison and ensure that she was okay. He tried to stand, fell back, and tried again. Successful on the second attempt, he staggered to his feet and braced himself against the building. He touched the back of his head and felt a bump already rising accompanied by a pain that made him lean over and vomit.

Breathing heavily, he wiped his mouth on his jacket as he glanced around. Seeing no one, he started walking towards the Liverpool Station in the hope that Madison had made it there safely. As he rounded the corner by the station he saw her standing on the corner by the Bank of England with her back towards him. Still a little woozy and not wanting to draw attention to either of them, he waited until he got close enough to her before speaking. Just as he started to say her name, he stumbled and fell into her.

Madison screamed. She had started to kick him to break free when Kyle was finally able to say, "Madison. Madison, it's me. It's me, Kyle."

"Oh," she gasped. "Kyle. What the hell?" She hit him with her purse. "Why did you do that?"

"Stop, stop. Seriously, I have been beaten up more tonight than in three months of basic training. I didn't mean to scare you."

"Well, you did," she said looking around. "Or someone did. Someone was following me."

"Yeah, someone was, but I think he's gone. I was worried about your meeting with Hawthorne, and I was in the neighborhood, so to speak, so I took a chance I'd run into you."

She only nodded as she tried to catch her breath.

Kyle put his hand on her shoulder. "Are you going to be sick?"

She shook her head.

"Good. I may be." He paused for a moment as he waited for the nausea to pass. "I chased your stalker, and got beaned by him," he said as he gingerly touched the back of his head again. The bump was bigger, but there was no blood.

"Oh my God!" she said, fear lighting her eyes. She held his face in her hands and looked into his eyes. "Can you focus on my face? Are you nauseated? Did you lose consciousness?"

"Yes, yes, no. I think. No trick questions now. Come on, my car is parked at Tower 42. I'll drive you home." He put his arm around her shoulders and turned her around to walk back to the building.

"Shouldn't we call the police?" she said as she glanced over her shoulder.

"I *am* the police. Someday that concept will actually take root. Not everyone gets a police escort, you know."

They walked for a block without speaking as Madison kept looking at him, a worried expression lining her beautiful face.

"So, how was your meeting with Hawthorne?" Kyle asked, changing the subject to get her mind off her scare.

"Unsettling. Seriously, are you okay to drive, or even walk?"

"I'm good," Kyle said, looking behind him. "Why unsettling?"

"What is it?" Madison asked, immediately tense again as she followed his gaze.

"Nothing. Tell me more about Hawthorne."

"Well," she sighed. "He gave me a song and dance about Chris embezzling money from the firm."

"Why song and dance?"

"Because he's the one, or so he claims, who oversaw the business affairs end of it. He said that just yesterday—at the funeral. That was weird in and of itself. And then he tells me that his partner was somehow stealing from the company, right under his oversight. So to speak."

"Okay, that's odd. Are we sure money was being taken out of the company at all?"

"Duncan said that, too, remember?"

"Uh-huh. Give me a minute. I'll catch up."

"He also alluded to Duncan being a seriously pissed off investor."

"Maybe he is," Kyle said as he did a three sixty search of their surroundings.

"I would be. But Duncan didn't say he was. He said quite the opposite."

"Because Duncan always tells the truth," Kyle said as he took one last look around before he opened the door to his unmarked sedan.

"Seriously, what have you got against Duncan?" she asked as she slipped into the front seat.

"Nothing," Kyle said as he closed her door, wincing at the noise.

"Maybe I should be the one to talk to Duncan then," she said as he got in and started the car.

Kyle's mouth twitched, but he kept his eyes directly on the road in front of him and said nothing.

"*And*," Madison continued, "he denied knowing Sydney."

"Duncan denied knowing Sydney?"

"Hawthorne."

"Oh." Kyle checked the rearview mirror to make sure they weren't being followed. "How is that relevant?"

"Well, he saw her in the bar tonight. He was clearly watching her, but he said he'd never met her and wouldn't recognize her in a crowd."

"I thought they spent a considerable amount of time together at the reception announcing Chris' and Jeff's new partnership."

Madison turned to look at him. "How do you remember that?"

"It was one of the few events with you guys I've been to in the past few years. And it was right before Sydney's accident. She looked stunning that night. Every man in the room was watching her."

"Really?"

"Yeah, really. Hawthorne in particular was tripping over himself all evening trying to get her attention. She was toying with me, er, him."

Madison smiled. "As Sydney has been known to do."

"Yeah, I don't know what's up with her these days."

"Did you sleep with her?"

"What?" Kyle's head snapped towards her, and a fresh wave of nausea flowed over him. "Where did that come from?"

"Just answer the question. Did you sleep with her?"

"I don't think that's any of your business."

"No?" she said, her tone indignant now.

"No. Did you sleep with Duncan?"

"I don't think that's any of your business either."

"Well, I do," Kyle said, his voice rising alarmingly

"Well, you're wrong," Madison said quietly.

Kyle sighed. "We sound like jealous spouses," he said, his voice calmer now. He passed his hand over his face. "Or kindergarten children."

"Yes, I know. We should stop that."

"I agree. I just don't want you to get hurt," he said softly.

"I don't want you to get hurt either." Madison swallowed hard. "But to get back to your original comment, I don't know what's up with Sydney either. She's always been bad, but it seems worse. But contrary to what everyone seems to think, I don't psychoanalyze my friends."

"Well, thank God for that. Plausible deniability should always be a goal," Kyle said as he pulled into a parking spot on Coleherne Court. "Sit tight for a minute." He got out of the car, surveyed the street, and came around to open her door.

"I'm fine now," Madison said, her face strained by the concern written across it. "It's you I'm worried about. But thanks for the rescue."

"You didn't need rescuing. You're the strongest person I know," Kyle said as he walked Madison to her door. He glanced around again, standing guard while she searched for her keys.

She opened the door, caught Morgan on his way out, and turned around. "Do you think the person who attacked you was after me, or you? Be honest. I can take it."

"I really don't know."

"I have to let Morgan out to do his business."

"I'll wait."

"I'm fine," she said as she put the little terrier down on a patch of grass.

Kyle shrugged. "Then it will be a boring wait." He leaned down as Morgan came over to him, wagging his tail and sniffing his feet.

"He likes feet," Madison said.

"They tell him everything he needs to know about where we've been," he said as he scratched the little terrier behind his ears.

"He likes you, too," Madison said. "He doesn't like everyone. Scottish Terriers can be stand-offish little dudes."

Kyle smiled and stood up, picking Morgan up and handing him to her. "How does he feel about Duncan?"

Madison sighed. "Goodnight, Kyle."

"Lock your door. I'll touch base in the morning."

She nodded. "Okay." He didn't move. "I said 'okay.'"

"I heard you. I'm waiting until you close the door, and I hear you throw the bolt."

"It's rude to close the door in your face."

"I'm not as wedded as you to polite societal conventions. Close the door, Madison. And get some sleep."

"Please call me if you decide going to hospital is a good idea. Because I think it is." She looked expectantly at him, but he just nodded. "Goodnight," she said again as she closed the door.

Kyle waited until he heard her throw the bolt before he called in the license plate number of the car that had followed them from Tower 42 and requested a visible police presence every couple of hours on Coleherne Court.

CHAPTER 17

Duncan arrived at Madison's flat at 7:00pm. She quickly checked her look in the hall mirror before opening the door. Unlike her mother, she was not a slave to fashion. But this was the first night she had worn her new black Reiss dress, over which she had donned a matching tweed jacket paired with black suede Christian *Louboutin* pumps. She wasn't convinced she could walk very far in the four-inch heels, but thought they were chic and daring for her.

Duncan had dated a string of stunningly beautiful women over the years, confidence-rattling photos of whom Madison had been continuously bombarded with in the tabloid press. She was sure there were psychological studies delving into the self-image neuroses of the daughters of beautiful women, but she had studiously avoided them.

She would just have to be satisfied working with what she had.

Madison opened the door and smiled broadly at Duncan. He looked very handsome in a solid black suit, hand-made Madison guessed by his tailor at Gieves & Hawkes, silver tie and black French cuffs. He looked, she thought with an inward smile, like tabloid bait.

"You look lovely, Madison," he said, kissing her hand.

She pursed her lips before she said, "We should have coordinated better. We look like we're in mourning."

"Well, in a way I suppose we still are."

She nodded. "I guess you're right. Now that I think about it, it seems somehow more respectful this way."

"I thought we'd go to Tintagel for drinks and then onto dinner, if that works for you."

Madison pulled her door shut behind her and locked it. "I haven't been there in ages, and I wanted to catch up with Gig, so that's excellent."

It took less than twenty minutes to arrive at the entrance to Tintagel, which was understated and easily missed if you were not aware of its existence. After graduating from university with them, Gil Stockton had taken over a classic London townhouse in Chelsea and transformed it into one of the most sought-after private clubs in London. The precariously steep stairs leading down to the entrance were the infamous cause of many sprained ankles and a few broken bones from patrons who had imbibed too much. But they had not diminished the club's popularity.

Tintagel's interior decor was reminiscent of the gentlemen's clubs from the Second World War, all dark mahogany, library-style paneled walls, and portraits of people Madison knew she should recognize but did not.

The restaurant, famous for old classics such as caviar, rare steaks and decadent chocolate desserts, was located on the left as one entered the club, with the private rooms, Avalon, Merlin, and Llamrei, located in the back, with an elegant black granite bar in the center.

The club had something of an old fogey feel to it that, rather than making it something its young patrons would avoid, made it retro chic. Its clientele no doubt contributed to its allure, and Gig had not hesitated in the early days to call upon his friends to help build its reputation. Popular among both the locals and the stars, including Prince William and Kate Middleton in addition to other young royals, the atmosphere at Tintagel was always described as friendly, refined, and indulgent.

Madison successfully navigated the stairs in her heels, and the doorman greeted them warmly. They were ushered in immediately, and the hostess led them to a booth in the back of the bar, where they had a view of everything going on. She bid them a good evening and noted that Gig would be with them as soon as he got off the phone. Madison looked around at the patrons of the club. Several were familiar faces and acquaintances she'd seen at the club before, but she didn't see anyone she would consider a friend.

A waitress came at once to take their orders, and Duncan ordered them Excaliburs, Tintagel's signature drink and Madison's personal favorite.

Made with a secret combination of oranges, brandied cherries, bourbon and Campari, the elixir had been concocted by Gig and Jules one bitterly cold evening in St. Andrews. It was fortunate that they had written down the recipe as neither was able to remember how they had ended up the next morning in St. Salvator's Quad, clad only in swim trunks and each snuggling a Skye Terrier puppy, much less the ingredients in a new drink. They had tried diligently to find the real owners of the pups at the time, but no one ever came forward and Gig ended up adopting both.

When the drinks arrived, Madison and Duncan clinked the custom made, cherry-red martini glasses and each took a long drink. She looked at Duncan mischievously, and said, "Do you think they had martinis in King Arthur's time?"

Duncan laughed. "What do you mean?"

"Tintagel? Avalon? Excalibur? They're very Arthurian. Didn't you know?"

He shook his head and shrugged. "I did not know. Jesus, I'm learning a lot of things about my friends I never knew. Who would have pegged Gig Stockton as a devotee of Camelot? See, I told you everyone has secrets."

Madison gestured around the club. "That one isn't exactly a secret."

Duncan leaned towards Madison. His voice was low and seductive when he said, "What secrets are *you* hiding from me?"

Madison looked at him for several long moments before she answered in an overly dramatic tone, "I've been in love with you since university?" She took a sip of her drink and smiled playfully. "Is that the right answer?"

Duncan furrowed his brow. "Is that the truth?"

Madison was spared having to answer him when Gig came up to their table. He leaned down to kiss her cheek and clapped Duncan on the shoulder before he sat. "I thought something may have been rekindled last weekend, but I was too polite to say anything."

"Good call," Duncan said. "Okay, Gig. What's up with King Arthur? I never made any connection between Tintagel, Avalon, and Arthur."

Gig nodded to the waitress across the club before replying, "Seriously, Duncan, are you really an Englishman?"

"Yeah, I am," Duncan said in mock defense. "I know who King Arthur is, and what Camelot and Excalibur are. What are Avalon and Tintagel?"

Gig looked at Madison and held his hands open in mock exasperation.

"You tell him," she said, laughing. "You're the expert here."

Gig sighed. "According to legend, Avalon is the place where King Arthur is taken to recover from his wounds after fighting Mordred at the Battle of Camlann. I also think it's kind of mystical, something like heaven." He looked at Madison. "Am I right?"

"I think of it that way; isn't there something about Arthur not really dying but just going to Avalon?"

Duncan looked at them both, seemingly amused. "I never knew." He took another long drink. "And Tintagel?" he said holding up his glass.

Madison and Gig said in unison, "It's the castle where Arthur was born," and then laughed. Duncan joined in briefly, and then they all three stopped immediately, with Madison feeling guilty that they were enjoying themselves so soon after Chris' death.

There was an awkward moment of silence, and they all looked relieved when Duncan's iPhone rang and he excused himself to take the call. The waitress arrived with Gig's Excalibur. He clinked glasses with Madison and said, "When in Rome—."

"Or Camelot."

"Or Avalon." He passed his hand over his eyes and briefly rubbed his temples. "Jeez, that reminds me again of Chris."

Madison reached over and patted his hand. She said gently, "How are you, Gig? I think we're all struggling to come to terms with his death."

"I'm okay." He shrugged. "I know that sounds heartless, but I don't know what else to say. This is all just ghastly." Gig looked around him and lowered his voice. "There are a lot of rumors going around about Chris now."

"I don't find that surprising."

"No, I guess not. I suppose it's the shock and people not wanting to believe something like this could happen to them. But there are murmurings that he didn't die of natural causes." He looked around again. "And the rumors are ugly."

Now Madison lowered her voice. "What are they saying?"

"They're talking about him screwing up his company, infidelity in the marriage, and payback being a bitch." He shrugged. "That kind of thing. Christ, wouldn't you think they could leave him with a little dignity at this point?"

"I hadn't heard that he was unfaithful to Annabel," she said softly, watching as Duncan walked slowly back to them, stopping at several other tables almost as though he were a politician asking for votes. She involuntarily cringed when a woman she recognized as a minor television actress put her arms around Duncan's neck and slowly kissed him. Madison could not tell if Duncan returned her passion, but she was sickened at the thought.

"You know that marriage had been a wreck almost from the beginning," Gig said following her gaze to Duncan and the actress. He jerked his thumb at them. "Georgina is a party girl, Madison. She's in here all the time. Take it for what it is."

"And what exactly is that?"

"A distraction. For both of them."

Madison picked up her drink and without taking her eyes off Duncan said, "So who was Chris sleeping with?"

Gig turned to look at her. "What makes you think it was Chris?"

CHAPTER 18

"What was Chris?" Kyle asked as he walked up to their table.

Gig smiled broadly as he stood and clapped Kyle on the back. "I can't believe I haven't gotten you in my club before now. It's good to have you back in the fold, mate."

Kyle nodded warmly to Gig as he shook his hand and leaned down to kiss Madison to cover his embarrassment before he sat. He knew he should have kept in touch with his university mates much more than he had over the years.

He said, "Madison finally convinced me that I had to see your masterpiece. I'm sorry I haven't been here before now." He pointed at her drink. "What's that?"

"Oh, ho, you *have* been out of the loop," Gig said, laughing as he slid his own untouched drink across the table to Kyle. "That, my friend, is our signature drink—the Excalibur. Once you've had one, you'll never go back."

Duncan returned to the table, looking somewhat sheepish, and sat next to Kyle, at whom he glared. Madison ignored him and changed the subject as the waitress replaced Gig's drink. "What do you think of Chris' partner?" she said directly to Gig.

"Hawkins? Hawthorne? Something like that. I think the man is pond scum. I only met him once, but I didn't like him." He looked uncomfortable and went on. "Chris had his number, though."

Madison repeatedly tapped her glass. "I can't help but wonder what number of Chris' Hawthorne had, though. There had to have been some reason why he stayed in business with him."

Duncan turned to Gig, and asked, "Have you spoken to Annabel at all since the funeral?"

"No," Gig replied. "I tried to call, but I just rang into voicemail. And she hasn't called back."

"The same for me," Madison said. "I wanted to try to see her tomorrow while she's still in London, but I haven't been able to reach her." She paused. "I think, all in all, that Annabel may be the key to figuring out what happened here."

Gig shook his head skeptically. "I don't know, Madison. I really think they had a troubled relationship, one full of secrets. I don't know what she knows. Hell, I don't even know that she wasn't involved." He looked down, staring into his drink as if embarrassed. No one else said anything.

Duncan finished his drink, put his glass on the table with a bang and said, "Should we order another round?"

"I can't, mate, sorry," Gig said. "There's a private party in the back I need to get back to. Order what you'd like, though. It's on me."

"I can't let you do that, Gig," Duncan said. "With all your friends who drink here, you'll be broke if it's always on the house."

Gig stood up and clasped Duncan's shoulder. "I mean it, Duncan. This week has driven home to me, to us all, how important friends are." He smiled and gestured around his elegant club. "What's Camelot without your friends?" He blew a kiss to Madison, nodded to Kyle and headed toward the back room. An exotic woman stopped him on the way, put her arms around his neck and whispered something in his ear. He smiled and shook his head, looking uncomfortable. He kissed her cheek as he removed her arms and continued on his way while she looked longingly after him.

Kyle tasted and then stared at his Excalibur. "Doesn't anyone else see anything vaguely phallic in naming an alcoholic drink, known to break down inhibitions, after a great big sword with magical powers?"

"Nothing vague about that at all," Madison replied.

"Freud saw something sexual in everything," Duncan said, shaking his head.

"I was not a student of Freud. Not all psychologists are, you know."

Before Duncan could answer, pandemonium broke out in front of the club. Horns were blaring, and people were shouting. It was clear, even from behind the dark drapes, that the paparazzi were outside.

"Are Kate and William here tonight? Do you think they're the private party?" Madison asked.

Duncan shook his head. "No, Gig would have told us if that were the case. It may not have been a planned visit, though."

At that moment, the door to the club opened. The noise and strobe-like flashbulbs invaded the club as Pippa Middleton rushed in. She looked dazed and disoriented as she stood alone for a moment while the doorman fought to close the door against what could really only be described as a mob.

"She can't be alone, can she?" Madison asked, concerned. She didn't know Pippa well, but they had met on a few occasions when she had been with her older sister. Madison was touched by how young and vulnerable she seemed as she looked around the darkened club for someone she knew.

"I doubt it. I'll go see if she's okay." Duncan stood at the same moment that Sydney Atwood and a man Madison did not recognize came through the back entrance to Tintagel.

Kyle tensed when he saw Sydney. She made her way through the club like a movie star greeting her public. He suspected that the subdued lighting of the club restored some of the confidence taken by the accident as he scrutinized her demeanor and tried to gauge her mood. Sydney looked gorgeous but it was the way she carried herself that put him on-guard. She pointed at people she knew and laughed and flirted with not only her companion but also seemingly everyone she encountered as she walked through the club.

"*Lady* Madison," Sydney said as she walked up, "this is Bill—something." She smiled brilliantly at her companion, and Kyle realized she had clearly had too much to drink.

Madison turned to Bill Something and smiled, almost apologetically. "How do you do?" she said.

He smiled and shrugged sheepishly. "Bill McNeil, Lady Madison. If you haven't guessed, we haven't known each other long," he said as he glanced at Sydney before shaking Madison's hand.

"Madison, please. It's a pleasure Mr. McNeil."

Kyle reached out to shake Bill's hand as well and realized that tonight was going to be one of the nights Sydney ignored him.

"Excaliburs for the group?" Duncan asked as he rejoined them. He and Bill McNeil nodded to each other, and Kyle wondered if they knew one another. Duncan exhaled. "I don't know how they have ever gotten used to the paparazzi. I'm afraid I'd deck one of them at some point."

"I've thought about it." Bill grinned, and Kyle realized he was an anchor on one of the evening news programs he infrequently caught on television. "But the negative publicity, not to mention the displeasure of the network, wouldn't be worth the thirty seconds of pleasure."

"There are so many things in life like that, aren't there?" Madison asked.

Duncan looked at her, his eyes widening. They all burst out laughing, with Kyle laughing the hardest. Madison could barely speak when she said, "I swear to God, Duncan; that's not what I was referring to."

"Uh-huh." He cleared his throat as they all attempted to stifle their laughter, which was, for the moment, beyond Kyle's ability. "Moving on," Duncan said as he looked at Sydney. "I didn't see any television news coverage about Chris. Did I miss it?"

Sydney's eyes were glassy now when she looked at Duncan. "I think there was something in the paper. But honestly, there was nothing newsworthy about it." She shrugged, took a drink out of Bill's hand and held it up in tribute to someone over Duncan's shoulder that Madison could not see. "I mean, it's very sad, of course. But Chris wasn't a public figure. He had a heart attack and died at a sporting event. That happens *all the time.*"

"Does it?" Bill asked before he was interrupted by a woman Kyle thought looked too young to be drinking legally. Sydney virtually sneered as the younger woman threw her arms around the anchor's waist, pulled him closer to her by wrapping her leg around his and snuggled under his arm as her friend snapped a photo. Bill smiled indulgently as he pointedly extricated himself from the woman's grasp, took a step closer to Sydney and kissed her neck. The fan pouted but she seemed to get the message as she flitted away.

"Careful," Sydney said witheringly. "You could get arrested for what you're even contemplating."

Bill winced and said to Madison, "You have my condolences. I'm sure you must all still be in shock."

"Oh," Sydney said looking at Madison and clasping her hand over her mouth in what Kyle thought was an attempt to stifle a giggle. "What did your mother say? She must have been *so* pleased to have this happen at Whiddenhurst."

"Yes, well," Madison said, nodding her thanks to the waitress as she set their drinks on the high top table they now all stood around, "it's never pleasant to be on the receiving end of the Duchess Treatment. She thought it in terribly bad form that I had the bad judgment, or taste, I can't remember which, to be present when something so untoward took place. On her property, no less."

"She didn't really say *that*, did she?" Duncan asked.

"Not in those exact words, no, but that was the gist. I think she was incredibly distressed about it, for all the wrong reasons." Madison stared into her drink, and they were all silent.

Duncan raised his glass. "To Chris."

They all raised their glasses and said in unison, "To Chris."

"Do they have any idea what caused the heart attack?" Sydney asked.

"I think they have several, but nothing conclusive by any means at this point," Kyle said, reluctant to go into detail the police did not yet want known.

Gig joined them again and reached out to shake Bill's hand. "It's good to see you again, mate." He turned to Sydney. "Syd—you're looking sharp."

Sydney's eyes sparkled. "You, too, Gig—as always," she said as Bill stood there awkwardly.

"I doubt anyone's in the mood for dancing tonight, but is anyone staying for dinner?" Gig asked.

"Bill and I are joining my father and his, um, wife for dinner at the Promenade," Sydney said. "I haven't had a chance to see him since the, er, Chris's death."

Duncan turned to Madison. "I would like to do whatever you'd like to do this evening, but I was thinking we'd dine at Babylon if that works for you."

"Anything is fine with me."

Duncan held out his hands and said to Kyle, "You are more than welcome to join us, of course."

"Thanks, but I have plans."

Gig nodded. "I'm sorry you won't be staying, but it's always good to see you all, however briefly. If you'll pardon me, my chef has threatened, again, to quit tonight, so I need to go placate him. I'm not sure what else, other than ownership of the club, I can promise him at this point but I've got to try." He blew kisses to the women and departed.

Duncan caught the eye of the waitress and raised his hand. She came over and smiled at him. Madison thought she was one of the most beautiful women she'd ever seen.

"Can you please bring me the bill?" Duncan asked.

"I'll get this," Kyle said reaching for his wallet.

"It's all been taken care of," the waitress noted. Duncan started to protest, but she put her hand lightly on his arm. "Gentlemen," she said quietly, "you know Gig wouldn't allow it. Have a good evening."

As Madison watched her walk away she said, "Does he even know any women who aren't gorgeous enough to be models?" She paused. "Present company excluded, of course."

Duncan leaned over and kissed her cheek. "Present company very much included. And no, I don't think he does. Gig loves beautiful women." He looked around the club. "And they apparently love him." She furrowed her brow. "It's a lonely life, Madison, full of meaningless encounters and shallow relationships."

"So you've been told," she said.

He smiled and slipped her arm through his. "So I just know." He leaned his head down closer to hers as they started to walk towards the door with Kyle following at a discreet distance. "But you saw his reaction to that woman. She was breathtaking, and he was polite. But not interested. I know that for certain."

They all collected their coats and Sydney and Bill left by the back door as Madison, Duncan and Kyle walked out the front. The paparazzi were still waiting outside the club, and they were met with a barrage of shouted questions and blinding flashbulbs before the photographers realized that they were not the royal couple.

Kyle again fought the instinct to flash his badge as Duncan, his arm protectively around her waist, guided Madison through the gauntlet to the next block. They stopped on the corner while they caught their breath after the assault and waited for the spots in front of their eyes to disappear.

Madison shivered. "Do they do this every night, just stake out locations where the royal family could possibly show up? I just don't know how they deal with that. I'm afraid it's not a life I could live."

"You should probably cut and die your hair then," Duncan said as he smiled and tapped her lightly on the nose.

"No," Kyle said as he kissed her cheek goodnight. "Don't do that. Don't let them win." He nodded to Duncan before watching them get into the Aston Martin the valet had just pulled up.

Kyle stood there alone on the corner and watched them drive away.

CHAPTER 19

Madison and Duncan pulled up in front of Babylon, a trendy new restaurant located above a former department store on High Street.   Madison knew that the restaurant, and the private club above, were owned by Sir Richard Branson. She had never been inside before and was amused that the interior design was so dramatic, and almost surreal with three themed gardens populated by over seventy full-sized trees and a flowing stream that appeared to be stocked with many varieties of fish she sincerely hoped were not on the menu. Live flamingos preened and a flock of ducks squawked at the patrons as they completed the impression of an adult amusement park.

They were welcomed by a maître 'd who clearly knew Duncan and promptly seated them at a small table with a lovely view of the roof top gardens. Madison thought she recognized several famous faces among the diners, including Sir Richard's daughter Holly sitting with her new husband, Fred Andrews.

As Duncan perused the wine list, Madison studied the menu. She had just settled on her choice when the waiter arrived with a bottle of a 1970 Petrus, which he elaborately presented for Duncan to study the label.

Duncan read the label and smiled up at the waiter. "I think you have the wrong table."

"No, sir. The gentleman over there," he said nodding towards another table, "sent this over. He also wanted me to convey to you that he was hoping he could join you for a drink."

Madison and Duncan both turned, and her heart sank when she saw Jeff Hawthorne lift his own wine glass in salute. Duncan nodded politely and turned back to her. "It would be rude to decline one drink."

"Yes, I know," she said.

"One drink?"

"Of course," she said reluctantly, knowing she could refuse neither of them without being impolite.

Duncan nodded and the waiter brought another chair to their already cozy table for two. He stood and shook Hawthorne's hand as he joined them.

Madison willed herself to smile as Hawthorne bent to kiss her hand before sitting too close to her. "Mr. Hawthorne, how are you?" she said.

"Jeff, please."

"Yes, course," she said with a stiff smile. "Thank you for the lovely bottle of wine. I don't have it often, but it's one of my favorites."

"How did I know that?" he said with a smile that made Madison shudder.

"To what do we owe the pleasure, Jeff?" Duncan asked as he swirled the tasting pour.

"I wanted to get back to you on the questions you asked earlier in the week," Jeff replied.

Duncan glanced briefly at Madison before he said, "I don't think dinner is the appropriate time for that, do you? We don't want to spoil Lady Madison's evening out, do we?"

Madison's eyes widened at Duncan before she caught herself and smiled too brightly at Hawthorne. "Yes," she said and then, unable to help herself, continued with, "I don't get out much, so this is a special evening."

Duncan choked on his wine and coughed. He looked down immediately to avoid her eyes as he dabbed his own with his napkin.

Jeff seemed blissfully unaware. "Ah," he said, "of course. This is such a lovely restaurant. It's very romantic, and I certainly do not wish to intrude." He stood and bobbed his head to Madison. "Enjoy your dinner—and the wine with my complements. Good evening."

Jeff Hawthorne did not return to his own table, and Madison wondered if he had finished his dinner or if he just decided against staying after that awkward encounter.

Duncan watched him depart before turning back to Madison. "He's a strange man. My questions were routine and certainly not in need of being accompanied by an elaborate gesture of," he said looking at the label, "a thirteen hundred dollar bottle of wine."

"That did seem a little over-the-top. What do you think that was about?"

Duncan shrugged. "He might be trying to convince us that everything is okay—or maybe just that he's a player and worth keeping around."

She smiled. "Perhaps he'll expense it—to his bankrupt company. Or *your* company," Madison said before she could catch herself.

"We haven't figured out the new structure yet, and that's part of what we needed to discuss. It certainly seems of concern to Jeff. I have a feeling he thought Grisham Investments would be all his now that Chris is gone, but that's not the case. But no matter how it works out, Chris carried a hefty amount of key-man insurance, so the company will soon be flush with cash."

Madison watched Duncan as the waiter served their appetizers and felt a chill migrate down her body. Her palms started to sweat. "How much cash?" she asked as casually as she could.

"A lot."

"Enough to recoup your losses?"

"Almost." He reached across the table and closed his hand over hers. "I am so glad you're here with me tonight, Madison. There is nowhere I would rather be, and no one I would rather be with."

Madison caught her breath. Duncan had unparalleled charm when he wanted to use it, and regardless of what had taken place between them, she was not immune to it. And that concerned her. Not only were the hurts of the past still lurking in her memory, but new suspicions had also been added.

She was far from sure with whom she was dealing when it came to Duncan.

When the waiter brought the bill, Duncan put his credit card in the folder without looking. "You may know that there's a private Members Club on the roof," he said as he smiled at her. "The views are pretty spectacular. Or, we could go back to my place for a nightcap."

She looked at him with a slight smile as she contemplated her options.

"Or," he said smiling, "we could go back to your place for a nightcap. Or, I could call for a car to take you home and we could avoid the whole potentially awkward goodnight scene. Lady's choice."

"Hmm," she said tapping her finger against her cheek and weighing her concern against her curiosity and a long-held attraction for Duncan. "I don't believe I've seen the new place."

He smiled.

"Don't look so self-satisfied," she said. "One nightcap. That's it."

"On my honor," he said, standing as he reached to pull out her chair.

Duncan's new flat was located in Belgravia, and it did not take long before they were pulling up before an elegant white façade facing the gardens at Eaton Square. He turned on the Aston's flashers, got out and came around to open Madison's door.

"They're renovating part of the building, so the underground parking is a hassle these days. It's full of construction equipment and white plaster dust. I'd rather you not have to go through that, so I'll just take you up and then come park the car."

"I'm not fragile, Duncan."

"No, but it's still dirty and dangerous. Indulge me," he said nodding to the porter who opened the door for them. "I'll be right back if you could just keep an eye on the car."

They took the lift to the third floor, and the doors opened onto the expansive marble entrance hall of a private flat.

"It's lovely," Madison said.

"You should tell my interior decorator. I admit I had nothing whatsoever to do with any of it. Open a bottle of wine. Make yourself at home. I'll be right back."

Madison stood in the entry hall a moment and looked around at the large, well-proportioned rooms. It was a sophisticated, masculine flat, and Madison thought that his decorator clearly knew with whom she was dealing.

From where she stood, Madison could see that the flat contained a drawing room with floor-to-ceiling windows through which she could see a large balcony. She walked through the room and tried to open the sliding glass door. When she could not figure out the overly complicated lock, she headed into the kitchen. A small wine cabinet sat snuggly under the green granite-topped island, and she reached down to view the selection. She chose a nice port and was searching for a corkscrew when she saw it.

Sydney Atwood's mobile phone sat on the counter beneath the wall phone. She recognized the device because of its cover, personalized with a photo of Sydney and her father taken at graduation from university. It was a rare nod to sentimentality that Sydney had replaced many times over the years with the same photo. Madison's hands started to shake, and her mouth went dry. She had gone against her better judgment and had let herself be vulnerable again to someone who clearly could not be trusted.

Madison sat at the island and waited for Duncan to return. He did so within five minutes.

She heard him walking through the flat until he got to the kitchen. "Ah," he said, "you found the wine. But probably not the corkscrew. I'll get it." He stopped cold when he saw her face. "What happened?"

"Nothing."

"Come on, Madison. We played that game before, and it didn't work. Being passive aggressive isn't going to get us anywhere good."

She nodded, her lips pressed tightly together. "Neither is screwing around, Duncan. I can't take that again. I can't come anywhere close to even trying." Madison stood. "I think I should go."

"Please wait," he said with a frustration bordering on anger slipping into his voice. He grabbed her arms. "I swear to God, I have no idea what you are talking about. And of course you can leave. I'll take you home. But not before you explain what has upset you."

Madison tossed off his hands and walked towards the counter. She held up Sydney's mobile and stared at him, hostility and pain distorting her pretty features.

"Sydney's phone?" he said, confusion shadowing his face. "I don't get it. Why would you care if I had her phone?"

"In your house? Has she been in your house, where she accidentally left her phone?" She slammed the device down on the counter harder than she had intended. "Or was it on purpose, kind of like marking her territory?"

"You are out of line, Madison. If you would like to have a calm, rational discussion I will be happy to do so. But accusing me of betraying something that isn't really there is not okay."

Madison blinked and stepped back. She shook her head and put up her hands.

"Okay, I didn't mean that. I'm sorry," Duncan said as he took a step towards her. "I didn't mean 'that wasn't really there.' Look," he said, closing his eyes and putting his hands over his face for a second, "this is important to me, and I feel like it's slipping away before it's really had a chance to begin again. And for nothing other than past mistakes. Please let me explain." He held out his hands. "Please."

She crossed her arms, her lips tightly pursed.

"Will you sit down?"

"I'm fine here."

"Okay. Okay," he said as he backed away and sat on Madison's vacated stool. He put his head down, running his hands through his hair as though he were giving himself enough time to get his story straight. "We were all out last week, just before Chris died. Chris, Annabel, Gig, Jules and I. We went to the opening of that new club. Sydney stopped by. Our mobiles were on the table, but when she went to use hers, the battery was dead. She asked to borrow mine. I didn't think anything of it, and somehow I ended up with hers. I don't know if I just absent-mindedly put it in my jacket or what. In all the trauma of Chris' death, I just haven't remembered to return it, and she hasn't mentioned it. But she has never been in this flat, or any flat I've ever owned. I'm not that stupid, Madison. Whatever else you think of me, you know I've always thought Sydney was hazardous to anyone's well-being—including probably her own. I don't have any tolerance for that."

Madison exhaled. She couldn't keep the quiver out of her voice when she said, "I don't believe you would have been willing to be without your mobile for one day, much less more than a week."

Duncan unclipped a device from his belt and held it out to her. "I have my Blackberry, which I use for work. I use the iPhone primarily for social stuff, and I haven't missed it."

Madison's anger gave way to tears and then to feeling foolish. She shook her head. "I'm sorry. I agree, that was out of line. I don't know where that came from. Except, well—."

He stood and took her hands. He said very softly, "I told you I would never lie to you again, and I won't. I see now that I have to earn your trust again, and I understand. But if you could give me the benefit of the doubt before you—."

"Freak," she said as she pulled her hand away and wiped her tears.

"Freak is a good word," he said smiling. "As a descriptor more than as a goal probably."

"I think I should go home."

"I'll drive you home now," he said holding out his arms. "If I can have just one hug before you go. I'm sorry for whatever I did years ago that produced your reaction tonight. I cannot tell you how very sorry I am."

She allowed him to take her gently in his arms. "You don't even remember, do you?" she mumbled, her face against his chest.

He sighed heavily. "I guess I don't. I'm sorry for that, too. I really am."

CHAPTER 20

In an effort to blow away the residue of the mind-numbing small talk at a reception to interest prospective recruits in the force, Kyle put down all the windows in the Range Rover, yanked off his tie, and started to drive home. Members of the Home Office had been at the event tonight and since the bulk of funding for the police force came from that office in the form of an annual grant, the Chief Inspector of Scotland Yard had deemed the affair "compulsory attendance." Kyle was perplexed as to why he was always required to attend these events; he loathed them to an extent he felt certain he could not hide. Nothing was further from detective work than brown nosing politicians as far as he was concerned.

He was driving past Eaton Place when he passed Sydney's Jaguar. Kyle instinctively ducked, even though he was sure she had not seen him. He didn't think she would even recognize his vehicle if she had. He briefly considered next steps, decided she was connected to an on-going murder investigation and executed a perfect U-turn just in time to see Sydney park illegally in front of a large white townhouse overlooking Eaton Place and run inside.

Kyle pulled into the next block and phoned headquarters. "It's Kyle Ward. I need an ID on an address. Eight-nine Eaton Square. Right. Belgravia." He pulled out a pen and pad he kept in the center console and was prepared to write down the name of the owner. When he heard the name, however, he put the pen down. His throat tightened and his voice sounded strangled when he said, "Thanks." Kyle disconnected the call.

He sat there for a minute in front of Duncan Rand's expensive townhouse as he mentally debated what to do. Kyle thought briefly about having her car towed because she was parked illegally but concluded that would be small, to say nothing of an abuse of power. He looked in his rearview mirror and tried to adjust it to see if he could still spot Sydney's car. He could not, so he put the Rover in gear and drove around the square again. He did not have a plan and wasn't sure what he was expecting to find as he approached the townhouse again and slowed. The flashers were blinking on the Jag, which meant Sydney expected her visit to be brief. That was less disturbing, but still odd. It was after eleven and no one in Kyle's experience went visiting "just friends" at that hour.

Kyle sat in the Range Rover for twenty minutes and had just concluded that he had learned all he would tonight about the relationship between Sydney Atwood and Duncan Rand when he saw her exit the building. She looked angry, livid, in fact, and he ducked below the sight line of the window. When he raised his head again Sydney was driving away. He waited until she got to the next block and then followed her. He reached into the back of the Rover and felt around until he found an old baseball cap, which he pulled low over his head on the oft chance she could recognize him in her rearview mirror.

They had not driven far when she pulled into a neighborhood he recognized and then parked directly in front of the flat he had been in just two days ago. Sydney was home. He was about to drive past when he saw a man in a dark coat and hat leaning against the entrance to her building.

Kyle was suspicious of all loiterers in disguise, as well as late night meetings. Both looked clandestine, which never amounted to anything good in his experience. He thought the man in the dark coat was almost caricature-like in his appearance, but being an amateur did not necessarily make him any less dangerous. Kyle pulled into an empty space several cars behind Sydney's and killed the engine. He drew his firearm from his shoulder holster and quietly opened the car door so he could move quickly if the situation turned bad.

Sydney kept her head down when she exited her vehicle. She was clearly agitated and looked eager to get inside. But even in that state, she was graceful and almost catlike, barely touching the sidewalk as she sprinted towards the steps. And then she looked up and stopped. Evidently she had seen the man in the dark coat and even from this distance, Kyle watched in amazement as Sydney crouched a little as though ready to spring into an attack. Then he thought for a moment she would run past the stranger into the safety of the lighted lobby and perhaps even push him away to give her time to escape. But he had forgotten whom he was watching.

At this distance, Kyle could not make out what she was saying, but the agitation and volume in her tone carried down the street. It was clear that she was yelling at the man as her arms flailed wildly. The man backed away, putting his hands up and then patting the air as if to placate her. He looked around nervously and took off his hat.

Kyle got his second jolt of the evening when he recognized Jeff Hawthorne. He had no idea what this confrontation was about, but it was evident who was winning. He holstered his weapon but did not pull away. Hawthorne did not look like a threat to Sydney, although Kyle thought it was probable that she was a threat to him at that moment. He watched as she continued to yell at him for the next ten minutes, advancing on him while she pointed her finger within inches of his face. Kyle barely recognized her as hostility distorted her face. She finished her tirade with a final stab of her finger that actually made contact with Hawthorne's chest and stalked off into the lobby of her building, leaving her stalker—*Or was he her victim*, Kyle wondered— looking pale and shaken. Hawthorne glanced both ways down the street, pulled a mobile out of his coat and made a call, which he continued as he hurried away.

Kyle rubbed his chin as he contemplated whether Hawthorne was worth following. He was clearly connected to Chris' world, but Kyle was most perplexed by the link to Sydney. Hawthorne did not strike him as someone on whom she would waste her time in any capacity and certainly not someone about whom she would get so exorcised. He was weak, and while Sydney toyed with weak young men in social settings, this was obviously different. This man knew where she lived. Had he been there before? What had he done that so enraged her? Was it anything more than just showing up outside her flat? If that had been a come-on of any kind, Kyle thought Sydney would have dismissed him with a cool humiliation and walked past.

He found that his mind worked better when his body was also in motion, whether that was running or driving, so Kyle decided to follow Hawthorne. He pulled out of his parking space and drove slowly as he kept to the block behind Jeff Hawthorne. Kyle was skilled in tailing a suspect without being seen, but it was harder on a deserted. Chances were high Hawthorne would make him, and he was prepared to drive on past if that happened. Unless he was the perp, Hawthorne was not yet aware that Chris had been murdered. And Kyle knew that people showed their hands a lot more readily if they didn't know they were being watched.

He abandoned his tail on Jeff Hawthorne a frustrating thirty minutes later when Chris' former partner entered a small, rundown townhouse in Notting Hill. Another quick call to headquarters told Kyle that the residence belonged to Hawthorne, and that he was six months in default on his mortgage. The Bank of England had started foreclosure proceedings on the property.

Glad that the tail had not been a complete waste of time, Kyle still headed home with more questions than answers.   But finding the answers was the part of the job he liked, and at least now he had a few more questions.

He did not bother to turn on the lights in his flat when he got home. He threw his coat on the chair and was headed to the much-needed respite of his bed when his mobile rang.   His training had been rigorous enough that he was incapable of letting the phone ring into voicemail, regardless of how tired he was.

"I'm tellin' ya, I am keeping score," the voice on the other end said before Kyle could even say hello.

He rubbed his eyes trying to place the voice. "DiCarla? What the—?"

"No, wait a minute, mate. I've got something for you."

"Shoot."

"Seriously, do you think detectives should ever say that, even in jest?"

"Clock's ticking, Jim. What'd you have?"

"I couldn't trace the formaldehyde or the sodium, naturally, because they're both easy to buy, no lot numbers, well, you got it."

"I got it. I assume you couldn't trace the oysters for the same reason."

"No, mate, that's why I called. Look, I don't eat oysters. I think they are disgusting, like boogers or—."

"Really?"

"Yeah, right. It's late. Anyway, these were special oysters. A guy in the lab recognized them. They're called Crasso—Crassostrea or something. I can spell it."

"That's okay." Kyle lay back on his bed and closed his eyes.

"Anyway, they're imported by this fancy little wine and spirits store in Tetbury. Supposedly the Prince of Wales likes them, but he was out of town this weekend. So they had a surplus."

Kyle sat up. "A wine store? I bet it sells champagne."

"Bingo. I traced the peach champagne back to that store. Believe it or not, it's a specialty item, really expensive. The customer bought two dozen oysters and two bottles of the peach champagne and several bottles of regular champagne. And a case of Macallan Scotch."

"Did he pay by credit card?"

"She, and yeah, but she used some dude's credit card—a Duncan Rand. He remembered it because it was one of those black American Express cards, and he had never seen one before. But the clerk also remembered the customer, because he said she was with a friend and they were two of the most beautiful girls he had ever seen. One was a blond, tall and leggy. The other was a dark-haired woman he had seen on television, maybe presenting the news but he wasn't sure of that. Guy said she was absolutely gorgeous, even with the scars on her face."

Kyle used his thumb for more pressure as he rubbed his temple to try to stop his pounding headache. "That's great news, Jim."

"Does it help?"

"A lot. Thanks for working so hard, and so late, on this one. I owe you a bottle of Macallan myself."

Kyle hung up the phone and fell back on his pillows. So Sydney and Peyton had bought champagne and oysters for Duncan—and the rest of the group. But was that so out of line considering that Peyton was in charge of catering the event, and Sydney probably went along for the ride?

Probably.

CHAPTER 21

The next evening, Madison waited impatiently in the line of cars idling in front of and down the street from the Royal Opera House. The buzz for the evening's production of La Boheme had generated considerable interest, and the fact that the Prince of Wales and his wife, the Duchess of Cornwall, were expected ensured that the ever-present paparazzi were out in force.

When her hired sedan finally pulled up to the front, Madison gathered the folds of her gown and got out, careful to not get tangled in the fabric while still attempting a graceful exit. She was meeting her parents for tonight's performance and since she never liked to show up unaccompanied and be subjected to her mother's icy disapproval, however silent, she had invited Kyle to be her escort for the evening. Madison knew on some level that it was cruel to subject Kyle to the inquisition her mother had so perfected that her victim seldom knew it was happening. It was almost bloodless. Years of detective work had taught Kyle the same skill, however, and in a perversely mischievous way, Madison was looking forward to the subtle battle of wills and wit.

Madison regretted her insistence on meeting Kyle at the opera house rather than her flat, but she was eager to avoid the appearance of a date. She was, however, just as eager to avoid lingering alone outside the Opera House, so after a quick glance around she had just turned to go in when she felt someone gently take her elbow. Relieved, Madison smiled and turned, expecting to see Kyle. She gulped, the smile slowly slipping from her face when she saw Duncan standing there, brilliant in his custom-fitted tuxedo.

"Duncan," she said, recovering sufficiently to offer her cheek for a kiss and paste her smile back on for the cameras. "I didn't realize you would be here. How lovely?"

"Is it?" he asked, his eyes questioning. "Perhaps. But *you* are undoubtedly lovely this evening. I don't think I've ever seen you look more beautiful."

"I think we're blocking traffic," she said with a small laugh. "We should go in. Are you expecting someone?" Madison shook her head and put her hand up as though to stop his response. "That was just small talk. I don't really think it's my business."

"I'm here with a client, Madison—someone in from Geneva who wanted to attend the opera this evening. I have season's tickets, and I thought I could use the opportunity to discuss a new deal."

Madison watched as Duncan's face inexplicably fell. And then she heard Kyle's voice behind her. "Ever on the lookout for a new opportunity, eh, Duncan? Madison," Kyle said, kissing her cheek, "you look beautiful tonight." He glanced at Duncan and then back to Madison. "I am truly honored to escort the loveliest lady here tonight. Shall we?" he asked as he offered her his arm. "Duncan," he said nodding, "enjoy the show."

She slipped her arm through Kyle's and waved casually to Duncan as Kyle steered her towards the entrance. Madison waited for him to comment on Duncan's presence, but he said nothing. "I didn't know he would be here," she said.

"It's none of my business."

"No? Am I mistaken that I caught a slight annoyance emanating from you?" she asked as they navigated the milling crowds. She had arranged to meet her parents in the Balconies Restaurant for drinks prior to the performance, and Madison followed as Kyle seemed to know exactly where he was going. "By the way, you look very handsome in that tux. I was worried you didn't have one."

"You were worried? Oh ye of little faith."

"So what, exactly, do you have against Duncan?"

Kyle said nothing as he clasped the hand linked through arm and put his arm around her waist to guide her through a particularly crowded area by the Will Call window. When they had cleared the space, she pulled him to a stop. "Seriously, Kyle, you two used to be friends, and now you appear at odds."

He shook his head. "We were never friends, Madison. We were just members of the same group of friends, but we were never friends."

Madison pulled her head back, blinking her eyes in surprise. "Okay. But you were not enemies."

"Nor are we now," he said.

"But—."

Kyle exhaled. "But I don't trust him." He looked away, paused for a moment and then looked back at her. "And I don't think you should, either."

"In what way?" she asked, her voice very calm.

"In any way, frankly. I think Duncan Rand is good at keeping secrets and good at compartmentalizing his life and great at putting people into those compartments that will best serve his agenda. Regardless of how it affects them."

Madison found her breath was coming quicker, and she was caught between the ideas of whether she should mount an angry defense of Duncan or give in to her own fears. The latter won, and her voice was composed when she asked, "Is he officially under suspicion of Chris' murder?"

"Confidentially? Yes," Kyle said, lowering his voice as he looked around him. When his look returned to her, she saw understanding in his eyes. "Why don't I think that comes as a surprise to you?"

"Because you are a good detective," she said as she spotted her parents across the lobby. They were talking to the Prime Minister and his wife, and, not wishing to interrupt them, she simply waved just to get their attention to let them know she had arrived. Her father smiled broadly, but her mother only nodded briefly and without pausing in her conversation.

"Tell me one thing I need to know about your mother before I meet her," Kyle said as he attempted to straighten his tie for the tenth time and without the benefit of a mirror.

"Well," she said pausing to think for a moment. She wrinkled her forehead at a memory. "Several years ago our butler Parker, whom you met the other day, took a six-month leave of absence to take care of his mother, who was dying of cancer. We had a temporary man come in." Madison glanced back again at her mother and felt an unsettling mixture of pride and aversion wash over her. The Duchess was a striking figure, beautiful, tall, slim and aristocratic. She carried herself with the bearing of a woman who had never once doubted her self-worth and would not tolerate anyone else who did either. Madison kept her eyes on her mother while she continued. "In what is now something of a legendary dinner party, one of the staff whispered to Mummy that the unfortunate butler had just committed suicide below stairs."

"Jeez," Kyle said with his eyes now also focused on the Duchess.

"Yes, very sad. But my mother's reaction was telling. Her face betrayed neither shock nor distress when she whispered back, 'Has everyone been served?' Informed that everyone had, she then politely excused herself from the table to attend to the matter downstairs."

Lifting a single eyebrow, Kyle shook his head. "What should I take from that?"

"That appearances are very, very important to Mummy."

Kyle just smiled uncomfortably and nodded.

"Are you ready for this?" Madison asked.

"They train us to always be ready, ma'am."

"That's the Boy Scouts," Madison said.

"Close enough," he said under his breath as they walked up to Madison's parents.

"Mother," Madison said, kissing the cool smoothness of her mother's cheek. "You look lovely, as always. Daddy," she said, giving her father a full hug. "I've missed you." She turned to Kyle. "Mother, Daddy, I'd like to introduce you to a friend of mine from university, Kyle Ward. Kyle, these are my parents, the Duke and Duchess of Abbott."

"How do you do, son?" Edward Abbott said as Kyle shook his hand with a very slight bow, a nod really, of his head.

"Your Grace," Kyle said, repeating the gesture and greeting with her mother. "I have heard about you both for many years, and it is a privilege to meet you."

Madison smiled to herself at Kyle's perfect execution.

"And we you, young man. Madison keeps many of her friends hidden from us," he said looking at his daughter with a fond smile. "I think she's embarrassed by us." Jacqueline Abbott smiled coolly but said nothing. "Come, Jackie, let's all sit down and enjoy a drink before the show." He nodded at Kyle and put his arm around his shoulders. "I find it prudent to be well-fortified before three hours of opera."

Madison's mother took her hand and slowed her walk, allowing Kyle and Edward Abbott to go on ahead into the elegant restaurant. "Is your father being gracious, or have I forgotten you ever mentioning a Kyle Ward? I like to think I keep up rather well with your friends."

"Yes, Mummy, you do, but primarily the titled ones. I have mentioned Kyle on many occasions, but it has been a couple of years now."

"I see. And who are Mr. Ward's parents?"

Madison sighed. "His mother passed away several years ago, but I think Daddy is rather a good friend of his father's. Kyle is a detective with the New Scotland Yard. He graduated from St. Andrews with me, Will, Kate, and the rest of the group."

"A detective," Jacqueline said slowly, with a level of incredulity Madison had never heard before in her mother's voice. "My word, Madison. Is it serious?"

Madison thought for a moment whether it would be fun to lead her mother to believe that they were quite seriously dating and had talked of marriage. But, she reasoned, it would likely make the rest of the evening tense to the point of unbearable so she said, "Not even a little bit, Mum. We are only friends."

Jacqueline Abbott audibly exhaled at that moment, and Madison suppressed a smile as they sat down for a pre-theater course of appetizers and drinks.

"Tell me what you do at the Yard, Kyle. I have long been a fan of Arthur Conan Doyle. Is it something along those lines?" Edward said.

Madison smiled indulgently at her father and winked at Kyle.

"As a matter of fact, sir, I am also a detective, although not in the same league as Sherlock Holmes. Fortunately, we have more forensic tools these days so I don't have to rely solely on my wits."

"I am fascinated by that," Edward said as he leaned forward. "Are you working on anything rather exciting at the moment?"

"Well—," Kyle said, glancing nervously at Madison.

Her mother visibly stiffened and her ramrod posture became even straighter, as if that were possible. Madison smiled and nodded to Kyle.

"There was the incident at Whiddenhurst last week, and I am looking into that."

"Please," Jacqueline said tautly as she stood, "I would prefer to not speak of this. The earl's death was tragic, but I am certain there is nothing untoward there. If you will pardon me, I would like to powder my nose before the opera."

The Duchess looked pointedly at Madison, who knew she was supposed to accompany her mother and chose not to. They all watched her walk imperiously down the hall.

"She doesn't like anything unpleasant," the duke said apologetically, furrowing his brow. "She is such an incredible lady on every level. But she never likes to speak of upsetting subjects. It's touching really."

The evening's production of *La Boheme* was very well done, and Madison was pleased to see that Kyle seemed to be enjoying the performance. She was distressed that she had timed things so poorly by ignoring her mother's unspoken invitation that she had to excuse herself before intermission, but she was able to unobtrusively slip out of the theater. She could never recall where the loo was in the opera house and, because it was prior to intermission, there was a shortage of attendants around to direct her.

Madison mistakenly turned down a small corridor that led to a coatroom. She was retracing her steps when she saw Duncan back into the same hallway. She was on the verge of calling out to him when Sydney Atwood also appeared. Madison gasped, and stepped quickly into the coatroom, hoping they had neither heard nor seen her.

"You are making a scene, Sydney. I wish you would stop," Duncan said, his voice tightly controlled and just loud enough for Madison to hear. "There are people we know here, and this is neither the time nor the place."

"If you hadn't refused to talk to me the other night, I would not be 'making a scene,'" Sydney said, clearly angry. "I have been trying to talk to you for days. Why haven't you been taking my calls?"

"Because I don't want to get involved. I don't know what's going on with you, but I don't think I can help. I am truly sorry you seem to be under stress, but this has nothing to do with me."

"Has nothing to do with you?" Sydney said, her voice rising. "You were the one who invited him to the charity match. You were the one doing business with him. You are the connecting factor to everything terrible that's going on. It has *everything* to do with you."

"I don't know what you're talking about. And I don't want to know. I admit I made a mistake. I'm trying to rectify it. But these kinds of confrontations aren't good for anybody. You have to see that."

"What I see, Duncan, is that you made a mistake and you think everyone else has to deal with the consequences. You would just prefer to float, unscathed, over the wreckage you've made of everyone else's life."

"I am done with this conversation, Sydney. Goodnight."

"I'll tell them, you know," she said, her voice no longer a whisper as Madison heard Duncan walk away. "I will tell them all, especially *her*, about everything you have been up to."

CHAPTER 22

The noise jarred Kyle awake far too early the next morning, and he reached blindly for the snooze button. He punched it several times before he realized it was his phone ringing and not his alarm clock. He and the Abbotts had been out later than he had expected. And he had enjoyed himself more than he had expected. Her mother was an iceberg he felt certain would never warm up to him, but her father had been personable and funny, in a somewhat aristocratic, politically correct way, but fun to be with nonetheless.

So the phone call was unwelcome.

"Ward," Kyle mumbled without picking up his head or checking to see who was calling.

"Get your ass out of bed, Ward. It's 8:00am."

"Who is this?" he said as he struggled to sit up.

"It's Peyton Taylor," she said softly. "Get up. Let's go for a run."

"Huh?" His head was still fuzzy with sleep but he was aware enough to remember that Peyton had not spoken to him in almost a decade. "Seriously, who is this?"

"Seriously, it's Peyton. Meet me in Hyde Park at the Lido Café Bar in thirty minutes. It sounds like you need some caffeine."

Kyle was about to respond when he realized Peyton had hung up. He had no idea what was going on and wanted nothing more than to go back to sleep. But he knew this was an opportunity of some kind and he did not want to miss it. He dragged himself out of bed and headed towards the shower.

He arrived ten minutes late. Peyton had really not given him enough time, and he wondered if she had done so as some kind of test. The park was quiet this early on a Sunday morning soggy with a light drizzle and shrouded in fog. He found the Lido Café and was heading towards the queue, which was, even in the rain, longer than he would have wished, when he saw Peyton.

She was standing down by the lake doing warm up stretches, and he watched as several men passed by looking at her with appreciative glances. Peyton did look good, slim and toned in a tight shirt and very short running shorts. Kyle thought she also looked about sixteen with her hair pulled back in a pony tail and wearing very little make-up. She saw him, waved and walked over to a nearby table and picked up two large cups of what he hoped was seriously caffeinated coffee.

Peyton smiled, and Kyle instinctively looked behind him to see to whom that was directed. Seeing no one familiar, he looked at her and pointed to his chest. "Me?" he mouthed.

She nodded as she smiled broadly and motioned him over with the coffee cup in her hand.

"It's raining," he said as he held out his hands.

"It's not raining hard. And it will stop. Don't be a wuss, Ward."

"Uh-huh. Okay, what gives, Peyton? You've hated me for so long now, I thought it was irreversible."

"Really less time than you think. But I've decided to let you off the hook. It's too hard to stay mad, and it's starting to get in the way," she said, handing him a large cup. "Alas, we never got to know each other well enough for me to know what you like in your morning coffee—or maybe I just forgot—so you have to doctor your own if it's anything other than black. There's the little stand where they keep everything," she said as she nodded towards the café.

He smiled. "No, this is good. Thank you."

Peyton looked away, seemingly entranced by the ducks gliding effortlessly on The Sepentine Lake, and he drank the hot coffee too fast. He winced, glad she had not seen such a stupid move.

"I love this park in the early morning before it gets full of tourist and screaming children. It's even better in the rain," she said before she turned back to him. "How are you doing, Kyle?"

"I'm good. How are you, Peyton?"

"I am excellent," she said as she watched two women jog past. "I guess there's no way I could talk you into a run, is there?"

"Absolutely none. I got up far earlier than I wanted to for you. That's about as much as I can manage at this point."

Peyton sighed. "Okay. Let's walk then." She turned and started off down a path that ran along the lake. He felt he had no choice but to follow.

"Contrary to what you think, I'm always happy to see you," he said, "but I am a little curious as to what this is about. I have a feeling it's not about you."

She turned to look him, her eyebrows raised. "What makes you say that?"

He shrugged. "I don't think you would have put yourself out there with me if it was about you. Why risk what you always perceived as rejection again?"

Peyton scratched her eyebrow as she continued to look at him as they walked. "I am impressed."

"I'm good at motives," he said as he shrugged. "It's what I do for a living."

"Okay, I didn't know that specifically, but I have heard that you are a good detective."

He was pleased to hear this, but did not want to pursue any topic that sounded self-aggrandizing. They walked for awhile in silence, Kyle too wary of saying anything that would put her off.

"It's about Madison," Peyton said.

"Okay."

"Or, more accurately, it's about Duncan."

Kyle finished his coffee and tossed the cup into the trash can as they passed. "I'm listening," he said.

"I don't know what's going on with the investigation into Chris' death, but I've heard you're looking into it. Was he killed?"

"He was," Kyle said softly.

"I was afraid of that."

"What makes you say that? Have you talked to Madison about this?"

"No. I didn't realize she knew anything about it. My concern for Madison is that Duncan seems back in her life, and the timing seems just a little too convenient." She gestured dismissively. "I'm not talking about being old friends. I'm talking about him trying to pick their relationship back up again."

"And you don't want that?"

"I think she was so devastated by their break-up, to say nothing of the reasons for it, and I don't want to see her go through something like that again."

"Maybe he's grown up."

"Duncan's issues are not a matter of immaturity. He's just selfish." She stopped walking and turned to Kyle. "Look, don't get me wrong. I like Duncan. He's brilliant and charming and witty. And he's a loyal friend in every aspect. And, of course, he's successful, but that's not really important."

"Sure it is."

"Yeah, well, maybe. But some of the characteristics that make him so good in all those ways are the same ones that make him lousy to be involved with. I don't want to see her hurt again."

"Okay," Kyle said as he headed over to one of the now damp park benches lining the lake. He hoped she would follow him this time, and she did. "But there's something else you're worried about. I've sort of been out of the loop with you guys for a couple of years, but ignoring that, isn't this something to be discussed between girlfriends? It's not the kind of cautionary message to be delivered by a ham-handed detective who could have a hidden agenda, which would ensure that anything meaningful was lost."

Peyton looked at him, her eyes wide and a smile playing at the corners of her mouth. "Do you have a hidden agenda, Kyle?"

"No. Jeez, I knew you'd take it that way. I'm just saying it could look like that."

She exhaled keeping her eyes on the lake. "Look, I've always known that you had a thing for Madison. I was some kind of poor man's substitute for her until you realized that just made it worse by comparison. So you went underground because you didn't know what else to do."

Kyle slowly closed his eyes and smiled a rueful little smile before he got up the courage to look at her. "I'm sorry. I didn't think you knew."

"I didn't think *you* knew. I still think I figured it out before you did." She shrugged. "And then hating you became kind of a sport, because, quite frankly, it was fun to watch you squirm. And you never failed to do so."

"Well—yeah—well. As for being a poor man's substitute, isn't your father one of the most successful property developers in New York? I can see you've lived like a spurned wallflower all these years."

She snorted as she looked at him slyly out of the corner of her eye. "Most men think I'm beautiful, Kyle."

"Most men are right, Peyton."

She turned to face him, pulling one knee up onto the bench and wrapping her arms around it. She rested her chin on that knee. "So back to Duncan. He was acting weird that day—the day Chris died."

"Weird like how?"

"Like he was nervous, except that Duncan isn't the kind of guy who ever gets nervous. So maybe he was just distracted. But he clearly wanted Sydney out of the way. She was being her normal self, all flirty—but with everyone, Chris and Jules, too, not just Duncan—and she really seemed to be getting on his nerves. When Hawthorne got there, he and Duncan were talking quietly and she kept interrupting them. So Duncan finally gave her his credit card to go pick up supplies to get away from her for awhile. So, of course, Syd went wild with the champagne fountain and all."

"Did you hear what he and Hawthorne were talking about at all?"

Peyton shook her head. "No, but I caught the body language and it was intense. Hawthorne's a slimy guy, and he seemed to be trying to placate Duncan in some way. I think Duncan was angry, but he's always such a controlled guy that it's hard to really tell. But it was all really strange, particularly in retrospect."

"How does this concern Madison, though?"

She sighed. "Doesn't the timing seem odd to you? They broke up ages ago, and he was pretty thoughtless of her feelings during the years since. And then, just when a friend of ours dies under mysterious circumstances, he wants to get back together with her, like, immediately?" Peyton shrugged. "I don't know. Maybe I'm just too suspicious of his motives because of the things he did before, but it just strikes me as odd. Like he wanted to distract her from something." She turned to look at Kyle. "Or maybe have a champion."

A couple walking hand-in-hand around the perimeter of the lake caught Kyle's eye. They were several hundreds yards away, but there was something in the man's build and gait that was familiar to him. Kyle watched as the man leaned his head down towards the petite woman as though he wanted to hear every word she said. Even at this distance, there was clearly an intimacy there. As they got closer, Kyle leaned forward and squinted to make sure he was not mistaken.

"What is it?" Peyton asked spinning around to follow his gaze.

"It's another really strange thing, maybe even more so."

She narrowed her eyes and put her hand over them, even though there was still no sun from which she needed shade. "Do we know those people?"

"Indeed we do. It's Jules and Annabel."

"Oh," Peyton said in a small voice. "I didn't know."

"I don't think anyone did."

CHAPTER 23

Madison stared at the invitation on her desk and wondered if there was any way she could get out of the event. The missive itself was beautifully crafted, and it was clear that Duncan had spared no expense. The same would, no doubt, hold true for the affair itself, which was to be held this evening in the Orangery at Kew Palace. The reception was for clients of Duncan's firm, Titan Investments, and it would undoubtedly be filled with glittering people made wealthy by Duncan's financial acumen, analytical prowess and willingness to go to the limit of finely calculated risk as he made the kinds of deals that made headlines. He was renowned in London, New York, Zurich, Tokyo and Munich for his ability to get into a deal right before its peak performance and get out before any downturn, and his party would no doubt have high profile attendees from all over Europe.

Quite apart from what Madison viewed as the questionable taste of holding such a conspicuous event so soon after Chris Grisham's death, she was still troubled by the argument she had witnessed between Duncan and Sydney at the opera. She had not spoken to either of them since, and she did not relish seeing them tonight. Madison was certain Sydney would be at the reception this evening, as would Jules. Duncan handled both of their investment portfolios, and he liked to have his high profile clients at his events.

She paused at that thought and wondered for an unpleasant moment whether Lady Madison Abbott was also a high profile person to have his event. She pushed the thought out of her mind, knowing that if she believed it, that would be the deciding factor in whether she attended.

If she had not agreed weeks ago to show up at the long-planned event, she would have made her excuses. As it was, Duncan had sent a car for her. It would arrive in less than an hour and she had made no progress towards getting ready. After several minutes of tossing his rubber duck for Morgan to fetch, she reluctantly mounted the steps to her bedroom to get ready.

Ninety minutes later, the rented sedan pulled into the drop off lane in front of the Kew Palace, and Madison carefully got out with the help of a liveried footman. She had to admit that the venue looked stunning, with the Orangery lit up in the distance, small white lights sparkling in the trees of the Queen's Garden and a live orchestra playing in the background. While she disliked arriving at events unescorted, she had declined coming as Duncan's date, with the attendant duties of acting as hostess, and thought bringing a guest too rude.

Madison eyed the gravel path and regretted the heels she had chosen. She sighed as she gathered the hem of her new gown as she also questioned her choice of the sheer white overlay for an outdoor event. Madison kept her eyes on the path so she could avoid ending up on her bum in a puddle of satin and organza.

She had just taken a few steps towards the Orangery when she looked up and saw Michael Rand standing before her and smiling broadly. Duncan's father was an older, slightly grayer version of his son and the most distinguished, as well as one of the most handsome, man she had ever known. He had been very supportive of her when her own father had been too devastated by Charles' death to be emotionally present for anyone. Madison had harbored a schoolgirl crush on Michael Rand while at university and had maintained something of an infatuation with him in the years since. She suspected that this was because Michael was a more mature version of Duncan, but the deeper meaning did not stop her from enjoying his company.

He walked towards her and took her hands in his own as he held out her arms. "You are undoubtedly the most beautiful vision here, Madison. I have missed seeing more of you."

She smiled warmly and kissed his cheeks. "I have missed you as well. I cannot tell you how thrilled I am that you are here this evening." Madison looked around at the crowd of expensively dressed and bejeweled attendees and lowered her voice conspiratorially. "I was wondering who I was going to talk to all evening."

Michael laughed as he turned towards the sound of the music wafting through the gardens. He pulled her arm through his and started towards a large white stucco building that blazed with the light that spilled out onto its terrace. As they walked through the flowering gardens, Madison had to admit it was a lovely event. The orchestra was set up on one end of the terrace of the Orangery. Small tables with pale salmon satin tablecloths and flickering candles were also set and liveried waiters circulated among the mingling guests, all of whom had beautiful views of the surrounding landscape. The Orangery's floor-to-ceiling Palladium doors were open and already there were over two hundred guests milling between the gardens and what Madison assumed were buffet tables and food stations set inside.

"My son is running late," Michael said conversationally as they slowly strolled along. "He said something about a deal cratering, and I have been tasked with being a fill-in host until he gets here. But I had specific instructions to look out for you and make sure you had a good time."

"That's kind," Madison said gently squeezing his arm.

"It's pure selfishness on my part. Do you know the history of the Kew Palace?" He asked as he waved and nodded to familiar faces, not once breaking his stride with Madison.

"Hmm. If I recall, Queen Elizabeth, otherwise known as the Virgin Queen, gave it to her courtier Robert Dudley, the Earl of Leicester, for, ahem, services to the Crown. He was, after all, her lover," she said, her eyes twinkling.

"Allegedly her lover," he said.

"Ah, I always forget that the Rand men are solicitors. I will admit that it certainly *proves* nothing, but she kept his final correspondence in a box by her bedside until she died. She wrote "His Last Letter" on it. I find that romantic."

"As do I," he said, patting her hand.

"Are you a romantic at heart?"

"Oh, I'm not sure about that. But I had a great love affair with my wife for almost forty years before she passed away. Maybe that's something."

They walked on in silence as Madison looked around to more fully take in the aesthetics. She saw a familiar figure and instinctively shrank back.

"What is it?" Michael asked.

"Jeff Hawthorne. He's done some business with Duncan, but I am surprised to see him here. And I would rather he not see me."

"Indeed," Michael said and subtly changed their direction to avoid running into Chris' former partner. "I am familiar with Mr. Hawthorne. I cautioned against that investment. But my son is loyal to his friends."

"To a fault perhaps," Madison said

"Sometimes we don't know where those fault lines are until we trip over them." He smiled. "We're lucky if we merely trip and don't fall flat on our—faces. Ah," he said nodding towards another guest walking towards them, "we are fortunate there's a doctor in the house."

Julian looked flushed from the heat of the crowd, and Madison wondered if he had already been dancing. He was seldom at a loss for companionship, however brief, and she noticed the appreciative looks from many women as he passed by. She thought that his tuxedo gave him an impression of elegance only barely containing an energetic ruggedness and an adventurous spirit. For the first time in all the years she had known him, Madison thought that Jules could be capable of great passion, which, depending on the situation, could mean pleasure or danger. She was actually embarrassed by the thought, and turned away for a moment to compose herself as Jules walked up.

"And here's Julian Marlborough. Jules," Michael said as he reached out to shake his hand. "If you can keep Lady Madison company, I can excuse myself to check on Duncan's status and see to the other guests before he arrives."

"I am happy to. Madison, what can I get you to drink?"

"Whatever the special drink of the evening is. These kinds of events generally have a theme. Did Peyton coordinate this?"

"Not that I'm aware of," Jules said, as he stopped a passing waiter carrying a tray of dark blue drinks. Within the very contemporary martini glasses small sugar cubes soaked in 151 proof rum burned brightly as they floated in the inky liquid producing a new drink their waiter called a Midnight Sky.

"Wow," Madison said as she looked at the flaming drink.

"Blow it out before you drink it," Jules cautioned.

"Thanks for that tip, doctor. It might not have occurred to me," she said as she gently blew on the cubes until they were extinguished. She shook her head. "Boy, there's nothing over-the-top about this, is there?"

"Duncan is a subtle kind of guy, love. You've always known that about him."

Madison sighed and tasted the drink, which was surprisingly delicious. "Do we know anyone here?"

"I think you and I will be the only members of our group here this evening. Sydney sent me a text, and she won't be able to make it."

"Well, that's—unfortunate."

Jules laughed. "Men don't trade platinum for tin, sweetheart. Even if it's just a chance for platinum. I don't know what's on Syd's agenda lately, but she's plotting all by herself. Duncan isn't that stupid."

"No?"

"No. Come on, let's have a dance and then see what kind of expensive food they've put out to harden our arteries and get me more patients."

Jules whirled Madison onto the temporary dance floor that had been laid down just off the terrace in the Queen's Garden. She relaxed into his arms as she watched the other guests circulate around them. She recognized several members of Parliament and one rather famous American actress whose name she could not recall. She still felt awkward about being here but had to admit it was enchanting.

They slowed to a waltz, and Madison gazed over Jules' shoulder as he pulled her closer. She stiffened. A woman who looked surprisingly like Sydney Atwood had just slipped into the crowd heading into the Orangery.

"Did you say Sydney is not going to be here this evening?" she asked.

"I did. I didn't speak to her, but she texted that she came down with strep throat or something. I think she just didn't want to attend. I gather there's a new someone she's been seeing for a couple of months that she doesn't want us to meet for some reason."

"Is he married? Would she be that reckless?" Madison thought she saw Jules blush as she watched embarrassment flicker across his eyes.

"I don't know," he said. "People do stupid things all the time. And Sydney wasn't ever really one for playing by conventional rules."

The waltz ended, and Jules and Madison joined the group of dancers as they clapped for the live orchestra. Madison glanced back towards the Orangery, but the Sydney lookalike did not reappear. Her small purse vibrated, and she looked sheepishly at Jules. "I know it's tactless, and I really only bring my mobile for emergencies, so do you mind?"

"I'm a doctor. I'd answer mine."

"Thanks," she said as she pulled out her device. "I don't think we can leave until we at least say 'hello' to Duncan, and I don't think he's even here yet." She glanced at the text and sighed. "He's still running late. He says he'll be here within thirty minutes." Madison looked up at Jules and squinted, pulling a face. "Should we be annoyed?"

"No," he said. "We should just overindulge and then we won't care if he's here or not."

"I like the way you think. I'd also like to find the loo first if you don't mind, and then I'll meet you back here."

Jules nodded towards the reception hall. "I think they're back behind the hall, near the kitchens."

Madison made her way through the beautifully decorated hall. Elaborate food stations of caviar and vodka, crab legs, shrimp and oysters, roasted meats of beef, pork and chicken, a bar where a chef prepared fluffy, made-to-order omelets, a chocolate fountain with fruits and little cakes, and several others on the opposite side of the hall from her path tempted the party-goers, and all had growing queues.

She made her way through the great room to the hall behind it and paused for a moment, not sure which way to go. Madison turned left but stopped just before she entered a door that was clearly the kitchen. A helpful steward directed her across the hall to the public loos. She made it a practice to drink very little at formal events to, among other reasons, avoid having to deal with her formal gown, but Murphy's Law generally came into play anyway.

Fifteen minutes later, Madison had put herself back together, checked her make-up in the mirror and walked out of the loo. Momentarily disoriented, she walked straight out instead of turning right and back towards the main reception hall, and she ended up in a small conference room.

It was then that she saw Jeff Hawthorne lying on the industrial grey carpet. He was curled into a partial fetal position, with both of his hands clasping his stomach, under which spread a rapidly growing bloodstain. Hawthorne's pupils were fully dilated, and he stared, unseeing, at the floor.

The similarities between the ways in which Hawthorne lay there, almost pathetically in a barren, commercial back room on cheap carpet and her beloved Charles as he lay in the luxurious

surroundings of his own home were striking.
Madison felt the room start to spin. A heated flush
started in her stomach and rose rapidly as her heart
rate accelerated. Her hands started to shake and a
wave of nausea took her to the ground just as she
turned away from the body and vomited into a small
wastepaper basket.

CHAPTER 24

He got the call on his mobile because the dispatcher made the connection between Duncan Rand's event and Kyle Ward's murder investigation. Kyle seldom used it, but tonight he felt justified in taking the flashing red light from his glove compartment and letting the magnet within secure it to the roof of the Range Rover as he sped towards the Kew Palace.

By the time he arrived, a Major Investigation Team, or MIT, was already on the scene. In addition to an ambulance and an unmarked sedan, the Forensic Medical Examiner's SUV and four uniformed police units were already onsite. A uniformed officer was waiting for him, and he walked over as Kyle shut down his engine.

"Do we know who the victim is?" Kyle asked, a little concerned that he would be attending the funeral of another of his friends.

"His name is Jeff Hawthorne. There are several people here who know him, including the woman who found him. She's pretty upset, but she's in good enough shape to talk to you."

Kyle was surprised to see Michael Rand, whom he had not seen for many years, walking towards him. "Detective," he said, reaching out to shake Kyle's hand, "you may not remember me, but I am Michael Rand, the father of a friend of yours."

Kyle did not stop walking but said, "Of course, I remember you, Mr. Rand. Is Duncan still here?"

"He will be here in ten minutes. He got caught in some unavoidable business conflict downtown and hasn't been here yet tonight."

"I see," Kyle said noting a large group of people looking very impatient. Undoubtedly they were quite agitated to find themselves caught in something not only horrific but that would also delay their departure from an event most of them were by now more than ready to leave. He addressed the uniformed officer when he said, "I assume you've cordoned off the scene and kept everyone away?"

"Yes, sir."

Michael Rand caught Kyle's jacket and pulled him to a stop. "Madison Abbott is the one who found him. Apparently, it was a gruesome scene. I think she's in shock, and she—."

Hearing Madison's name Kyle shook himself free of Michael's grasp and took off running as he headed towards the officers clustered over by the Orangery.

She was sitting at an elegant table with an elaborate flower arrangement, fine china and crystal that seemed incongruous if not perverse under the circumstances when Kyle entered the main hall. Madison did, indeed, look in shock as she stared, seemingly unblinking, at an indefinable point at the far end of the hall. She seemed to sway a little in her chair, but she was calmly answering the questions being asked by another detective.

Kyle put his arm on the man's shoulder to pause the interrogation and saw that Madison's beautiful white evening gown had an angry slash of blood across the front. "Are you hurt?" he asked trying to keep his voice calm.

Madison looked up and at first did not appear to recognize Kyle. Relief finally flooded her stricken features, but her eyes were clearly still haunted and her voice husky when she simply said, "No."

"It would be foolish of me to ask how you are," Kyle said. She just nodded slowly. "I need to see the scene. And then I'll come back, okay?" She nodded again. He turned to the detective. "Hold up until I get back, okay?" He lowered his voice and turned away from Madison before he said, "Watch out for her. Don't let anyone bother her."

Kyle joined both the uniformed and plain-clothed officers mingling around the hall leading to the small conference room. A police photographer was snapping photos of every aspect of the victim and the room. Kyle flashed his badge at the Medical Examiner. "Detective Chief Inspector Ward," he said. "What do we know?"

"We know he's dead, and has been for no more than two hours. Single edged stab wound to the liver, four-inch knife. Probably bled out in less than a minute. I'll know more with the full autopsy."

"You're good. How can you tell it was a four inch knife at this point?"

The ME rolled the victim onto his back and nodded. "He left the knife. I have no idea how it ended up under him. Maybe they struggled. Maybe the vic pulled it out himself in a really misguided effort to make things better, which, of course, would have only made him bleed out faster. Anyway, the perp was probably surprised and left in a hurry before he had a chance to retrieve it."

"Anybody hear anything?" Kyle asked the junior detective on the team.

"Not that we've found yet. We still need to question everybody, but there was a lot of noise. The kitchen is right here, and they were getting ready for a big dinner with a lot of people. There was an orchestra, too."

"So a guy gets stabbed in the middle of a party for a couple of hundred people and nobody sees or hears anything?" Kyle rolled Hawthorne over once more and scrutinized the knife. "This come from the kitchens here?"

The detective shook his head. "Don't think so. This is a pretty fancy knife." He looked at his notepad. "It's a Japanese made—. It's a— I'll spell it. Kikuichi Hammered Santoku knife. The chef recognized it. Very expensive, but not all that rare. He said it was unlikely but not impossible that an industrial kitchen or caterer would have one, but you can buy them pretty easily if you just have the money."

"Great, that narrows down the list of suspects to about two hundred considering this crowd," Kyle said. "I can't see somebody bringing his own knife to a fancy event just in case anybody pissed them off to the point they needed to be killed. I'd say this one was strictly spur-of-the-moment with little to no planning involved. Hawthorne argued with somebody, or threatened them; the perp grabbed a knife," he gestured towards the kitchen, "and killed him."

"Yeah, that sounds like a reasonable assumption to me. This guy have any enemies?"

"Legions from what I've heard," Kyle said as he rubbed his chin, not taking his eyes off Hawthorne. "So we're checking prints on the knife? I think you'll find Hawthorne's there, too. I'd like the team to split up and interview the crowd. You can ask people to come forward if they saw anything. Take everyone's name so we can check for connections with Hawthorne, but if they didn't see anything, we don't have to delay them further. I know this kind. There will be hell to pay if we keep them much longer."

Kyle returned to the main hall where Madison was still sitting, flanked now by Michael Rand and Julian Marlborough. Kyle nodded to the latter as he pulled out the chair next to Madison, turned it around and straddled it so he faced her. "What did you see?" he asked gently.

"Nothing. I mean other than Jeff Hawthorne lying on the floor stabbed—," she gulped and looked up at Kyle. "Was he stabbed? I didn't see a knife but surely someone would have heard a gunshot?"

Kyle nodded. "He was stabbed. The knife was left. Anyway, go on."

Madison exhaled. "I stumbled into the room by accident. I didn't hear or see anything, or anyone. I just took a wrong turn trying to find my way back from the loo." She shook her head and ran her fingers through her hair. "I have no idea why he would have even been in that room. It had nothing to do with the reception. Unless—."

"Unless?"

"I don't know. Unless he went in there to talk privately to someone."

"Who might he have been talking privately to?"

Madison sighed heavily and shook her head again. "I really don't know, Kyle. I didn't see him talking to anyone I knew all evening. But I—well, I—I thought I might have seen Sydney heading into this building earlier. But it was just a flash, and it may not have been her. I guess it's really unfair of me to say it was her. It was so brief and the woman was quite far away."

Kyle looked at Michael Rand. "Did you see Sydney Atwood tonight?"

"I did not. She was supposed to be here, but she let Duncan know at the last minute that she couldn't attend."

"And me," Jules said. "She sent me a note as well."

"That was comprehensive," Kyle said. He looked at Madison. "Did she tell you?"

"No."

"And Duncan was not here the whole evening. Is that right? Has he arrived yet?"

"He has," Duncan said, looking like something out of a James Bond film striding up to the table wearing a white dinner jacket, white shirt and black bow tie—and looking more anxious than Kyle had ever seen him look before. "Can someone tell me what the hell is going on here?"

"Your partner Jeff Hawthorne has been murdered," Kyle said, looking directly at Duncan and trying to gage his reaction.

Duncan's eyes widened momentarily, but he did not flinch when he returned Kyle's look and said calmly, "He wasn't my partner."

"Really? I had heard that you two did a deal together where you got hosed. Where were you tonight, Duncan?"

"I was at my offices downtown. I have witnesses."

"You have witnesses, huh? Why would you need witnesses?"

"Because I'm being questioned by the police about a murder," Duncan said, his tone sharp but not defensive. "Look, I was delayed by a two billion dollar deal that was falling apart. I was in communication with a lot of people about it. There are phone records and about ten people on the conference call that delayed me who can attest to that."

Kyle just nodded. "It's standard protocol that we check, so I'll need their names."

"Of course," Duncan said. "You'll have them tonight."

"And it would be good for you to not leave town for a couple of days," he said, gesturing to the group, "all of you."

"Does that include me?" Madison asked.

Duncan looked surprised that she was there, and he came immediately to her side and took her hand. His eyes widened when he saw her dress, and he knelt by her side. "My God, Madison. How did—?"

"She found him," Kyle said still staring at Duncan. "Were you planning on leaving town, Madison?"

"I would like to go home, to Whiddenhurst. Will that be a problem? I can be reached there and will return to London right away if you need me to."

Duncan stood while keeping ahold of Madison's hand. "I'll take you home myself. We can leave tonight."

"No," Kyle said. "I'd like you to be available for further questioning."

"I *will* be available," Duncan said tightly. "But I'm taking Madison home. If you want to stop me, arrest me." He pulled Madison to her feet, removed his jacket and placed it carefully around her shoulders. Duncan turned back to Kyle. "You have all my numbers, Kyle. I will return to London within two hours if you need to speak with me in person." Duncan looked around. "Dad, do you mind handling things here while I take Madison home? I don't know if they need to talk to everyone at the party or not, and I think one of us should be here. But I think Madison has been through enough tonight."

Kyle watched Duncan lead Madison out of the Orangery, annoyed that he was being so defiant—or was it merely arrogant?—under the circumstances. But Duncan was right about one thing. Short of arresting him, Kyle really could not demand that he remain in London. And he had no probable cause whatsoever to arrest him.

Julian and Michael left to go deal with a group of by now very unhappy guests. Kyle idly wondered, as he pulled out his mobile and dialed headquarters, whether this would negatively impact Duncan's business or not. He was not wholly displeased at the thought that it might.

"Ward here. I need you to put a trace on the mobile number for a Duncan Rand. I need to know everywhere he went today, particularly in the hours between six and ten pm. Tomorrow? Okay, thanks."

Kyle returned to the conference room in which Jeff Hawthorne had had his final and fatal encounter. He had not liked the man in life, but taking a knife to the gut and bleeding out alone on cheap carpeting in some back room while a party raged around you seemed an especially sad way to die.

The MIT team was wrapping up, and the emergency medical technicians had already bagged Hawthorne and strapped the body onto a gurney, which they would then transport to the Coroner's Office in Bromley for autopsy. The Forensic Medical Examiner came to stand by Kyle as they watched them go.

"You probably know that England and Wales have one of the highest autopsy rates in the world," the FME said.

Kyle narrowed his eyes and looked directly at him. "No," he said, irritated. "I didn't know that. Where do you get this stuff?"

He shrugged. "It's my job." And he followed the EMTs out of the building.

CHAPTER 25

Duncan guided the Rolls to a stop and double-parked before Madison's flat. She had an overwhelming desire to get out of London and had it not been for her dog, she would have departed without even an overnight bag with the knowledge that she could find what she needed either at Whiddenhurst or in Tetbury.

"Can you please go in and get Morgan?" she asked. "His travel bag is a large Harrods canvas bag, the one with the Scotties and Westies on it, in my kitchen. I'll get his car seat out of the Cygnet."

Duncan studied her face for a moment before he took her keys and entered the flat. She heard Morgan bark but knew the little terrier would do no more. She kicked off her heels and walked half a block in her stocking feet to her car, where she removed Morgan's small black car seat from the boot. Madison returned to the Rolls and thought her poor little dog would be lost all alone in the vastness of its back seat. Kyle had been right. It did look like a hearse.

She was struggling with the seatbelt when Duncan returned carrying the Harrods travel bag, a pair of sweat clothes, and a bottle of water as the twenty-five pound Scottie did his best to pull him along so he could get to

Madison. Regardless of the situation, Morgan's enthusiasm always made her smile and she crouched down to pet him. It was only when her little dog became inordinately interested in the blood on her dress that she recoiled and hurried to lift him into the vehicle.

When they were all back in the car and securely buckled in, Duncan handed her the bottle of water and the sweat clothes and started the car. "I think you need to change your clothes and take one of these."

She looked at the prescription bottle in his hand but was unable to read the label. "What are they?"

"Valium. It's a low dose, but it can help."

"Do I strike you as an hysterical woman? I found a dead man tonight. He was still warm, so I just narrowly missed a murderer. I have his blood on my dress. And I haven't even shed a tear."

"Exactly. I think you're in shock, and that's going to wear off before we get to Whiddenhurst. And I think it will be brutal when it does. I also think you really need to change your clothes."

She stared at him a moment, handed the bottle of water back to him, removed her seatbelt and turned so he could unzip her dress.

"It would have been a great idea to have done this at your flat," he said, as he tried to unzip her with one hand while she held the top of the dress.

"I don't want to be in the intimacy of a flat with you at the moment."

"Yeah, because this is so much less dangerous."

They got the dress unzipped and she wiggled out of it, balled it up and threw it in the backseat. "Are these windows darkened?"

"They are, but there's no one around."

Madison struggled into the sweat clothes she didn't realize she even owned and found them to be warm and comforting. "Where did you find this?" she asked as she fought with the childproof cap on the Valium.

"In your medicine cabinet. I didn't know you were on Valium."

"I'm not. They're my mother's."

"She doesn't strike me as the type to pop Valium."

"She wasn't—before Charles was killed. She doesn't like to ever appear as if anything gets to her, even the death of her son. But she needed help for awhile to attain that. And then I think it just became something she wanted to always have ready just in case emotions loomed." Madison gave up and put the bottle down for a moment with a resigned sigh. "Who do you think killed him?"

"Do you want some help?" he asked reaching for the bottle.

"No," she said jerking it away from him. "I got it." She tried once more and was able to twist off the lid. Madison tipped two pills into her hand and washed them down with the bottled water. As an afterthought, she said, "How many should I have taken?"

"I'd start with one."

"Oh. Well, I—."

Duncan looked at her with concern and then amusement. "Maybe you'll sleep all the way there." He punched the button for seat heat. "You can put the seat almost all the way back."

"I don't want to sleep before you tell me who you think killed him."

"Hawthorne? I don't have any idea."

"Did you?" she asked in a defiant tone.

Duncan stared straight ahead, his upper lip disappearing into a thin flat line as he gripped the steering wheel more tightly. "Is that you or Kyle Ward asking?"

"Is there a different answer depending on who's asking? And while you're at it," she said yawning and having some difficulty now in keeping track of her thought process, "what have you got going on with Sydney?"

"I don't have anything going on with Sydney. I've told you that before, and it has not changed."

"She was there tonight, you know. She told everyone she wouldn't be, and then I thought I saw her."

Duncan looked at her, taking his eyes off the road for several seconds. "Are you absolutely positive?"

"No. I guess I'm not absolutely positive. But I think I saw her. Really, what kind of games are you two playing?"

"Where is this coming from? What makes you think *we* are doing or playing anything? It has been an absolutely dreadful week and instead of supporting one another, we seem to be at each other's throats."

"I saw you two together at the opera, Duncan. There was clearly something going on between the two of you. And it was not anything good."

"It wasn't what it looked like."

"I have found, in my experience, that when people say that, it is almost always far worse." Madison yawned again. She could not recall the last time she had taken a sedative, and she had forgotten that she did not like the deadening of her neural processes. She supposed that was the point, but her thoughts and emotions were all slipping just out of her reach.

"Sydney isn't stable," Duncan said quietly. "And I can't be part of her world anymore. She wants something from me that I can't give her, and she isn't letting up. I tried to tell you last week that I thought the accident pushed her over the edge."

Madison leaned back and pulled Duncan's jacket over her. She closed her eyes. "Do you know how many women I talk to in my practice who say their significant other is always saying they're 'unstable' when they really just want to control them? It's called gas lighting. I've seen it for years."

Duncan was silent for a long time. Just before she slipped into a restless sleep, she heard him softly say, "That's not what is happening here."

Even in the twilight of the Valium, Madison felt the texture of the road change from asphalt to gravel beneath the tires of the car, and she instinctively knew they had arrived at Whiddenhurst. She opened her eyes as they drove through the massive iron gates of the estate and punched the button to bring the seat back into an upright position. As she watched the rolling hills come in and out of her sightline in the moonlight, Madison waited for that first glimpse of the house, which would be lit even this late at night. Regardless of what hurricanes of change blew through her life and upended her world as she knew it, Whiddenhurst remained the same, a stalwart fortress of safety and familiarity to which she would always return to regain her footing.

"We're here," Duncan said softly. "I called Parker while you were asleep and told him we were coming and asked him to prepare two rooms. He said he would stay up but I told him that wasn't necessary. I hope that's okay with you, but it's after midnight."

"Of course, it's fine," she said, still coming to and realizing the effects of the Valium had not worn off. "I don't think Mummy and Daddy are here. Am I wrong?"

"Yes, you are. They arrived earlier this evening. Parker will have told them we are on our way, but I'm sure they're asleep at this hour," he said, bringing the car to a stop in the front courtyard. "I guess there are no bags to get, but I'll bring Morgan if you'd like."

Madison awoke the next morning to a thunderclap that rattled the windows and sent Morgan burrowing under the covers. If crossed, the little Scottie would undoubtedly take on a fox or even a dog more than twice his size but thunderstorms terrified him, and he always undertook frantic efforts to get as close to her as possible when they broke. The heavy velvet drapes had not been completely closed the previous night, and Madison saw the rain pelting against the glass as lightning streaked across the grey sky in violent slashes that perversely reminded her of the previous night's murder.

She vaguely recalled arriving home last night, but nothing after, including how she had gotten into her pajamas and bed and wondered wryly if Duncan had played any part in that. Madison was still fuzzy headed, and she dozed for another hour, drifting in and out of a light, troubled sleep as she relived the events of last night. She finally woke again to a knock on her door. Assuming it was Sara, the housemaid who looked after guests at Whiddenhurst, Madison called for her to come in. The young woman timidly pushed open the heavy door as she balanced a tea tray with one hand.

"Good morning, ma'am," Sara said shyly as she placed the tray on a massive, roll-top desk that had always stood in Madison's room. "It's a miserable day today, and they don't expect it to clear all day," she said as she turned to Madison and smiled. "You may want to consider staying in bed the entire day."

Sara Mitchell had worked for the Abbotts for five years and in all that time Madison had never been able to draw her out and into a conversation about even the most commonplace subject. She took it as a positive sign that Sara was taking steps this morning to at least talk to Madison, even about something as mundane as the weather.

"If it were only an option, I would. But first," Madison said, throwing back the heavy covers and slipping into her shoes, "I need to take Morgan out. He doesn't stand on ceremony, and if I don't adhere to his schedule, he will be forced to make due with my mother's handmade Aubusson rugs." She pulled him out of his hiding place under the covers and kissed his nose. "And if we are both to maintain our welcome here, I think it's a good idea to not let that happen."

"I can take him," Sara said eagerly. "I have always wanted a dog of my own, but living here—." She shrugged and smiled shyly. "But your father has been good enough to share his Labradors with me, and we go on long walks together. I'll take good care of him, I promise. I know how important he is to you."

"That's kind of you, Sara. If you really don't mind—."

"I don't," she said, scooping the little dog out of Madison's arms. "Oh," she said, looking back at the tea tray. "I should pour your tea first."

"No, no," Madison said, laughing. "I am perfectly capable of pouring my own tea. And Morgan can't wait. It will take you another fifteen minutes as it is to get downstairs and outside, and we're already pushing it."

Eager to see her father, Madison forewent the tea all together, showered and dressed quickly. Knowing she would be seeing her mother as well, she did a quick survey of her look, which she immediately knew would not pass muster. She brushed her long hair into a sleek ponytail, added a smart blue blazer to her outfit and hastily applied mascara, powder and lipstick. The Duchess held strong opinions about women leaving the house—or even their bedrooms—without make-up.

Madison thought about and quickly rejected knocking on Duncan's door as she walked past it. She knew her mother would have a breakfast tray in her room this morning, and she wanted her father to herself. Lured by the smells of coffee, bacon and something sweet already drifting down the hallway, Madison was quickly descending the staircase when she saw Parker in the front hall.

He looked up and smiled warmly at her. "Good morning, ma'am. I hope you slept well."

"I did, thank you. I'm looking for my father this morning. Is he in the dining room?"

"No, ma'am. He was feeling a little tired this morning, so he decided to sleep late."

"Oh," she said, trying to keep the disappointment out of her voice. "I hope it's nothing serious."

"I think not, ma'am. Mr. Rand is already in the dining room. I believe he is waiting to breakfast with you."

Madison entered the dining room and realized how hungry she was. She had not eaten anything since lunch the previous day, and she disregarded her normal self-consciousness against piling her plate with as much food as she wished.

Duncan looked at her plate and smiled. "I wish we had done something worthwhile last night to work up that appetite."

"Shush," she said reaching over to grab one of the newspapers displayed before him. Duncan got up and filled his own plate, as Madison glanced at the headlines in the *Financial Times*. Her heart sank, and she quickly pulled the other papers towards her. *The Times* and *The Daily Telegraph* all carried versions of the same story. She quickly scanned the first several paragraphs of all of them before she looked up. Duncan was staring at her across the table, his gaze unwavering and his expression inscrutable.

Madison swallowed. "Is this what the conference call was about last night?"

"In part, yes." He sipped his coffee but left his breakfast untouched.

"So the takeover of Chris' company is complete."

"In theory, yes. The legal papers are being drawn up today, but we have binding oral agreements all around."

Madison's heart started to beat faster. "So less than one week after Chris' death you take over his company—at the exact same time his remaining partner is getting himself killed at *your* event."

"I know how this looks."

"Do you? What does it look like to you?" she asked, keeping her voice low so the staff did not overhear her.

Duncan exhaled. "Chris' company was vulnerable to takeover, Madison. It had assets, investors, and employees, and someone was going to make a move if I didn't. Because of my deal with Chris, I had the right of first refusal, but it was going to time out quickly," he said, his voice very calm and clearly in control. "Hawthorne had neither the money nor the brains to be able to do it himself. I invited him to the event last night so I could tell him that." He nodded, putting out his hands in a placating gesture. "Not in that way, of course."

"But somehow he ended up getting killed instead. Did he fight you on the plan so you killed him?"

"I didn't *have* to kill him, Madison," he said, his voice breaking a little in frustration. He shook his head and passed his hand over his eyes. "Not that I would have, under any circumstances. I just want you to understand that Hawthorne wasn't a consideration from a legal or ethics standpoint. He didn't have the power to foul up this deal."

"And Chris? What about him? You couldn't have taken over his company if he hadn't died."

Duncan sighed. "No, you're right. That wouldn't have happened. But I was just trying to salvage a bad situation for everyone here. You can't believe I would have killed, well, anyone but certainly not a friend just to gain control of a failing company. Why? What would be the possible reason?"

She shook her head and stood abruptly. "I don't know. I honestly have no idea what you're capable of, Duncan."

"I'm sorry to hear that," he said coolly as he stood. "If you will pardon me, I really do need to return to London this morning to sign some papers. I simply wanted to make certain you got home okay last night. Please give your parents my regards." He came around the side of the table and kissed Madison's cheek. "I hope you will reconsider your conclusion about me at some point."

CHAPTER 26

Kyle looked up from the morning papers as his mobile started playing *Chelsea Morning*; a photo of Madison looking up at him through eyes that were clearly amused flashed on the screen. She seldom called him and never at work, which was fortunate. Her ringtone was not something the hardened detectives of Scotland Yard would ever let him live down.

He answered on the second ring. "Madison, I've been worried about you. How are things?"

"Not good," she replied, her voice dull but clearly controlled.

"What happened?"

"Did you read the papers yet this morning?"

"I did. I know you want to see the best in Duncan, and I'm sorry."

"It gets worse. Someone let my horse, Jaipur, out of his stall last night, or maybe early this morning. The grooms found him wandering on one of the far edges of the estate where the stone fence is fairly low. He could have jumped it and been gone, or seriously hurt. It runs along the road there."

Kyle heard her voice break. He asked, "Are you sure he didn't just get out on his own?"

"Not possible. Aside from the sentimental value of them, all of the horses in that stable block are prize-winning stallions, including Jaipur. The stalls and stable are constructed so they can't get out, and they can't hurt themselves." Her voice dropped so low Kyle could barely hear her. "And there was a note."

"Oh, Jesus," Kyle said as he stood and began pacing the perimeter of his small living room.

"It was fastened to his bridle, which means it had to be someone he wasn't skittish about who could take the time to attach it to him. It said, *A lot of people have already been hurt. You could be next if you keep asking questions.*

Kyle stomach dropped. "Don't touch the note without gloves. If you can keep the bridle on Jaipur, do that; if not, use gloves to remove it. I'll be there as soon as I can." He paused and swallowed hard before he said, "I assume Duncan is still there?"

"No," she said, and her voice was back to being emotionless. "He had to return to London to finalize the deal you read about in the papers—the one that gives him complete control of Chris' company."

Kyle made excellent time on the M4 as he pushed the Range Rover close to 90mph. It would be embarrassing if he were pulled over by a member of a local constabulary, but he could make the case that he was investigating a threat, out of his jurisdiction to be sure, but one he was certain was related to Jeff Hawthorne's murder. His jaw was clenched as he relived his decision to not arrest Duncan Rand last night and instead let him take Madison to yet another situation where she could be in danger. It was true that he could have only delayed him at headquarters, and Duncan would have been furious and no doubt would have filed charges of false arrest. But Kyle was not at all certain that Duncan himself was not the danger, and the delay would have prevented her from being in a potentially perilous situation with him.

She was sitting on the stone wall lining the circular courtyard in front of the house when he arrived. Her hair was pulled back into a ponytail, and Madison looked far younger than her twenty-nine years. She snapped her fingers and called Morgan to her and out of the way as Kyle parked off to the side.

"They won't have it towed, will they?" he asked in a weak attempt at trying to lighten a mood that was anything but.

Madison's smile seemed sad as she pushed herself off the wall. "Thanks for coming, Kyle. I guess I should have stayed in London, but I wanted to feel safe again." She clasped her arms about her and rubbed them as if trying to generate warm. The rain that had dogged Kyle all the way from the city had stopped, but in its wake was a distinctly chillier day. There was water pooled about the courtyard, and the surrounding tree branches hung low, their leaves heavy with dripping moisture.

Madison glanced over her shoulder at the great manor house which looked, at least to Kyle, foreboding against the backdrop of intimidating looking grey clouds that threatened to drop another shower on them any minute. "I'm not sure Whiddenhurst is my sanctuary anymore," she said sadly.

"It is the people in it who make a place a sanctuary. And it's people who threaten that," Kyle said following her gaze to the house. "It's nice, and big, but it's just a house. It can't protect you from people you let into it."

"So you think it was Duncan," she said, her voice heavy with resignation.

"I didn't say that."

"But you do," she said, her voice almost cold now.

He nodded. "I think you do, too. I'm sorry, Madison, but everything I've seen points to that. We're waiting for the analysis on the prints we found at the scene to come back, as well as some tracking information. But so far, all evidence points to him."

Madison looked defeated as she gave a barely perceptible nod. She did not meet his gaze as she pointed down a gravel path branching off the courtyard and started to walk in that direction. "The stable block is this way," she said. "I thought you might want to have a look around."

On each side of the path sat a stone pier on which stood a massive, granite eagle poised to take flight. Kyle looked more closely at the eagles as they passed. They looked threatening with their sharp beaks and piercing talons in which each eagle held a snake.

"What's up with the killer birds?" he asked.

She glanced back at the piers. "They're part of our family crest. Eagles are a symbol of power and strength, and of the protector. Snakes symbolize wisdom."

His smile was quick and then replaced with a serious look. "So they're crushing wisdom with their power and strength?"

Madison laughed. "I think the intent is that while the Abbotts are powerful, they try to operate with wisdom in all things." She paused. "I think, however, that I am a perfect example that proves that we do not."

"You are being too hard on yourself."

"What will you say if I tell you I don't think he did it?"

Kyle did not immediately answer. He rubbed his bottom lip as they walked and carefully constructed his answer. "I think," he said slowly, studiously avoiding the need in her eyes, "that you are too invested in believing he didn't do it. It clouds your judgment."

Madison did not reply, and Kyle was relieved when the path curved and the stable block came into view. He looked at the freshly painted buildings sitting in neat rows, with tidy, landscaped paths running between them and thought that the Abbotts' stables were more luxurious, and no doubt more expensive, than most people's houses.

A young man came out of one of the stables as they approached and walked over to them. He doffed his hat to Madison, and she said, "Kyle, this is Jimmy Caine, our stable manager. Jimmy, this is Detective Ward from Scotland Yard."

Jimmy looked suitably impressed, and Kyle stepped forward to shake his hand. "What can you tell me about the disruption here last night?" Kyle asked.

"Well," the stable manager said, his hands hung loosely on his hips as he looked around the area, "not much actually. And I think it may have been this morning. Jaipur was soaked for sure, but he didn't look like he had been out all night. I live just over there," he said nodding towards a small cottage sitting several hundred yards away. "I check on the horses every night before I turn in, and last night my last call was at about midnight. Everything was fine and locked up tight. I had to run into town this morning to get de-wormer for one of the colts, and I think that must be when it happened."

"I agree that makes the most sense," Madison said. "Otherwise, someone would have seen, or heard, something. No one else was out early this morning because of the storm. It had already started by the time I woke up, the first time, at around 6:00am."

Kyle rubbed his chin as he calculated the distance from the cottage to the nearest stable. "Anybody have a beef with the Abbotts, Madison in particular, that you know about?" he asked the stable manager.

"No, sir," Jimmy said. "Everybody here is loyal to them. And no one working on the estate would like to see a fine animal like Jaipur hurt. It just wouldn't happen."

"Okay, thanks, Jimmy. Mind if I look around?"

The stable manager glanced at Madison and then back to Kyle. "Not at all, Mr. Ward. I'll stick around if you have any other questions."

Kyle nodded towards the nearest stable. "Is that where Jaipur is kept?"

"Yes," Madison replied. "He's in there now. His groom took off his bridle before I could get to him. It was wet, and Jaipur was wet, and he thought he was doing the right thing by toweling him off. It's still in there, but the note is back at the house. My father was pretty upset, but he thought going to the local police would be a waste of time. He's been meeting all morning with the security people to increase protection on the estate." She bit her lip and paused in what looked like an effort to control her emotions. "We had pretty serious security before—because of Charles. So I think the prevailing thought is that it was somebody familiar with the estate whose presence would not have raised suspicions."

"I don't disagree," Kyle said. "I'd like to walk the perimeter of the stable just to see what I can see, and then I'll come inside. Don't touch anything, okay?"

"Can I check on Jaipur? Daddy didn't want me walking down here alone, so I haven't seen him yet."

"Sure. Just—."

"Don't touch anything," she said. "I got it.

Madison turned to go into the stable with Morgan trotting along at her heels, while Kyle started his standard perimeter walk of the scene. He knew that with the storm, there would be no footprints and all other trace evidence would likely have been washed away as well. But you couldn't always tell. People did stupid things, which is usually how they got caught.

He hadn't gotten far when he heard Madison's steps behind him. Kyle turned around immediately. "Is the horse all right?"

"Yes. But there is something you should see."

Kyle followed her into stables that were just as neat and clean on the inside as the out. Rows of recessed lighting on the ceiling produced a soft, warm glow. Several of the stallions nickered at the stranger in their mist and one very large chestnut-colored beauty stamped his feet and snorted as Kyle passed. Madison spoke softly to the horses as she walked by.

One of the most beautiful animals Kyle had ever seen stretched his neck to reach Madison as she approached, and his coat glistened even in the subdued lighting.   The blue-black stallion was at least seventeen hands high, and Kyle saw the power in the animal's physique. Jaipur would be a worthy opponent to anyone trying to harm him.

Madison stroked the horse's nose, and said, "Are you thinking that he had to have known who bridled him because he could have fought—and maybe even killed—a hostile stranger in his stall, let alone one trying to put a bridle on him? In a raging thunderstorm no less? He's sensitive to storms and is generally more agitated and harder to handle then."

"That thought crossed my mind."

She slipped a halter over Jaipur's magnificent head before she opened the door to his stall. Kyle had grown up around quarter horses, not high-strung stallions, and he hesitated.

"He won't hurt you, Kyle," she said with a touch of amusement in her tone. "Just don't come up behind him when he doesn't know you're there. Look over there," she said and pointed to a small fawn-colored object lying partially buried in the straw on the floor of the stall.

Still reluctant to put himself anywhere near the hooves of the massive stallion, Kyle squinted at the object. "What is it?"

"A mobile phone," Madison said.

"Are you sure?" he asked as he pulled a plastic evidence bag out of his back pocket and stepped into the stall, taking care to keep himself as flat against it as he could. Jaipur seemed uninterested as he buried his nose in the green plastic feeder hung on the far wall of his stall. Kyle knelt and looked closely at the object, which he could now see was in an expensive-looking leather case. He searched his pockets for something with which he could pick up the device without obliterating any fingerprints. He found nothing, but Madison seemed to know what he needed as she pulled the silk scarf from her neck and handed it to him.

Kyle picked up the phone and held it up to see it more clearly. "Who the hell has a leather case for his phone?"

Madison pointed to initials engraved on the case. "DBR. Duncan Bradford Rand."

CHAPTER 27

That afternoon after lunch, Madison started the drive back to London with Kyle. Duncan had been thoughtful enough to leave Morgan's car seat, and she strapped him into the back of the Range Rover. Madison had long-standing plans to meet Sydney and Peyton at London's hottest new club, LouLou's, and while she had decided to cancel the date when she left for Whiddenhurst the previous evening, she reconsidered after Duncan departed. She wanted to see Sydney, although she was not entirely sure why and was certainly not looking forward to it.

Neither she nor Kyle spoke for the first half of the trip. While he was not given to diatribes, Madison knew he was convinced of Duncan's guilt in an ever-growing list of crimes and she was disinclined to hear a logical presentation of the evidence against him.

After more than an hour, Madison sighed and reluctantly said, "Okay, I can't take it anymore. The unspoken words in this vehicle are so heavy I can barely breathe, and I'm worried about the well-being of my dog. Just," she said pantomiming strangling an imaginary person in front of her, "say it."

"There is an official, on-going police investigation here, several, in fact, and I'm not at liberty to discuss the case," he said, clearly trying for an authoritative tone that just sounded absurd to Madison.

"Oh, knock it off, Kyle. You just don't want to argue in an environment you can't leave."

He turned to look at her. "Where did you get that? Have we ever argued?"

"No, but you're a man and no matter how big and strong, they tend to flee in the face of conflict with a woman. Remember, I do this for a living."

"Speaking of, why have you not being seeing patients this week?"

"It is my vacation."

"Wow, you *do* know how to have fun."

"I don't think he did it."

"So you've said, repeatedly. I just can't tell if you're trying to convince me or yourself."

Madison nodded as she considered what he was saying. "You have a point. But it's just too, I don't know, convenient. If you're going to commit a crime, or whatever that was with Jaipur, would you be so careless as to drop your mobile?"

"He's not a professional, Madison. People slip up in unfamiliar circumstances."

"Considering the week, I'd say this is getting pretty familiar. You'd think he would be good at it by now. There was really no slip up regarding Chris. You don't seem able to prove that one."

"Not yet anyway. And remember, if I had not been there in all likelihood no evidence would have been preserved and that would have been a perfect crime, if that's not an oxymoron."

"I think it is. But I really don't think he did it."

Kyle smiled. "You know, he's sort of a friend of mine, too. I'm not thrilled at seeing Duncan go down for this, but we have to face facts. He looks guilty."

"Or someone is trying really hard to *make* him look that way."

"You have to look at who had something to gain by Chris' and Hawthorne's deaths. Duncan turned a multi-million dollar loss into a gain of a entire company, one in which he no longer has to deal with, at best, an incompetent partner."

Madison chewed the inside of her lip as she protectively squished up her shoulders. "I get that. But I think there's got to be something we're not seeing."

"Every rookie detective makes the mistake of talking himself out of the obvious for one reason or another. I think," he said as he put his hand on her shoulder, "that you should try to separate out your personal feelings and look at it from a more objective viewpoint."

They went back to traveling in silence, each apparently lost in his own thoughts. Madison had been conflicted about Duncan in the years since their relationship ended, and she struggled now to find a middle, unbiased ground on which to stand and view his actions. When she was in his company, she believed him and could not conceive of him doing anything dishonorable, or even under-handed, in a business deal, much less anything illegal and brutally violent.

But when he was not with her, and was, in fact, God knows where, doubts came flooding in. It had been many years since they broke up, and Duncan could, if confronted, excuse away his actions with the thoughtlessness of youth. But Madison had known Duncan to be insensitive to the point of cruelty. His extraordinary success was based, in large part, on his ability to be so single-mindedly focused on his goal that he could compartmentalize everything, and everyone, else to the degree of being inconsequential.

Madison shivered. She of all people knew that the characteristics she was mentally scrolling through could describe a classic sociopath. Or they could simply describe a successful capitalist.

She had not realized she had been drumming her fingers on the center console until Kyle said, "I'll talk about anything you want to if you agree to stop doing that."

"Sorry. It's a habit I picked up in grad school." Madison chuckled. "Freud did cocaine. I just drum."

"What's up with that?"

"Have you ever heard of the Hare checklist?"

"Hmm." Kyle scratched his eyebrow. "I vaguely recall hearing about this. I don't remember if the guy who developed it—."

"Robert Hare."

He nodded. "Right. I don't recall if he was in law enforcement himself but the checklist is some kind of standard inventory used to figure out if suspects are, something. Crazy, maybe?"

"Apart from the fact that we don't use the word crazy in my field—although frankly, sometimes it just applies—you're right. The Hare checklist is used to identify sociopathic, or psychopathic personalities."

"Okay."

"So on the checklist, the top score is forty. Most of us probably fall somewhere between five and fifteen. Someone you have to be wary of would be somewhere in the low twenties. And a *really* damaged person, the victim of abuse or trauma—or possibly genetics since we don't really know—would probably be somewhere around thirty. Those are the basics." She gestured toward Kyle and nodded her head. "It's been criticized, of course, but it has its uses. In law, the cutoff point for a dangerous psychopath is twenty-nine."

"This is all fascinating, but where are you going with it?"

"I am just wandering." She sighed as she unscrewed the cap on her bottled water and stared straight ahead for a couple of minutes, lost in thought before she continued. "But there was a study a few years back by an American who suggested that the traits that make a person a psychopath, or sociopath—lack of empathy, remorse, loving kindness—were on the higher continuum for some of the world's most successful CEOs. With the implication being that in order to excel in a business environment," she said as she shrugged, "or maybe even in any environment, it helps to have some of these tendencies. After all, if you are going to throw thousands of people out of work because it's more beneficial for the company to shut down certain operations, it is better to not get torn up over it, right?"

"Everything in life is a continuum, Madison, from lying to shading the truth to the end justifying the means. But there are still absolutes, particularly when it comes to murder."

Madison turned to him and cocked her head. "Are you sure? Isn't justifiable homicide in the case of self-defense or preventing greater harm to, say children, a grey area?"

Kyle smirked. "Maybe. But we hear excuses of one form or another all the time in my field. Like people trying to justify really bad behavior because something awful happened to them as children. A lot of people had crummy, even abusive, childhoods and don't end up breaking the law or hurting other people."

She smiled. "Hang 'em high. And put their heads on a stake at Tower Bridge so everyone else gets the message, too."

He nodded. "Okay, okay. I know that there are sometimes extenuating circumstances. But I do believe there are some absolutes. You have to have boundaries and laws and moral absolutes, or society would devolve into anarchy."

"And, of course, there are absolutes, both in law and in psychopathy. The main absolute in the latter is a literal absence of all empathy for anyone, including animals. In all my years of study and practice, I've only met one person who qualified."

Kyle glanced over at her, one eye almost closed in a squint with a slight smile playing about his mouth. "Is he a mutual friend of ours?"

"Patient confidentiality precludes me from commenting on him, or her."

His tone turned serious so quickly, it startled her. "What about Jules?"

Madison turned to look at him. "What *about* Jules?"

"He's the one with the most opportunity, and the most knowledge, to have killed Chris." He raised his eyebrows. "And Hawthorne, for that matter. That's the thing about being a doctor. You know effective ways to kill, quickly and without being able to trace it."

"Maybe. But doctors typically score pretty low on tests like Hare. They are, by nature of their professions, usually very empathetic and caring personalities. They, for lack of any kind of better phrase, feel people's pain and want to help them get rid of it. That's generally why they go into the medical field."

"Even surgeons?" Kyle asked. "Who from everything I've always heard really only like to cut, fix it and get out, and generally dislike the 'dealing with the patients part?'"

Madison bit her lip and rubbed her neck as she considered what she had also heard. "That's still a pretty big leap from that to killing, particularly an old friend. And what could possibly have been the motive?"

Kyle kept his eyes on the road. "I'm working on that. Did you have any idea that Annabel and Jules were, er, involved?"

Madison turned to him. "In university? Yes."

"Recently?"

Madison swallowed hard. "No, that can't be. Annabel was married."

"Oh, Madison," Kyle said, shaking his head.

CHAPTER 28

They arrived back in London, and Kyle helped Madison bring Morgan and his things into her flat. "Do you see any irony," he asked as he lifted the terrier out of his car seat, "in the fact that the humans travel back and forth to London with nothing but the clothes on their backs, but your dog has his own luggage?"

"I see tons of it," she said and smiled down at the little dog as his tail wagged with the rhythm of a metronome. "You were more than good to come get me and to make sure we were okay. I owe you—."

"Nothing. You owe me nothing more than to keep yourself safe tonight. If you need me, call my mobile and I'll get there as quickly as I possibly can." He turned and opened the door of the Range Rover before she could say anything. "Lock your door, Madison. I mean it. Until we really figure out what's going on, I think you're in danger."

Kyle was surprised at the churning in his stomach that started as he drove away from the flat on Colherne Court. Madison seemed to be the one person all the disturbing events of the past week had in common, and he could not help but think the person, or persons, behind them would come after her again. What he had not yet figured out, of course, was why.

In an effort to make headway on that problem, he drove straight to his office in Westminster. The guard at the car park garage recognized Kyle and the parking sticker in his window, but he flashed his shield anyway. He never entered the garage without remembering the bomb that terrorists had exploded in the underground garage of the World Trade Center in the 1990s before actually succeeding in bringing the buildings down in 2001. Scotland Yard would be a natural target for the same kind of terrorist act.

Kyle walked into his office, threw his jacket over the back of his chair and made his way to the break room. He needed caffeine, and there was always a hot, albeit not always a new, pot of coffee there. He didn't care about freshness, and he poured a mug of coffee that was almost sludge-like in its consistency. He hadn't slept through the night since Chris' murder, and he'd take caffeine in virtually any form.

When he returned to his desk, Kyle booted up his computer and collapsed into his chair, absently rubbing the bridge of his nose. He took the two evidence bags from his pocket and placed them by side-by-side on his desk. Pulling a pair of latex gloves from his top drawer, Kyle snapped them on and removed the iPhone from its bag. Thinking it would almost certainly be password protected, he slid the arrow on the bottom of the device and was surprised when it opened to the welcome screen of multi-colored apps. There were those that were to be expected of someone in Duncan's position: stock market, weather, newsstand, iBooks, a dictionary, wine notes and two restaurant reservation systems. His music consisted of several symphonies and classic rock bands, as well as numerous workout playlists. He tapped the mail application and got nothing; Duncan clearly did not access his email on this device. Similarly there was nothing to be found under recent calls or in voicemail, although those could be easily deleted.

Kyle tapped the camera roll and scrolled through several photos of what he thought looked like thoroughbreds standing in various winners' circles with people Kyle did not recognize proudly holding up various trophies. The last photo was of Madison's horse, Jaipur, taken not in a winner's circle but in the same location Kyle had first seen him today, his own stall at Whiddenhurst. The horse's eyes were wide with fear and glowed red with the photo flash. With the juxtaposition against the black of his coat, Kyle could not help but think that, however trite, he looked like something the devil himself would ride back into hell.

Disappointed in the lack of anything of importance on the phone, he turned his attention to the note he had convinced Madison's father and his security people to relinquish. Leaving it in the see-through evidence bag, he picked it up and read again: *A lot of people have already been hurt. You could be next if you keep asking questions.*

If Madison had been asking a lot of questions of the possible suspects in this case, Kyle was unaware of it. This was assuming, of course, that Madison was even the targeted recipient of the note. Whiddenhurst's stables were renowned, and they were expansive. Leaving a threatening note on one black horse, regardless of how valuable—assuming the perpetrator even knew that—without addressing it to anyone specific struck Kyle as amateurish at best and staged at worse. The block letters were obviously cut out of magazine and newspaper articles and carelessly glued onto cheap copy paper, and they were reminiscent of a tactic not used for decades. In an era of laser jets that were almost impossible to trace, this method actually increased the chances that forensics would be able to find a fingerprint on the note.

Kyle scratched his chin as held the note at arm's length, looking for anything of significance that too close examination tended to miss. He saw nothing other than a crude scare tactic. Doubting fingerprint analysis would turn up anything useful, he still sent it to the Scenes of Crime Branch at New Scotland Yard where, after various elimination and checking procedures, any prints would be coded for search on either the Police National Computer (Scenes of Crime System) or the Automatic Fingerprint Recognition System (AFR).

He returned to his desk and sat idly scrolling through the unread emails of the past twenty-four hours he had deemed non-urgent. Kyle knew he was killing time in an effort to avoid an unpleasant task. He was more reluctant to make the call he needed to make than he ever remembered being in his life. But it was already past the time he should have made it, and Kyle knew he was coming dangerously close to dereliction of duty. He picked up the phone and dialed.

Annabel Grisham answered on the fifth ring, and her voice sounded overly nasal, as though choked in tears.

"Annabel, it's Kyle Ward," he said softly. "I was hoping I could talk to you today. Do you have some time?"

"Kyle, yes, of course. I've been expecting your call," she said and he heard her blow her nose. "I beg your pardon."

"I know this is a difficult time, but I think we should have a chat. I can come to you."

"No," she said quickly. "Don't come here. I haven't been out of the house in days, and I'd rather come to you. Are you at your office?"

"Ah, well, yes," he replied, grimacing as he looked around the office. It was stark and cluttered at the same time, with absolutely no effort having been put into making it a more hospitable place to work. The best it could be described as was utilitarian, and he did not want to put Annabel through that. "But you don't want to come here, really. How about the Goring Hotel? Does that work?"

"That works for me. They have a lovely afternoon tea in The Veranda."

"Oh, well, yeah, sure. I'll meet you there." He hung up and rested his head for a moment on the heel of his hand. Expensing a receipt for tea in The Veranda would undoubtedly earn him ridicule for the rest of career.

Annabel had already been seated at a small table on a balcony overlooking the admittedly beautiful, private gardens of The Goring when he arrived. For some reason, he was surprised to see that she looked remarkably composed and, apart from looking even thinner than usual, Annabel looked, well, serene.

"Thank you for coming here," she said smiling slightly as she looked out over the brilliantly blooming garden. "I was going a little stir crazy in that house all alone, with everything," she said as she closed her eyes, "reminding me of Chris."

Having seen her the day before walking with Jules in Hyde Park, he was troubled that she had twice mentioned that she had not left the house. Kyle took a deep breath as he sat and said, "Can you think of anyone who would have wanted Chris killed?"

Annabel slowly took her glance from the gardens back to Kyle. Her voice was quiet when she asked, "Would have wanted him killed—or would have wanted him dead?"

Not given to goose bumps, Kyle was surprised when they popped up on his arms. "I—well, I should have asked about both. Who would have wanted him killed?"

She blinked very slowly and then shook her head. "I know of no one who would have wanted him killed." Annabel sighed wearily before she continued. "Chris had some real professional challenges, and he—flailed at times. But I don't think he ever angered anyone to the point where they would have wanted him killed." She smiled sadly. "He was a very kind man when he wasn't hating himself so much."

Kyle swallowed hard, remembering the promise of his old friend. Chris had been so delightful in university, with such big plans to bring wealth and prestige back to his family's name. And now, he was gone.

Kyle's voice was gentle as he asked, "So who wanted him dead?"

Annabel pursed her lips and ran her hand through her hair as she tilted her head away from Kyle and stared out at the gardens again. "I'm not sure. I have a feeling that his, er, absence makes things easier for some people."

He nodded, trying to understand. "Would you be one of those people?" he asked quietly, trying to quell the anxiety now raging in his gut.

She raised her eyes slowly to look directly at him; they welled but no tears fell. "No. But—."

No, but almost always meant yes in Kyle's world so he leaned forward and waited.

"Nothing. I don't know what I was thinking," she said as she brushed off her previous words.

Kyle leaned back in his chair. "How are you doing financially, Annabel? Did Chris leave you in good shape?"

"No," she said as she picked up her spoon and stirred her tea again. "He had two rather large insurance policies, totaling about five million pounds."

"That should be okay. Isn't it?"

"It would have been," she said, dropping her gaze to her teacup, her shoulders curling inward, "if he had kept up the premiums."

Kyle searched her face but a veil of protection had descended and she showed no emotion. "You didn't know," he said, and it was not a question but a disheartening realization that his friend had kept his wife in the dark on something of such importance.

She shook her head. "That my husband didn't want me taken care of if something happened? And that he didn't hold me, or our marriage, in high enough regard to even tell me? No, I didn't know."

"How are you coping?"

"How am I coping?" She smiled tightly. "Well, it's easier when you don't have a choice, isn't it?"

Kyle looked out at the gardens and kept his gaze on the lavender plants swaying slightly in the breeze. "What about Jules?" he said casually, and he heard her sharp intake of breath.

"What *about* Jules? I haven't seen him since that retched polo match."

He turned back to look at her now. "That's the thing about lying, Annabel. It makes you look guilty of something. And in a murder investigation, it's really never a good idea to look guilty."

Annabel wrapped her arms around her and sat back. "How did you know?"

"I didn't know. I guessed. But I didn't *know* until you just confirmed it now."

She smiled ruefully. "But something tipped you off." She sighed. "What was it?"

Kyle cocked his head, his lips pressed tightly together in sympathy. He said quietly, "A look exchanged at the polo match, a walk in Hyde Park. No one having an affair ever believes their actions are so transparent to others in regard to their true feelings." He winced as he shrugged. "But they always are."

Annabel rubbed her forehead. "So where does this leave us?" Her head popped up and she looked at Kyle with widened eyes. "Or me. I meant me."

"Did you kill your husband, Annabel?" Kyle asked, looking directly at her.

"No," she said with a heavy sigh. "But I would be extremely disappointed if Scotland Yard took my word for it." She held her hands out. "What can I possibly do to prove a negative? I was there. I was having an affair. I would have thought I benefited by his death, because I didn't know he hadn't kept the premiums up. Honestly, I know it looks bad."

Kyle grimaced. "Don't forget that Jules was his treating physician at the last."

"Oh, Jesus, God, I hadn't even made that connection," she said. Annabel looked up at him, blinking rapidly. "You don't really think

Jules would have done something so stupid, do you?"

"I don't know. Do you?"

Annabel swallowed. "He doesn't love me, Kyle. You know Jules. I was a distraction—or the one person he didn't have in university. Or just a convenience." She shook her head. "I don't know exactly what I was. But murder?" She screwed up her face and shook her head again. "I just don't buy it. He and Chris were friends." She waved dismissively. "Women are disposable pleasures in our group. To risk losing his medical license—to say nothing of prison. Just to get laid? Be real."

Kyle rubbed the back of his neck, distinctly uncomfortable with the naked emotion in Annabel's eyes as well as the straightforwardness of her observations.   "You would know better than I. I'm just trying to ask the right questions."

Annabel turned her head towards the gardens again. "I don't know what the right questions are, frankly, and I certainly don't have any answers for you. But I did not kill my husband. And I do not believe Jules did either. Our affair was wrong, undoubtedly." She turned to look at Kyle. "But in some, perhaps perverse way, I think Chris would have understood. We were both looking elsewhere for something we could not give one another."

Kyle pulled his head back, his lips pressed flat. "Are you telling me you think Chris was having an affair?"

She bit her lip and paused before she said, "I'm sure it sounds self-serving, but yes. I think he had been having an affair for six months or more. Jules and I have only been—involved for less than a month." Annabel shrugged. "Maybe it was revenge—or just self-preservation on my part to have a soft place to land when everything collapsed." She said, shaking her head. "I honestly don't know. But I'm not the one who started it."

"That sounds—."

"Childish."

"Yes."

"I know." She crossed her arms, rubbing them as though to keep warm. "I'm embarrassed by that. But I can't say it's not true." She cocked her head in acquiescence. "But that doesn't mean I killed Chris. I am simply not capable of something so unequivocal." She turned her face away from Kyle and blinked rapidly. Her voice was almost indiscernible when she said, "You should talk to Jules. He's always been so much stronger than I ever could be."

CHAPTER 29

As she watched Kyle drive away, Madison guided Morgan back inside. Doing as she had been cautioned, she locked the door and threw the bolt before she leaned against the door and closed her eyes. The event on her schedule for tonight was to celebrate the opening of the hottest new club in London, and she had absolutely no interest in going. If she had been able to get out of the commitment she had made as a favor to the owner, she would have cancelled after the polo match. Even she agreed with the Duchess that attending a social event at a nightclub so soon after the death of a friend would be deemed in poor taste by the press, but she felt obligated to make an appearance.

Nevertheless, Madison was ready and looking presentable by the time Peyton arrived at the agreed upon eight pm. Peyton would be the designated driver this evening as she was also scouting the place as a possible venue for her events company. Peyton in her serious, professional mode was not nearly as fun as the "social" Peyton, but Madison was not in any frame of mind for fun this evening.

She and Peyton arrived at Sydney's flat a harrowing fifteen minutes, following a high-speed race through the city. Sydney was notoriously late, and that night was no exception, so they were obliged to park the car and come upstairs and wait.

As the lift took them to her third floor flat, Peyton asked, "Have you talked to Sydney lately?"

"No," Madison said tightly.

Peyton looked at Madison, her eyebrows drawing together. "Humph. Nor have I," she said. "She's been off the grid entirely since the—polo match."

"In more ways than one," Madison replied as the old-fashioned lift doors opened and she struggled with the wrought iron gate.

"Is there something I should know?" Peyton asked.

"Undoubtedly," Madison said as she finally won the battle with the gate and they stepped into the elegant hallway. "But I don't know it yet myself."

Sydney answered the door breathless, as though she had been running. "Acckk," she said, smiling brilliantly as she opened the door further to her guests in only a bra and panties. "I've been out of town for the past four days, and I haven't had time to get it together. Forgive me."

"Yikes, Sydney," Peyton said putting her hands in front of her face and closing her eyes as she dramatically turned away. "A little modesty, please."

"Oh, come off it, Pey. How many people have you taken your clothes off in front of?" Sydney said sarcastically as she stood back to let them in.

"Women? None. Go get dressed," Peyton said nodding towards the bedroom.

"Make yourself at home. Pour a glass of wine. Give me twenty minutes."

Peyton sighed as Sydney disappeared back into her bedroom. "This gets tedious after awhile."

"Hmmm," Madison said, distracted now as her eyes swept Sydney's flat. They settled on a baby grand piano on which sat picture frames of all sizes and colors. She walked over to the instrument and lightly ran her hand over the keys. "When did she get this—and these?" she said nodding to the photos.

"Her interior decorator did it a couple of months ago. It was a real spree. Her timing was kind of odd considering the job situation, but you know Sydney."

"I'm not sure I do," Madison said as she picked up a photo of a breathtakingly beautiful woman who resembled Sydney but was more striking, with an ethereal beauty Madison thought would be mesmerizing in person. The dark-haired woman in the photo was laughing, with one hand resting lightly on the head of a little girl who was hiding her face against her skirt. "I've never seen any of these. Who is this woman?"

Peyton walked over and looked at the photo in Madison's hand. "That's her mother," she said quietly.

Madison was shocked. "She never talks about her. I always had the impression that she was out of the picture after her parents' divorce."

Peyton raised her eyebrows, lightly scratching her cheek as she nodded. "You could say that. She died young."

"Oh," Madison said. "I thought—. Well, I thought Sydney said—."

Peyton took the photo from Madison and gazed at the laughing woman. "She killed herself—in front of Sydney—not long after this photo was taken. Her husband left her for another woman, and she couldn't handle it."

They both turned suddenly at Sydney's approach, and Peyton quickly hid the photo behind her before she blindly replaced it on the piano.

"I'm ready," Sydney said cheerfully. "Thanks for waiting."

The drive to LouLou's Club was brief. Madison saw the undulating streams of light before they got there and she couldn't believe she was patronizing a venue that had what she considered Hollywood style klieg lights in front of it. And indeed, she was not. The lights belonged to a nearby video rental store, and Madison sighed with relief when they pulled up in front of a fairly nondescript white building in Shepherd Market in the heart of Mayfair.

Peyton stepped out of the car and handed her keys to the valet. "I'm pretty sure this is it," she said to Madison as she squinted at the building and sighed. "English life is a series of unlabeled doors. Everyone splashes their names across everything in the United States."

"And that," Sydney said taking Peyton's arm, "is why we all live in England."

A young couple walking by the entrance saw Madison and started to twitter excitedly. She smiled back trying to place their faces. They had just started to approach her when Peyton turned back. She took Madison's arm, leaned towards the animated couple and said conspiratorially, "She's really flying under the radar tonight, so if you could use your discretion, I know the prince would be grateful."

Wide-eyed and speechless, the young couple just nodded. Peyton waited until they had crossed the street before she burst into laughter.

"That," Madison said, pulling her arm away from Peyton, "was just mean."

Peyton smiled and flitted ahead as they were waved in by the doorman and entered the club. Madison took in her surroundings. This establishment was different than the traditional clubs of her parents' generation and, indeed, even her own. Gone were the heavy furniture, framed photos of notables, and dark, cloistered spaces. LouLou's was dazzling, possibly sublime. It consisted of a collection of rooms that seemed light, bright and glittering, perhaps even debonair. She smiled as she passed a giraffe's head and neck rising out of the floor, a bar made of shells, and an illuminated peacock. Madison was not certain that elegant hedonism was not a contradiction in terms, but this club was the essence of it.

Judging by its patrons, it was clearly a gathering place not exclusively for the upper class like many of London's private clubs. LouLou's was obviously willing to accept those who were self-made and in many ways epitomized the confident nonchalance towards excess that came with that distinction. Madison liked that aspect of it right away.

They were immediately shown a table, and the general manager came over to greet them, paying special attention to Peyton who had adopted a friendly but professional demeanor.

She was clearly here on business as she said, "If you can arrange for a bottle of your finest bubbly, please."

"No!" Madison and Sydney said in unison.

Peyton looked at them with surprise and then recognition. "Oh, right, sorry. Can you have crack babies sent over instead?"

The drinks arrived within five minutes in their signature test tubes.

"These are deadly," Peyton said as she picked one up. "I can have exactly one."

"It's the vodka," Madison said eyeing them with trepidation.

"It's the champagne," Sydney said with a subtle smile. "Champagne can be so lethal."

Madison's eyes widened but she made a great effort to keep the smile on her face. She picked up the glass tube and turned it around in her hands as she said, "Does anyone else find it a little inappropriate that we should be treating crack babies so irreverently? I mean, it's a serious problem in a lot of areas. I do some pro bono work—."

Peyton hung her shoulders, sighed heavily and glared at Madison, raising one eyebrow. "You are going to have to leave if you're going to be such a downer."

"Okay," Madison said smiling. "If you guys want to celebrate a social traves—."

"To Chris," Sydney interrupted as she held up her drink.

"To Chris," they repeated and clinked their tubes. Sydney downed her drink in one gulp, while Madison and Peyton sipped the potent cocktail. Sydney raised her hand signaling the waitress for a replacement, which she immediately gulped as well.

Peyton's eyes flickered between Sydney and the tray of drinks with obvious concern. "Slow it down, Syd. I may need to do business with these people. In that vein, if you'll excuse me, I need to go speak with the manager." She stood and looked down at Madison, "I haven't seen the owner, and I'm sure he's crazed but I'll try to find him to let him know you made it."

Madison nodded and watched Peyton make her way gracefully through the club, effortlessly slipping out of the embrace of a stumbling young man and skillfully dodging the sloshing drink of another.

"So," Madison said far more cheerfully than she felt as turned to Sydney, "where did you go?"

"St. Bart's," Sydney replied as she downed a third crack baby. "Chris and I went there several months ago, and we had a great time. So I wanted to escape again. To be honest, it wasn't as fun this time."

Madison almost dropped her drink. "You went there before with *Chris*?" she asked wondering if she had heard her correctly.

"Chris? Don't be silly. I said Bill. Bill, the actor," she said elongating the title. She shrugged. "You met him at Tintagel the other night, remember? We had such fun the first time, but the relationship was new then. Even so-so sex is interesting with someone new, just because it's different. But after awhile, if it's not good sex, nothing makes it interesting." She took another drink of her fourth crack baby, but did not bolt that one. "Not even St. Bart's."

Madison wrinkled her nose, pursed her lips and looked at everything in the club in feigned interest before her gaze returned to Sydney. "So, how long have you been dating Bill?"

"Not long." Sydney shrugged. "He's just a distraction. I'm not actually sure he can spell his name without any help, but it's kind of fun when everyone in the room turns to see him enter. That used to happen to me, but those days are over."

Madison had not seen Peyton return to the table until she said, "The pity party routine is getting a little old, Syd. You have got to move on. Look around the room, sweetheart. Men were falling out of their chairs when you walked by."

Sydney pouted, but said nothing. She finished her drink and waved for yet another. Madison swallowed hard as she watched her friend. There was something distressing in Sydney's demeanor tonight, an undercurrent of anxiety, or menace, but she could not put her finger on exactly what it was causing her concern.

"We should have invited Annabel," Madison said regretfully as she twirled her own drink between her palms again. "I think it would do her good to get out." She gestured around the club. "Although admittedly, this might be a little much so soon."

"I thought about it," Sydney said. "But she's been feeling under the weather lately. I mean physically not just emotionally, and she didn't want to go drinking. You know it's not good for her."

"True," Madison said as she finished her drink. "It's not good for any of us. But a drink or two socially on rare occasions is probably okay."

"What do you mean?" Sydney asked, a tight smile bringing out the lines in her forehead, which, unfortunately, highlighted her scars. "Annabel has only one kidney. She lost the other to kidney disease in university, so I don't think she's supposed to drink at all."

"She has only one kidney, yes, but she never had kidney disease. Annabel donated her

314

kidney to Chris. They knew each other before that, but that's really how they got so close."

Sydney blanched and swallowed hard. "Chris had kidney disease?"

"Yes," Madison said, not sure why she was so frustrated with Sydney. "Don't you remember? He had polycystic kidney disease as a child. You should ask Jules for more detail, but it's a bad thing to have. I think the cysts kind of take over the kidneys, and it can lead to kidney failure. The transplant of a healthy kidney saved his life."

Sydney rubbed absently at her arms. "How could I have gotten that wrong all these years?"

Madison shrugged. "I don't know. It was a really big deal when we were in university. The recovery period was pretty long. I know you were there. You probably just had too many other things on your mind." She put her elbow on the table and leaned her chin on her hand. "I've often wondered if that's what really sapped his confidence. He was so smart—."

Peyton put her hand in the air to signal a passing waiter. "Paging, Dr. Abbott," she said in an official tone. "We need another round."

Susan Leigh Shallcross

CHAPTER 30

Kyle stepped aside to let the young man pass
through the doors of the Royal Brompton
Hospital. No more than twenty years old, he
was holding his arm, and Kyle realized with a
wave of nausea that it was not only broken, but
also had a bone protruding through the skin.

The soon-to-be patient smiled broadly and
said, "Motorcycle accident. Still a blast, man."

"Yeah," Kyle said concerned for a minute
that he was actually going to be sick. He had
never been able to understand the fact that dead
bodies, no matter how gruesomely dispatched,
presented no issue for him, but live ones with
gaping, oozing wounds hit him like a physical
blow every time. Considering that there were no
emergency services at the heart and lung
specialty hospital where Jules practiced, Kyle
thought it likely that the young man would be
circling back momentarily, so he hung back to
put enough space between the daredevil and
himself that he ran no risk of further
conversation.

The nurse at the admitting desk was
undeniably very pretty, but Kyle almost laughed
when she batted her eyes at him. He did not
realize that women actually did that anywhere
but the American movies.

316

"I am looking for a Dr. Julian Marlborough in Cardiology," he said. "Can you tell me where I can find him?" Kyle knew he was taking a chance just dropping by one of London's busiest hospitals but he had been passing through the area and thought it might be better if Jules were a little unprepared for his visit.

The young nurse practically giggled at the mention of Jules, and her face turned bright red. Kyle was almost embarrassed for her, and he smiled kindly. "I can page him," she said. "If he's not in surgery or seeing patients, we might be able to find him."

"That would be great if you have time, thanks."

Less than ten minutes later Julian Marlborough was striding down the hall, looking slightly annoyed. He was approaching the admitting nurse when Kyle stepped in front of her. "It was me," he said, holding up his hands. "Don't blame her. I said it was police business." Kyle winked at the nurse, but fury clouded Jules' handsome features.

"You pulled me out of a meeting with the Chief of Surgery, mate."

"I'm sorry about that. I didn't think you'd answer the call if you were in the middle of something important."

Jules smiled, his eyes mischievous. "I wouldn't. So I owe you a big one. What's going on?" He reached over to tap the desk in front of the young nurse and put his hand up in acknowledgement as he nodded to her, which sent her immediately into a deep flush again.

"I was hoping I could catch a little bit of your time," Kyle said. "I know you're busy, but I was in the neighborhood. There's been a lot going on, and we haven't really touched base since Hawthorne died."

Jules winced. "Yeah, right. So catch me up," he said as he gestured for Kyle to follow him down the hall.

"We're still investigating the second murder—."

"*Second* murder?" Jules stopped walking and turned to Kyle, his mouth slack-jawed. "Who was the first one?"

Kyle stopped too. He rubbed his eyebrow and with a slight scowl on his face said, "You saw Chris' tox screen."

"No, I didn't," Jules said as he turned and held open the door to a sterile looking doctors' lounge. "I thought it hadn't come back yet. It usually takes a couple of weeks, and I have, admittedly, not checked."

"He died of cardiac arrest due to acute sodium poisoning."

Jules' face was inscrutable as he stood back and let Kyle pass him. "Acute sodium?" He grimaced and shook his head. "That can't be right. The sodium bicarb is standard procedure in cardiac arrest and isn't enough to be acute under any circumstances." Jules strode over to a coffee machine and lifted the pot. He gestured to Kyle with it.

The entire lounge smelled like burned coffee and Kyle thought the brown liquid swirling around in the pot in Jules' hand had an unpleasant viscosity to it, even for him. "Thanks, no," he said. Kyle watched the doctor pour himself a cup and take the chair opposite him. His brow was furrowed and Jules stared at an invisible spot on the floor, which was, given the industrial atmosphere of the room, remarkable clean. After two minutes of unbroken fixation on the floor, Kyle waved his hand in front of Jules' face. "Yeah," he said. "It was enough in this circumstance to push him into failure. The champagne Chris was drinking had twenty times the normal level of sodium in it, so the bicarb—."

"Put him over the edge," Jules said stoically as he looked directly at Kyle. "It would have. Frankly, that's sodium overload for anyone. And someone with Chris' medical history—." He shrugged and nodded. "Yeah, it would have taken him from infarction to arrest like that," he said, snapping his fingers.

"And it did," Kyle said calmly, not taking his gaze off Jules.

Jules sat back, rubbing his chin. "I'm sorry to hear that. Was there some kind of manufacturing error with the champagne? Sodium is a preservative in wine and champagne."

"No," Kyle said shaking his head very slowly while still looking at his friend. "We ran down the lot numbers and talked to the manufacturer. This was added after-the-fact."

"That would have tasted disgusting." Jules scowled. "But he was drinking that revolting peach champagne anyway, so he might not have noticed."

"It's curious that you did, though?"

Jules cocked his head. "That I did what?"

"Notice that he was drinking peach champagne. With everything that was going on, it strikes me as peculiar that you noticed what he was drinking."

Jules smiled slightly, his dark eyes intense. "I'm a physician, remember? I tend to notice things like that."

"Like that?" Kyle asked, his voice smooth. "You mean like what your lover's husband drinks? If I remember correctly, there was some insinuation that champagne wasn't a man's drink."

Jules eyes did not even flicker and his face betrayed no surprise. Still smiling, Jules nodded very slowly. "I do believe you have that right, mate. It kind of begs the question that if I wanted him to drink the poisoned—if you will— champagne, why would I taunt him into not doing so?"

Kyle shrugged. "I think reverse psychology is pretty accepted. You say he isn't a man if he drinks peach champagne, thereby almost guaranteeing he'll prove you wrong by showing you how confident he is in his masculinity."

Jules laughed. "That would be flawless reasoning except for the pscyho-babble bullshit involved. You know me, Kyle. I call a spade a spade, and I am not capable of the patience being so manipulative requires."

"But you are capable of sleeping with your friend's wife?" Kyle said, allowing a distinctly unpleasant tone to slip into his voice.

"Yeah," Jules said gruffly, as he stood and started pacing. He threw his coffee cup in the trash, and opened the refrigerator. Pulling a soda from the shelf, he popped the top and drained what must have been half before he continued. He did not meet Kyle's gaze when he said, "I'm not proud of that. Chris and I may not have been in sync in terms of our view of life, but he was a friend. And it was a low move to be f—, er, shagging his wife."

"So why were you?" Jules was silent, so Kyle continued. "If I were a cynical man, I would guess that the getaway for you is so much easier if she's married."

Jules' jaw visibly clenched and his eyes narrowed. Kyle thought for a minute he was going to take a swing at him and he stood to be on more even ground.

And then Jules relaxed. All rigidity went from his body and he slumped back onto the sofa. "You know," he said, shaking his finger at Kyle, "I see your point. If it had been any other woman, I would have even agreed with you." Jules puffed out his cheeks and exhaled slowly. "But the truth is, I have loved Annabel since university. And I never told her, and she married Chris. I didn't even try to resist when she came to me for a little comfort when she thought he'd been screwing around. That marriage had been a disaster from day one."

Kyle sighed with a greater sense of relief than he liked to acknowledge as he sat back down. He said, "So you thought you'd help her out of it by getting rid of her husband using," he shrugged, "I don't know, say your medical knowledge to do something undetectable?"

Jules sighed. "First of all, as a detective, you know there's no such thing as undetectable or we wouldn't even be having this conversation. Second—or maybe this one should be first—I took an oath that guaranteed I would do no harm. I get off too much on saving lives, Kyle."

He winked. "I admit it. I have a God complex. And finally—."

"Finally?"

Jules took a minute before he answered. "I think she still loved him. I could never have hurt her like that." He shrugged, seemingly a little surprised at his own answer. He pulled his head back and snorted. "Jeez, I never thought I could be selfless."

"Yeah, mate, get in line on that. So where do you go from here?"

Jules scratched his ear as he thought. "I don't think it's going anywhere. I was a port in a storm—maybe a way to get him to notice her again. Or maybe just a way to get him back for hurting her so much. But Annabel needs someone who doesn't leave her bed in the middle of the night to go fix somebody else's heart, if you know what I mean."

Kyle watched his old friend for a moment before he stood. He extended his hand to Jules. "Thanks for your time. I'll give you a call if I have any more questions."

Jules stood, his powerfully built body towering at least two inches above Kyle. "So I assume Jeff Hawthorne is the other murder you're still investigating?"

"Yeah."

"Am I under suspicion on that one, too?"

Kyle smiled. "Should you be?"

"No," Jules said, putting his arm around Kyle's shoulder as they walked out of the doctors' lounge. "I didn't know Hawthorne at all." He shook his head and dropped his arm to open the door. "But from what I've heard, if anybody needed killing, Jeff Hawthorne would definitely be the guy."

"Seriously, Jules, do you *know* what I do for a living?"

"I call 'em as I see 'em, Kyle. I keep telling you that."

CHAPTER 31

The lift came to a halt on the second floor, and Madison quickly squeezed through the crowd inside before she missed her stop. Her office was in the London Medical Centre and yet had, by necessity, the look and feel of a cozy living room. It was designed to make her patients feel at ease and as far from a clinical atmosphere as possible to avoid the impression they were under a microscope, possibly to be deemed unfit to live in society. Several of her regular patients had confessed this particular fear to her, and Madison was aware how antithetical that was to any kind of therapeutic progress.

Because she was still considered on holiday, her appointment calendar was clear. This meant that she was free to catch up on the paperwork and email that had accumulated while she had been out of the office for an entire week.

Madison was relieved to be safe in the cocoon she had created for her patients, and she slid down into the cozy leather chair before the massive, ornately carved mahogany desk that was her one concession to her mother. The Duchess disapproved of Madison being a psychologist—or "in trade" as she, incorrectly, called it. Her mother had been to her office exactly once, and then only to supervise delivery of the desk. In general, Jacqueline Abbott subscribed to the "stiff upper lip" school of thought and believed *whining* about one's troubles to be a waste of time. Consequently, she also refused to listen to Madison talk about her studies or patients.

The last time Madison and the Duchess had spoken of *her job*, her mother had referred to her patients as overly emotional and self-indulgent. Madison retorted that as an alternative she could refuse to listen to their concerns and instead simply prescribe copious amounts of Valium and a string of houses around the world that they could redecorate every other year to avoid dealing with any emotional trauma. On that occasion, mother and daughter had faced each other in the foyer of the Abbott's newly redecorated London townhouse, eyes blazing and arms firmly crossed. In that moment, they had, without a word spoken, somehow agreed to never again discuss Madison's chosen profession. And they had not.

And when Madison had recently overheard her mother telling a new acquaintance that her daughter spent much of her time volunteering at a London hospital, she just sighed and let it go.

Madison spun her desk chair to face the credenza and bookcase behind her. She opened the bottom cabinet and smiled at the scent that drifted out. It even smelled like university. It may have been the old books or the files that had not been opened in years, but the cupboard was like a perfect time capsule of her years of education.

Flipping through the files, she stopped far too many times on articles she had thought important enough at one time to keep, papers she had written, and correspondence with experts in her field of research.

Madison smiled as she pulled out a little stuffed Scottish Terrier in a small St. Andrews University jumper. He had been a gift from Duncan many years before. The smile slipped from her face and her eye twitched when she remembered that the stuffed animal was left at her door with a brief apology for missing dinner with her and her parents scrawled on a post-it paper-clipped to the dog's collar. The note she had torn off and shredded, but she could not bring herself to throw away the Scottie.

She slipped out of her chair and onto the floor so she could reach further into the cabinet and pull out the files she was looking for. During her senior year at university, she had been assigned to do a psychological review on someone she knew, with the subject's permission. It was, of course, more of an exercise in process and research than a true analysis of her chosen subject.

Madison had chosen Sydney Atwood, who had laughed in delight at the prospect of being the center of attention in any regard, including a research paper. She recalled that Sydney had been cooperative and responsive, earning her an A for the project and in the class overall.

Seeing the file she was after, Madison reached in and pulled it out, bumping her head on the credenza in the process. She sneezed as she blew the dust off the file, realizing she had not touched it in over eight years.

Eagerly opening the folder, Madison gasped at an eight by ten, professional, color photo of Sydney staring out at her, her enthralling violet eyes crinkled in the genuine happiness of a brilliant smile. No matter how many times she told Sydney and everyone else how striking she still was, Madison had to admit she was taken aback by the beauty of the woman in the photo. Of course, it was not simply Sydney's accident that had changed her appearance. They had all aged in the intervening years, and the daily incremental changes generally went by unnoticed. But the comparison between the Sydney of their university years and the woman they all knew today was striking.

Madison sighed and continued to flip through the pages in the file, which for some reason she could not recall, included Sydney's university transcripts; they showed a brilliant journalism student well on her way to first class honors. Sydney had won several awards for her writing and was considered a very talented, and persistent, investigative journalist.

By the time she came to the actual review and its analytical report, Madison's throat was dry and her eyes watered, whether from the dust of the files or the subverted promise of Sydney's career she could not be sure. She massaged her temples as she opened the report and reviewed the basics on Sydney. Madison gulped when she read: *Parents: Divorced. Father: Reginald Atwood, III, 55, Remarried, Corporate CEO. Mother: Anne Scott Atwood, 45, Divorced, Small Business Owner.*

Her stomach flipped, and Madison felt a cold sweat break out on her neck and roll down her back. She clasped her hand to her mouth and sat there a moment, thinking that perhaps Peyton had been mistaken.

Madison turned quickly through the rest of the report, not sure what she was looking for. She winced at the amateurish quality of her research and the conclusions she had drawn, which were that Sydney Atwood was generally a confident, well-adjusted young woman who carried few if any discernible scars from her parents' early divorce, other than, perhaps, a slight propensity to avoid committed relationships with the opposite sex. Madison remembered that not only was that not uncommon among children of divorced parents, but also that it was not unusual among university students in general.

Still sitting on the floor, she tapped the folder, trying to recall where Sydney had said her mother was when they had graduated from university. Madison vividly recalled her subject's idolatry of her father and her animosity towards her stepmother, but she did not remember the excuse Syd gave for her mother's absence. It had been nothing that caused any of them to doubt her.

Madison reached up and carefully pulled her laptop down from her desk. She quickly booted up and launched Google. Chewing her lip for a moment, she thought about exactly what she was looking for and decided to search for an obituary. An article on the death of Anne Atwood came up first and, indeed, the coverage of her life and its passing took up the entire first page of search results. Realizing that Sydney's mother had been more high profile than she had realized, she deleted that search and just typed in her full name.

The images of the Atwoods marching across the page of the next Google search told a detailed story themselves. Anne Atwood had, indeed, been just as beautiful as her daughter, and perhaps even more so. Her husband, while clearly older than she, was handsome and distinguished looking. Their marriage had been called the "society event of the year," and the birth of their daughter, whom her father called "his princess," was covered extensively. There were articles on the parties they had attended and the vacations they had taken around the world, as well as one report dedicated solely to the twenty-five thousand pound playhouse built for Sydney on their estate in Berkshire.

There had also been a very public fight at The Savoy in London, where Anne Atwood, almost unrecognizable now in baggy clothes, her face gaunt and her eyes haunted, had been snapped shouting at her husband. Several reports in the tabloid press detailed accusations of Reginald's infidelity and subsequent separation from his wife.

And then it was over. Anne Atwood was dead, at age thirty-one. There were several articles about her death, but they were vague. There had been some kind of hunting accident on the family estate in Berkshire, but the details were sparse. Foul play was not suspected. If she had her math right, and Madison would be the first to admit that wasn't her strong suit, she thought Sydney must have been about eight at the time. She swallowed hard.

Her iPhone chimed, and Madison jumped, spilling the contents of the Sydney file on the floor. She reached for her purse and dug out the phone. Madison saw who the text was from and her hand flew to her chest as she looked around her office feeling, quite irrationally, that she was being watched.

It took her a minute to decipher the cryptic text from Sydney: *Tonight. Movie premiere. South Bank Theatre. Station tickets. U in?*

Madison blinked at the message several times, trying to think of a measured response that did not provoke Sydney in any way or fuel her suspicions. She wanted to talk to her but knew that a movie premiere would likely not be an appropriate place. Although at that moment, meeting her in a public place with other people around sounded like the more prudent course of action.

Slowly and deliberately, Madison typed two words: *I'm in.*

CHAPTER 32

The chime sounded as Kyle was standing in line at Starbuck's. He pulled his mobile out and checked the text. He shook his head at the message, perplexed by both the number and the content before he realized it must be a mistake. He had recently, and annoyingly, begun getting marketing text messages, and he thought this must be one of them: *Tonight. Movie premiere. South Bank Theatre. Station tickets. U in?*

Certain it was a mistake, he typed back: *Who is this?*

Kyle rolled his eyes at the response before he saw the barista looking impatiently at him as she awaited his request. He ordered a Venti American drip before stepping aside and rereading the message: *I'm disappointed U don't remember. Syd.*

He scratched his head. Kyle had never been to a movie premiere in his life and was not particularly interested in changing that—ever. Nor was he interested in dating Sydney. He had learned that lesson. But there was clearly some agenda here, and it was more than the movie or seeing him. Kyle was eager to know what her game this evening was and to know if it somehow tied back to Chris' murder. He could not shake his unease with the fact that she had been Duncan's choice to buy the champagne at the polo match. On the other hand, he thought Sydney might just be bored. Or she might be challenging him. With more than a little apprehension, he responded: *In.*

The skies were dark and drizzly as Kyle parked at South Bank, an impressive riverside complex located just minutes from Trafalgar Square, Covent Garden and the Houses of Parliament. From there, he made his way to the National Theatre, which consisted of three theatres with an international reputation for producing award-winning shows.

Sydney had said she would leave his ticket at the Will Call window and Kyle stood outside for more than ten minutes trying to figure out how to get there without walking the red carpet. Not only was he a detective who sometimes needed to be undercover, but he was also simply constitutionally unable to pull off what he thought was a pompous display of narcissism—captured on film. He had just strategized on an obscure route inside when he saw Sydney alight from a limousine directly in front of the theatre.

She stood for a moment as she smiled and waved to the assembled crowd, obviously practiced in the art of allowing the photographers to get a good shot. Kyle had to admit that she was good at it and she looked poised and captivating. But he felt he knew her well enough now to recognize that this was just a performance and one completely devoid of sincerity. She did not remotely care about anyone in her audience, even though they were cheering wildly for her.

When Sydney saw Kyle, her eyes widened and her smile somehow became even more brilliant. She was seemingly delighted to see him. Sydney waved even more enthusiastically to him, and he realized he had just lost his opportunity to slip into the theatre unnoticed. She walked straight towards him as the photographers' cameras whirled and snapped in a stomach-churning strobe lightshow.

Sydney took his hands in hers and kissed both his cheeks. She whispered, "You clean up good, Ward. If you smile it will make a better photo than one where you look like you're about to spray the photographers with sick."

Kyle self-consciously pulled at his tie before he managed a weak smile. Sydney took his arm and waved again to the crowd as they started to walk together down the by-now soggy red carpet.

He kept smiling, knowing full well that he must look like an idiot. Kyle tried to not move his lips much as he asked, "What is this about? I've never seen anything like this before."

"This kind of thing goes on all the time, darling," she said, doing a much better job than he of smiling and speaking under her breath. "You've just been living in a dingy little police station. Welcome to the show."

"Do we know the movie?"

"It will be," she said, actually winking at and then pointing to someone in the crowd, "something almost unbearable. It's some kind of nature documentary in honor of Prince William's animal conservation charity Tusk Trust. I suggest," she said, stopping as she dropped his arm and turned around to face the crowd and photographers one last time as she waved animatedly, "that you drink heavily."

They had just stepped inside the theatre when Kyle heard the decibel level of the roaring crowd go up significantly. He looked back to see William and Kate disembark from a Jaguar XJ. They stepped onto the red carpet and the photographers' flashbulbs went off with no respite. It was like watching two people trying to walk in a jerky, slow motion through one of the fun houses of Kyle's youth. He was pretty sure that analogy was more apt than the couple trying to navigate the gauntlet would be comfortable with.

"This is just disturbing," Kyle said, almost mesmerized watching the spectacle.

"It's a rush," Sydney said waving off his comment. "Like drugs—or sex." She smiled wickedly at him. "Lighten up, Ward. This is supposed to be fun. Let's go find Madison."

Kyle felt a jolt. "Madison's here?" he asked, cringing at the enthusiasm in his voice. He saw Sydney watching his reaction too closely. He cleared his throat and said more casually, "I mean sure; where are we meeting her?"

"In purgatory," she said, her voice enticing and disquieting at the same time.

"What the hell, Sydney. Is this some kind of game?"

She pulled her head back and looked confused. "What do you mean? If you'd ever been to one of these things, you would know that waiting in the hot lobby with a bunch of over-dressed people trying to impress one another before the film starts is called purgatory." She laughed. "Depending on the quality of the movie, you are either about to go to heaven or to hell." She picked up a glass of white wine from a passing waiter. "I don't know about you, but watching wild animals in Africa, however endangered, is not my idea of heaven."

"Humph," Kyle grunted as he declined the wine. He thought it judicious to stay as intellectually sharp as possible in this setting, and in this company.

"There's Madison," Sydney said waving. "She looks beautiful tonight, doesn't she?"

"Yes, Sydney," Kyle said exasperated. "You all look beautiful tonight."

She looked at him out of the corner of her eye. "As always, right?" She brushed up against his arm and smiled as Madison walked up. "Darling, I am so glad you could join us at the last minute," Sydney all but cooed. "It's something of a command performance by the station management, and I simply loathe these things. Apparently, the real anchors are busy actually doing their jobs tonight presenting the news, so I am the fill-in."

Madison gazed at Sydney with a look Kyle could not place, something of a mixture of affection, pity, and wariness with a touch of loathing like a cherry on top. It clouded her pretty face and gave her an unpleasant, strained look.

"Sydney," Madison said, kissing her old friend's cheek, "you were very generous to invite me this evening. Thank you for that." She turned to Kyle and went to hug him, but Sydney subtly moved closer to him thereby preventing any contact other than a light kiss on the cheek. Kyle looked at Sydney with confused irritation, but she only smiled.

"We should have another glass of wine, mingle a little and find our seats. *Showdown in the Serengeti* is sure to be standing-room only," Sydney said before she stopped a waiter to swap out her empty glass for a full one.

"Is that really the name of the movie?" Kyle asked. "And is it possible people will actually have to stand throughout it?"

"No—to both," Madison said, not looking at him but keeping her eyes fixed on someone in the crowd.

Kyle followed her gaze as it tracked Sydney, who now seemed to be flirting with a Member of Parliament he recognized but could not name. "I had no idea you were coming tonight," he said.

"Nor I you," Madison said as she turned to him and smiled unenthusiastically. "Is this a date?"

"Between you and me?"

She laughed. "Between you and Sydney?"

"Oh," he said turning to watch Sydney again to make certain she was still too far away to hear their conversation. "No, it's not. I think it's some kind of game, but I can't tell who the players are." He pressed his lips together. "Or maybe I should say pawns."

"You and I for certain. I just don't yet know if she wanted to watch my reaction to you or yours to me. Or—," she said, her voice slowly drifting away as she spotted someone else in the crowd. He watched her eyebrows come together in a deep furrow as she squinted through the mass of people milling about.

"Or—?" he started to ask. But at that moment, he saw Duncan Rand emerge from the throng. And he was clearly not alone. A tall young woman who looked remarkably like Madison, albeit several years younger and not quite as pretty, was hanging on his arm, seemingly entranced by everything he said as she gazed adoringly at him.

"Or that," Madison said staring at Duncan, her voice cold and flat.

Kyle looked around for Sydney and he spotted her leaning against the far wall, her arms crossed and her head pivoting between Duncan and Madison as though she were watching a match at Wimbledon. The smirk of satisfaction on her face told him Madison was right. He caught Sydney's eye, and she winked at him.

Duncan stopped cold in the middle of the crowd when he saw Madison. He had been leaning down as though he were listening attentively to his companion as she talked non-stop, gesturing excitedly and laughing quite a bit. Her face lost that animation when Duncan stopped and she looked back at him, consternation darkening her previously attractive face. When she pouted, Kyle was reminded of a petulant five-year old who was not getting her way. He almost expected her to stamp her foot and start wailing.

Madison nodded tersely to Duncan and started to turn away. He pushed the crowd aside as he hurried to her side, the preschooler trailing sullenly behind him. Duncan pulled at his collar as though it had suddenly started to chafe, or as if he could no longer breathe, and Kyle almost felt sorry for him—but not quite. As he watched Madison's dismay, he felt his suspicions that Duncan's recent overtures towards her were designed exclusively to win her over to his side and make her doubt his guilt in the recent murders were confirmed.

"I don't care to be part of this," Madison whispered to Kyle as she turned her back to Duncan. She shook her head and pushed her hands out dismissively. "His business is his own, and, frankly, is none of mine."

Kyle glanced back to where Sydney had stood minutes before and saw that she was gone. He had started to search for her in the crowd when he felt someone take his arm, slowly running a hand up the inside at the same time. Kyle was not surprised to find Sydney at his side. She reached over to take Madison's hand to stop her fleeing at the exact moment Duncan arrived at the group.

Kyle shook his arm free and looked at Sydney in disgust. "What kind of game are you playing here?" he said hissed, low enough so only she could hear. "Contrary to what you seem to think, this is not remotely funny."

"Oh, I don't think it's funny, sweetheart," she said as she lightly tapped his lips. "I just think full disclosure is in order here, and—."

"And you wanted me here to witness it."

"That would be the meaning of *full* disclosure, Kyle," she said sweetly. "Lady Madison, Kyle Ward," she said, her voice now back to its normal volume but tinged with a cloying sweetness, "I'd like to introduce you to Beth Hawthorne, younger sister of the late Jeff Hawthorne."

Duncan glared at Sydney, his hands clenched by his side. He looked at Madison, desperately trying to get her attention, but she refused to meet his eyes. She stepped toward Beth, and Kyle admired her class when she offered her hand and coolly said, "Ms. Hawthorne, how do you do? I am Madison Abbott. You have my deepest sympathies on the passing of your brother."

"And benefactor," Sydney said quietly to Kyle as she sipped a sickeningly pink drink. "It kind of makes you wonder if she would have been the new owner of Grisham Investments if Duncan hadn't scooped it up so soon after Chris' death, doesn't it?"

CHAPTER 33

"Lady Abbott," Beth Hawthorne said, shaking her hand enthusiastically. "I've heard so much about you all these years—."

"It's Lady Madison," Sydney interrupted coolly.

Beth blinked and put her hand to her mouth. She glanced at Duncan who clearly could not meet her eyes. "I—I'm sor—."

"There is no need to be sorry," Madison said, as she mustered a smile for the nervous young woman. She looked reproachfully at Sydney before she said, "I am delighted to meet you, Beth. I'm certain you and Duncan will have a wonderful time at this event. If you will pardon me, however, I think it's time we all took our seats."

"Don't be silly, Madison," Sydney said looking at her watch. "We have thirty minutes. Kyle and I will take Beth to meet some people, while you and Duncan catch up."

Kyle shot a worried glance at Madison. She clutched his arm and whispered, "Under no circumstances are you to introduce Beth Hawthorne to the royal couple."

"Well, I—," he started to say as Sydney took his hand and began to tug him away.

"*No circumstances*," Madison said gritting her teeth. "And no pictures."

She watched them go before she started to turn away herself.

"Madison, please," Duncan said as he grabbed her arm.

Her look was withering as she glanced at his hand on her arm and then back to his face. He quickly released his hold on her. "I would like to powder my nose before the film, Duncan. If you will pardon me."

"I won't. Please, just give me a minute to explain."

She closed her eyes, trying to suppress an overwhelming desire to tell him what she really felt and knowing it was not an appropriate sentiment for so public a place. "There's really no need, Duncan. You owe me nothing. I'm sure she's—lovely."

"She is a child. And a spoiled one at that."

"You two should get along just fine, then," Madison said with a tight smile.

"I won't let you go until I can explain," Duncan said as he wrapped his arm around her waist and steered her toward a more private place. He picked up two glasses of white wine on the way. "She's just a—."

"Business associate," Madison said, nodding slowly as she took one of the glasses from his hand.

Duncan sighed. "Yes. Well, no—."

Madison smirked. "Quite frankly, Duncan, I am embarrassed for you. We have had this conversation in one form or another about fifty times, and it is simply a ridiculous one. If you are doing business with a twenty-year-old, then more power to you. Really, it is none of my concern."

Duncan looked at her with something alarmingly close to pity. "So why are you here, Madison? Did Sydney invite you?"

Madison glared at him. "You were always so adept at blaming others for your own failings. I am certain you think it is my fault that I'm here to witness your—whatever," she said gesturing towards Beth Hawthorne. "Or Sydney's fault because she invited me. Not yours that you are still playing the field with a string of women. Just let it go, Duncan. It really does not matter to me anymore. I told you several years ago that I wish you only the best."

Duncan glanced around to make sure no one else was listening. "I take that to mean 'yes.' Did she also invite Kyle? Did she want witnesses?"

"Witnesses?" Madison whispered. "To what? You have really lost your mind, Duncan."

"To the fact that I'm a lying, cheating bastard who seduced Jeff Hawthorne's sister so when I killed him, I could more easily take over his company."

Madison pulled her head back and blinked several times as she looked directly at him. He returned her gaze without flinching. Her voice was calmer when she said, "I think there are already legions of witnesses to the fact that you're a lying, cheating bastard." She swallowed hard. "I just don't get the connection with Hawthorne's sister and taking over the company." She threw out her hands. "Why is it relevant that I see that?"

Duncan glanced around and lowered his voice. "It's complicated."

"Of course, it is," she said, crossing her arms.

He sighed. "I meant from a legal standpoint."

"I'm listening," she said, her tone harsh. Even still, she was as touched as she was surprised by the entreaty in his eyes.

"Chris and I had an agreement that if he were to—."

"Die."

"Yes, if Chris were to die, I would have the right of first refusal to buy the company. You know that part. But Hawthorne still had a major stake in Grisham Investments. I held the majority interest but he still had enough voting interests to make a difference. I don't know who ran it into the ground the first time, but I didn't want to take a chance on that happening again by having any of the same people continue to be involved."

"Christ, Duncan, do you realize this is making you look more and more guilty?"

"I do. I fully do. And I think that's by intent."

"So are you telling me that with Hawthorne out of the picture, his sister now holds a substantial interest in your new company?"

"That is exactly what I'm telling you."

"And the only course of action you saw was seducing her into—what, selling her interests to you or just letting you run everything without her interference?"

Duncan nodded slowly. "Something like that—without the seduction part. She wanted to meet Wills and Kate, so—."

Madison raised one eyebrow only. "So being the magnanimous guy that you are, you offered to take her to the premiere and then to bed in exchange for her voting rights. Everyone is right about you. You can craft a win-win deal like no one else can."

Duncan rubbed his mouth, dropped his head and looked at her, his eyes searching for something she could not identify. "No," he said. "But I can see how you might think that's the case."

"So what was the outcome? Did you talk her into it?"

"Yes," he said, still looking directly at Madison, his eyes narrowing a little.

"Good for you," she said, feeling the familiar anxiety that Duncan's self-serving scheming always caused. "I guess that means you don't have to kill her now."

Duncan grabbed her arm and directed her into the corner. Years under the Duchess' tutelage pasted a smile on her face so no one would think there was a *scene* taking place. "Why would I have told you this if it weren't true? It's not like what I *have* told you makes me look good, Madison."

"Being an opportunist isn't quite the same thing as being a murderer, though, is it? The former gets you exactly what you want; the latter gets you life in prison."

"Who's going to prison for life?" Kyle said casually as he walked up behind Duncan.

Madison exhaled, only now realizing how unsettled she had been by Duncan's admission. She unclenched her hands, and they ached with the exertion of having been so tightly clasped for so long. Even in a crowded venue with the news media all around, she felt there was a threatening undercurrent in Duncan tonight, and she wanted to get away from him as quickly as possible. She reached for Kyle's arm.

"I think we all are going to the Tower if we interrupt the film after it's started. Duncan," she said, nodding politely, "it was a pleasure to see you. Please give my best to your friend. Enjoy the rest of your evening."

Duncan's voice had an almost frantic plea to it when he said, "Can I see you later? I'd like to finish this conversation."

"I think we have finished it, and I have a prior engagement, but thank you. Goodnight."

Kyle led her away, and she was grateful for his momentary silence that allowed her to regain her composure.

"What was that about?" he finally asked, his voice quiet as he stared over her shoulder and not directly at her.

"It was about Sydney stirring up trouble, I think. And—.

"And?"

"And more suspicions about Duncan cropping up. I am coming over to your side and beginning to doubt his innocence."

"I think you have doubted it all along, Madison. You have just refused to admit that, because the consequences of admitting it are too hard for you right now."

"So why haven't you arrested him?"

"A lack of concrete evidence. It takes longer to build a case when there is no physical evidence. But I'm working on it."

"Where did you leave Sydney?"

"She was introducing Beth Hawthorne to some people, and it was too painful to watch. She is definitely a piece of work."

"Which one?"

"Sydney. Beth is just an empty-headed little thing floating through life on someone's arm."

Madison winced and dropped Kyle's arm.

"That's not what I meant," he said. "She's just along for the ride, and will find someone to tote her freight. I gather it was her brother before, and she's looking for a replacement."

"In Duncan?"

"I doubt it. I don't know what that was about, except that Sydney was trying to make some kind of point." They joined the crowd queuing up to go into the theater, and Madison did not reply. Kyle took a deep breath and continued, "So did Duncan and Sydney ever have a thing?"

Madison's head snapped towards Kyle. "What makes you say that?" she asked.

He shrugged and put his hands up as though to stop her. "I'm just asking. I thought I saw them together a couple of days ago, and I was just wondering. Her little performance tonight suggested there's something going on there. I thought you said she had been seeing someone but hadn't told anyone who it was."

"Did I?" Madison said, distracted now by the image of Duncan and Sydney together rampaging through her mind.

CHAPTER 34

She declined his offer to drive her home after the show and against his better judgment, Kyle watched Madison step into a hired sedan and depart the South Bank Theatre. He turned and headed towards the car park. In the midst of vowing to himself that he would never again attend either a movie premiere or a film on African wildlife, or any wildlife for that matter, Kyle was dismayed to see Duncan's Rolls pull out of a parking space and follow Madison's sedan.

Kyle had just picked up his pace on his way to his own vehicle when he felt his mobile vibrate. "Ward here," he answered without slowing.

"Kyle, it's Seth. We did an analysis of the records for the mobile you sent down."

"And?"

"And there weren't very many calls made or received over the past month, just a couple from Mr. Rand's office, and several between him and a Madison Abbott, and about the same number between him and a Sydney Atwood. And one to the deceased, Jeff Hawthorne, on the night of his murder."

Kyle nodded, remembered Seth could not see him and said, "Not a surprise. They all knew each other. Go on."

"Well, the gem here is—wait, do you know how mobile phones work?"

"What?" Kyle said, not certain he understood the question as he took the stairs in the garage two at a time.

"No, wait, it's important, because this is way cool. In each cellular service area, dozens of cell phone towers maintain bi-directional communication with nearby wireless phones. When a cell phone is turned on, its signal is received by two, three or more nearby wireless towers known as 'cells.' That's why they call them 'cell phones' in the United States."

"Seth—."

"Yeah, yeah. When the cell phone user makes or receives a call, the cellular network analyzes the phone's position and determines which tower, or cell, is best positioned to provide wireless service. As a result of this overlapping service coverage, any mobile phone that is turned on maintains connections with several nearby towers. The phone does not have to be actively engaged in a call to be connected to cells, but it does have to be turned on; phones turned off will not register with the cellular carrier's network and cannot be tracked."

Kyle tried to keep the impatience out of his voice when he said, "What part of this do I actually need to know here?"

"The cell towers around Kew Palace about the time of Hawthorne's murder picked up Duncan Rand's mobile when he claims to have been at his office downtown. And then the towers in Gloucestershire picked it up again that evening and all the next day before you brought it back as evidence."

Kyle stopped before his Range Rover to absorb the impact of this information. "So he lied," he said.

"So he lied," Seth agreed.

And Duncan was at that moment following Madison home. Kyle disconnected the call, jumped in his vehicle, jammed it into gear and gunned it for the exit. There was a line of cars waiting to pay, and he leapt out, ran to the attendant and flashed his badge. "Look, I hate to do this, but I need to get out—fast. How can we make that happen?"

The attendant motioned to him to exit via the entrance, and Kyle pulled out directly into the slow-moving traffic from the premiere. Knowing it could take hours to work through the throng, he pulled his portable LED dash light out of the glove compartment, suctioned it onto the dash and flicked on the flashing light. By the time he made it through the traffic and was making speed on his way to Madison's flat, he was at least twenty minutes behind Duncan.

Kyle arrived on Colherne Court with an anxiety level he had not experienced since his first days on the force. He slowed the Ranger to a crawl as he looked for a parking space. Seeing that Duncan's Rolls was, indeed, already parked out front, he gave up the search and double-parked, blocking him in. Kyle left the dash light flashing to guard against being towed and ran for Madison's flat. He drew his service revolver and banged on her front door, determined he would break it down if there was no response.

The door was spared violence when it was opened seconds later. Kyle was surprised to see Duncan standing there, his eyes widened when he spied Kyle's drawn weapon.

"Where is she?" Kyle said as he threw his full weight against the door to open it wide enough so he could push past Duncan into the flat.

"She's not here," Duncan said calmly as he regained his balance and shut the door.

Kyle turned and glared at him. "I'll just have a look around if you don't mind."

"Of course," Duncan said, his hand sweeping the room.

Kyle searched the whole flat with Morgan scampering for his attention the entire time before he returned to the living room. "Where is she?" he asked again.

"I still don't know, Kyle. I'm worried about her, too."

"Why are you here?"

"I will tell you anything you want to know if you will just holster your weapon. I find it threatening," Duncan said as he walked into the living room. He sat and patted the sofa as an invitation to Morgan to join him.

Kyle did holster his revolver and watched in dismay as the little terrier jumped up and sat down next to Duncan. "Let's start with how you got in if she's not here."

Duncan was preternaturally calm when he replied, "I used my key."

Kyle's head dropped and he looked at Duncan with a mixture of horror and suspicion. "She gave you a key?"

"Yes. It was years ago. I just never gave it back and she never asked."

Kyle's eye twitched. "And so you just let yourself in?"

"I did. I was worried about her, and I thought that something might have happened when she didn't answer the door. I lost her in traffic on the way here, and I thought there was no way she had not beaten me here since she left the theatre first."

Kyle continued to glare at Duncan. He could arrest him now, but he was reluctant to do that before he found out if Madison was safe. If Duncan had harmed her and was arrested, it would not be to his advantage to come clean.

"Come off it, Kyle. What do you think I did in the past thirty minutes—kill her and hide the body somewhere in the vicinity?"

"You don't hide the bodies, do you? You leave them out in plain sight."

Duncan stood up so quickly and with such an aggressive stance that Kyle took a step back and reached for his weapon again. "If you have an accusation, make it, Kyle. I'm tired of all the innuendo."

"Duncan Rand, you are under arrest for the murder of Jeff Hawthorne, and you should know you are a person of interest in the murder of Chris Grisham. You do not have to say anything, but it may harm your defense if you do not mention when questioned something which you later rely on in court. Anything you do say may be given in evidence," Kyle said as he reached for his handcuffs.

"Don't bother," Duncan said as he glanced at the cuffs. "I'm not dangerous, and I will be happy to accompany you to the station, or whatever it is you call it. But I don't think either one of us wants to leave before Madison gets here and we can be sure she's safe."

Kyle had to admit he had a point, but it was not normal to sit around someone's living room chatting casually with a man he believed was a murderer. There was certainly no police procedure on that one. He pulled out his mobile and started to call for back-up to come get Duncan so he could wait for Madison.

"You must think you have some kind of evidence against me, or you wouldn't be making an arrest," Duncan said calmly. "What is it you think you know?"

"Other than Hawthorne, who is, of course, dead, you are the only one with the motive. And you dispatched him at your event. We traced your mobile back to the scene of that crime when you claimed to be in your office downtown."

Duncan turned his head to the side and had such a genuine look of confusion on his face that Kyle doubted himself for a moment.

"My . . .mobile?" Duncan asked as he started to reach into his pocket. Kyle cocked his pistol. Duncan immediately put his hands out. "Okay, you do it. Reach into my left pocket. My mobile is there."

Kyle stepped over and, still holding his cocked weapon, patted Duncan down and then reached into his pocket. He pulled out a Blackberry and looked at it curiously for a minute. "You must have two," he said.

"I do," Duncan replied, his hands still in the air. "But I haven't seen the other one for a couple of weeks." His eyes widened with a realization Kyle did not yet understand. "Oh, Christ. Oh, Christ."

"What? What?"

Duncan dropped his hands and looked directly at Kyle. "Sydney had the phone. We accidentally switched our phones, and we haven't switched back. I—she—. Kyle, the reason I followed Madison tonight is because Sydney was acting so weird. She's been acting so crazy since Chris' death. And whatever game she was playing tonight seemed designed to hurt Madison. I just wanted to make sure she didn't, and when I couldn't reach Madison on her mobile, I came here." He swallowed hard.

"You don't think Sydney—?" Kyle asked, once again trying to absorb the impact of what Duncan was saying.

"I don't know. I really don't know," Duncan said, shaking his head as he started to pace. "I always thought Syd played mind games with people, you know, just to stir up trouble. But since the accident, she really seems to have been sliding more and more off the deep end. She showed up at my flat a couple of nights ago—late, after midnight—spouting something about how she thought Hawthorne had killed Chris and that he was after her now. She couldn't—or wouldn't—say why she thought that. But even more disturbing than that, she was almost manic and rambling, pacing the floor and wringing her hands." Duncan stopped his own pacing and stared at Kyle with an odd look on his face. "Anyway, it was unsettling, to say the least. When I asked her to leave, she asked if she could stay the night, and she—."

Kyle exhaled slowly as he glared at Duncan.

"Well, whatever, but she did finally leave," Duncan said as he ran his fingers through his hair.

"Did she follow Madison from the premiere?"

"I don't know. I didn't see her. But I thought she might try to meet her here, which is why I came. And yes, it was wrong that I let myself in, but I had to be sure."

Kyle typed a quick text to Madison on his mobile. He also called her and rang immediately into voicemail. "No luck," he said looking up at Duncan, even more worried than he was before. "Where did she go if not home?"

Duncan shook his head as he shrugged.

"Would she have gone to your flat?" Kyle asked, even hoping by now that this was the answer.

"No," Duncan said tightly. "She was really, *really* pissed off at me tonight. I'm not sure she'll ever speak to me again, much less come by for, well—just come by."

Kyle smiled in spite of the gravity of the current situation.

"You can gloat later," Duncan said. "I think we need to find her. Can't you use whatever technology you used to find where my mobile was hanging out to find her now? You're with Scotland Yard for God's sake."

"Yeah," Kyle said as he punched a number on his mobile.

"Make it fast," Duncan said as he headed for the door.

CHAPTER 35

Madison had watched Sydney depart after the film, and on the spur of the moment directed her driver to follow her. She was eager to talk to her, in part to find out what game she had been playing tonight, but even more importantly, to see why she had lied about her mother. And to find out, if she could, what else she was lying about.

Madison had been just seconds behind her, but Syd was already out of sight by the time she arrived at her flat. Her palms were sweaty as she took the elevator up to the third floor. Taking a deep breath, Madison rang the bell.

Sydney answered immediately and smiled. "I wondered if I'd be seeing you again tonight," she said as she stepped back to let Madison in.

"Why did you think you would?"

"I thought," Sydney said as she kicked off her shoes and walked over to the drinks cart, "that you might want to commiserate after finding out what a lowlife your precious Duncan really is." She started filling a highball glass with ice before she looked over her shoulder at Madison. "A shoulder to cry on if you will. What can I pour you to drink?"

"Ginger ale," Madison said wanting to be as clear-headed as possible.

"Rookie," Sydney muttered as she popped the top on a can and poured the soda.

Madison walked over to the piano and picked up the framed photo of Sydney and her mother. "She was very beautiful," she said. "I'm so very sorry to hear of her passing."

Sydney placed Madison's drink on the coffee table and sat on the sofa. She closed her eyes for a moment and then looked at Madison through narrowed lids, a mocking smile creeping into her mouth. "Ah—is that what this is about?"

Madison put down the photo and walked slowly towards Sydney. She sat in the chair as far away from Sydney as was possible, tucking her handbag next to her as she reached for the drink. "Why did you lie about it?"

Sydney shrugged. "I didn't want to be the kid whose mother offed herself. I have found that, in general, if your mum is a candidate for the psych ward, people tend to think you are crazy, too. Too much stigma for a little kid. And then it just became impossible to end the lie without suffering through your friends' condolences, pitying looks, wary concern, curiosity about why I lied, et cetera. So I just went with it."

"Do you think that's healthy?" Madison asked carefully.

"Healthy?" Sydney scoffed. "Who the hell is healthy, Madison? God, you and Duncan have been doing this perverse little dance for a decade now where you can't be together *or* stay apart. Kyle's been in love with you just as long but has *never* said anything. Peyton shags everything that walks. Chris was cheating on Annabel. Annabel's loved Jules for a long time." She took a long drink. "Don't talk to me about healthy, doctor."

Madison was jolted by many of the claims Sydney had just made but one in particular stood out. If true, it confirmed what she had suspected for several days. She said, "Chris was having an affair?"

Sydney just looked at her, something close to pity contorting her exquisite features.

Taking a chance, Madison asked softly, "How long were you two involved?"

Sydney swallowed hard and a shadow flickered across her face and was gone. "Is that relevant?"

"I suppose not. I was just wondering. Did Annabel know?"

"Annabel," Sydney said snorting, "neither knew nor cared what her husband was up to in any regard. That marriage was over before it even started."

"And yet they stayed together."

"Only because he was a gentleman who couldn't end it."

Madison hands were sweating again, and she wiped them on the cocktail napkin her drink was resting on. Her mouth was so dry she was barely able to speak. "That must have made you very angry—his inability to end it to be with you." She started to take a drink and paused with her lips on the rim. She looked over the glass directly at Sydney. "What's in the drink?" she said.

Sydney smiled, and goose bumps popped out on Madison's arms. "Nothing."

Madison put her drink down. She flinched at the maniacal hint in Sydney's laugh. *How had she missed that all these years?*

"You're being paranoid, Madison," Sydney said as she lit a cigarette and threw her head back, blowing smoke into the air. "I don't have a reason to kill you."

"What was your reason for killing Jeff Hawthorne?"

Sydney's eyebrows went up for a brief instant, but she quickly regained her nonchalant demeanor. "Oooh, I *am* impressed. How did you know?"

Madison smiled ruefully. "You were the one who had Duncan's phone, not Duncan. I had forgotten about that until this evening. That was a little too obvious, don't you think?"

"Jeff Hawthorne," Sydney said as she again exhaled and blew a perfect smoke ring, "was unanticipated. Almost an accident, really, being that it wasn't planned and I had no intention of killing him that night."

"Touching," Madison said wondering if she could get to the door before Sydney.

Sydney sniffed. "He was pond scum, Madison. You know that. Hawthorne was blackmailing Chris, and then me. He had Chris in a corner over our affair, so he couldn't get rid of Jeff even when he found out he was embezzling money. And then that little weasel had me. He thought I killed Chris. His departure from this world was not a great loss to anyone."

"And Chris? Was he pond scum, too?" Madison asked calmly as she shifted in her seat and readjusted her purse.

Sydney's brow furrowed, and Madison was surprised to see a flicker of pain flit across her eyes. "No," she said. "Chris was not pond scum. And that very definitely was an accident."

"Because you were really after Annabel," Madison said quietly.

"Yes," Sydney nodded as she crushed out her cigarette in a flower arrangement on the table in front of her as she stood up and started pacing.

"So it's okay with you to kill people you think deserve it?" Madison said trying to keep Sydney talking as she started to slide out of her chair to be in a better position to run.

"Don't be such a child, Madison. Annabel didn't *deserve* anything." Sydney shrugged. "Her elimination was just a means to an end for me. It was unfortunate, but she was in the way and she simply would not get out of it."

"So you really wanted to marry Chris, is that it? A philanderer?" Madison inched her hand slowly towards her handbag. "You watched him cheat on his wife, and you thought he would never cheat on you?"

Sydney sighed and walked slowly towards her desk. "Yes, because it was different with us. He never loved Annabel. You know that. He has been *miserable* for years—for *years*. He needed help in getting out of that marriage."

"You don't seem upset that you killed your lover, Sydney. Have you ever thought about that?" Madison slipped her hand into her handbag and felt the reassuring coolness.

Sydney opened the desk drawer. "I regret the mistake, of course. But I can't change that at this point," she said coolly. "I can, however, change the current situation, which you seem intent on pursuing. I left the note on your horse hoping to scare you off, but you are relentless. Why, Madison? Are you trying to prove something? If you bring Chris' killer to justice, will that make you feel better about your helplessness in finding and bringing Charles' killer to justice? Christ, have you ever considered how much *you* need help? You're so hell-bent on fixing everyone else that you don't even see that you are the one who is struggling."

Madison took the mention of Charles' name as she would have a physical blow and she swayed, losing her focus and thus her advantage for a moment as she considered the truth of what Sydney was saying.

"How did you know, by the way?" Sydney asked casually as she rummaged for something in the desk drawer, just out of Madison's sight.

"I didn't know actually," Madison said as she struggled to regain her composure. "But I suspected. You seemed so intent on causing trouble for Duncan that I came to believe you were trying to frame him. He was the natural suspect without your efforts. That was clumsy of you."

Sydney nodded as if in acquiescence. "Granted," she said. "I'm new at this."

Madison was starting to feel confident that she could talk Sydney into surrendering. She slowly stood and took a step in Sydney's direction, thinking that walking towards her rather than away would calm her down. And then Madison saw the syringe in her hand.

"Don't be absurd, Sydney," Madison said, her eyes revolving between the syringe and

Sydney's face. "You've lost the element of surprise here, and you can't believe I would sit still for this."

"Ah, but you're not a fighter, Madison," Sydney said coolly as she walked unwaveringly towards Madison. "You never have been. One little mention of Charles and you are on the verge of fainting. You let life happen to you and talk and talk *and talk* about it while you think the answer is actually there. You don't take action. It's weak," she spat.

Sydney was not moving aggressively. Madison let her get only four feet away from her before she pulled the gun out of her handbag. Gasping, Sydney stepped back and almost hissed. And then she laughed. "A gun, Madison? Jesus, how trite can you be?"

"Because poison is so much better," Madison said evenly.

"It's cleaner. And far easier to hide."

"Knifing someone is neither."

"I *told* you. That was not planned," Sydney said, her voice tinged with anger now.

"Oh, well, then, that makes it all okay."

Sydney started to advance on her again. "I just told you you're not a fighter. Charles was the fighter and when he went, you just crumbled into a ghost of your former self. You really should have made an effort at that point to go with him, you know—put everyone out of your misery."

"Stop right there," Madison said, hating the quiver in her voice as she took several steps back. But she did cock the gun.

Sydney just laughed again, and the look in her eyes was truly frightening. She turned around and started to walk away, and for one second Madison thought she had given up. But Sydney pivoted again, let out a primal scream and ran at Madison, her arm held over her head as she gripped the syringe, her thumb on the plunger.

Madison fired twice in rapid succession, and Sydney went down. She stood there staring at the crumbled figure at her feet and the spreading pool of blood as it darkened the carpet beneath Sydney. Madison was instantly taken back to the night of Charles' death. But this time she did not falter, and she did not sink to the floor herself.

Still concerned about getting too close, Madison looked at her friend as she lay in a fetal position and tried to determine if she was breathing. Being uncertain, she kept the gun trained on Sydney as she backed away towards the phone on the end table.

Madison had just lifted the instrument from its cradle when she heard the sound of a massive weight being thrown against the door to the flat. Still giving the wounded woman a wide berth, she had just started towards the door when she heard it splinter, crack and give way completely as Kyle and Duncan fell into the room.

CHAPTER 36

Kyle pushed Duncan off of him and found himself staring at the body of Sydney Atwood. He instinctively recoiled and stumbled away as he got to his feet and stared in dismay at Sydney. She lay perfectly still, her arms wrapped tightly around her stomach, and Kyle could not tell if she was still alive.

"I would have opened it," Madison said calmly.

Duncan, too, had pulled himself off the floor and now rushed to embrace Madison, burying his face in her hair. Kyle thought he may have heard a muffled sob but was too disgusted at the thought to look. He looked at Madison, stunned to see a pistol in her hand.

"We heard gunshots and thought we didn't have much time." Kyle nodded towards Sydney. "Is she dead?"

"I don't know," Madison said as she extricated herself from Duncan's grasp and kicked the syringe lying on the floor in front of Sydney into the corner of the room. "If not, we need an ambulance."

Kyle knelt and felt for a pulse in Sydney's neck. It was weak, but it was clearly there. He nodded to Duncan who went to dial 999.

"What happened here?" Kyle asked as he looked to see where Sydney was injured. There was one wound in her arm, and one in her upper stomach area. He thought it may have missed anything vital, because although she was unconscious, she was still breathing. He made a tourniquet for her arm with his belt, grabbed a throw from the sofa and applied pressure to the bullet hole in her abdomen. Madison just stood there, her gun still pointed at Sydney, her eyes wide with fear.

"I don't think she's a threat anymore," Kyle said.

"You didn't see her," Madison replied. She gulped. "There's some kind of dynamic where crazy people don't always feel pain in the heat of, well, their craziness, and can keep going on the adrenaline for awhile."

"Crazy people? Is that what they taught you at university in Bedside Manner 101?"

Madison's hand started to shake and the gun wobbled alarmingly. "She tried to kill me, Kyle," she said, her voice almost breathless now.

"Duncan, if you could spot me here," Kyle said calmly as Duncan dropped to his knees immediately and took over applying pressure to stop the bleeding. Kyle stood and took the gun out of Madison's trembling hand. "You should sit down. I'll make you a drink."

"No! Do not touch anything. She keeps poison—in her flat!" Madison said as her voice rose with every word. "God only knows what's in that syringe," she said pointing to the corner. "She poisoned Chris," she said breathing so heavily now that she sounded on the verge of hyperventilating. A flush rose in her normally pale cheeks. "And she stabbed Hawthorne. She was unrecognizable tonight," Madison said, starting to shiver now. "I mean, like sociopathic, no empathy," she said shaking her head as she wrapped her arms tightly around herself.

Kyle was slightly concerned that Madison was sliding into shock. The irony was that she would be the one he normally consulted in such a situation, which left him uncertain what to do. Seeking to change the subject, he methodically turned her gun over in his hands.

"You have a Glock?" he said as his eyes widened in surprise. He decided against admitting to her that he was secretly impressed. "That's a serious piece—meant to do serious damage. Do I even want to know how you got a gun?"

Madison took two deep breaths and exhaled. Her voice was calm and measured again when she answered, "I'm legal. I have a special permit to carry one. When they didn't find Charles' killer, we all thought I might be next, so my father made sure I had a gun and knew how to use it."

"Lucky."

"Oh, yeah, that's me," she said as she suddenly sat down hard as if her legs had just given out.

Duncan looked up from where he sat on the floor, tamponading the wound on a still unconscious Sydney. "We are all lucky you weren't hurt. I never would have forgiven myself if something had happen—."

The pounding on wall next to the splintered door interrupted Duncan, and Kyle went to greet the EMTs. Duncan moved aside so they could take over from him as they checked Sydney Atwood's vitals. They hung an IV drip of some kind, lifted her and strapped her onto a gurney. Madison, Duncan and Kyle all stood silently as they watched them try to save a friend who had taken at least two lives herself and attempted to take at least one more this night. It was only as the emergency personnel started to leave with their patient that Madison asked in a very low, hyper-calm voice, "Will she live?"

"It is hard to say, ma'am," the lead paramedic said as they started to roll the gurney out through the wreckage of the door. "But we will do everything we can for her."

"I guess they have to do that, don't they?" Duncan said quietly as he stared after the departing crew.

"Yeah," Kyle said as he also stared after Sydney, who had not moved of her own accord since they had broken down the door to her flat.

"I wasn't trying to kill her," Madison said. "I was just trying to *stop* her."

Duncan turned to Kyle. "Isn't that what everyone says when they shoot someone?"

Kyle nodded. "Yeah, nobody ever means to kill anyone else. They're always just trying to *stop* them."

Madison's eyes widened. "Are you kidding me? You guys think I was trying to kill Sydney?" She swallowed hard. "Seriously?"

Duncan snorted nervously and passed his hand over his face. "No, Jesus, we don't think that," he said. "Just trying to break the tension on an unbearable reality here. Seriously, Kyle, how do you ever get used to the absolute terror of situations like this?"

"Well, to be fair, the murders I investigate are generally not those of my friends." Kyle glanced sideways at Madison. "Or ones involving gunplay with quiet, unassuming daughters of the aristocracy. This one has been an entirely new experience and, frankly, not one I wish to repeat."

"I'd like a drink," Madison said as her hands started to shake again.

"Me, too," Duncan said as he started to walk towards Sydney's drinks cart and immediately stopped. He turned back and said, "We can go to my flat?"

"Too weird," Kyle said as he dialed his mobile.

"I need to wash up," Duncan said as he looked at his hands for the first time and horror slowly spread across his face at the sight of Sydney's blood. "I swear I don't know how Jules does it."

"Gets his hands dirty, you mean?" Kyle asked as he held the phone to his ear and listened to it ring.

"Who are you calling?" Madison asked as she carefully stepped among the ruins of the door. "I don't think I can bear to be in this flat another minute."

"I thought it would be a good idea to have the crime scene secured and to turn over a gun used in the commission of a possible felony before we leave."

Madison nodded. "I am free to leave, though, right? Do I need to come down to the station or anything?"

Kyle looked at her and knew for certain the new lines around her eyes were there to stay. "I will need a statement but we can do that in the morning."

"Thank you," she said, relief evident in her voice.

As Duncan returned to the living room he said, "I think it's probably a good idea if you're not alone right now."

Kyle's head snapped towards Duncan, annoyed that he would use this opportunity to weasel his way back into Madison's life completely.

"I will be okay, but thank you. I really just want to go home."

In unison, Kyle and Duncan said, "I'll drive you."

Madison looked back and forth between them. She sighed heavily. "That's kind of you both. But I would prefer to take a taxi."

Kyle shook his head. "I'm not sure that's a good idea, Madison. I think you're in shock, and I would be more comfortable if—," he said as he glared at Duncan, "one of us took you home. Please."

"No, thank you—really. I am okay. I am really going to be okay."

"Madison—?" Duncan said, a clear plea in his tone.

She smiled sadly. "I am okay. I am *always* okay. I promise."

As Kyle and Duncan stood there together, they watched helplessly as she turned away from them both. She picked up her purse, squared her shoulders and walked out the door.

ABOUT THE AUTHOR

Susan Leigh Shallcross has been writing short stories and articles for over twenty-five years and is the author of the Lady Madison Abbott Mystery Series. She was formerly the director of marketing and communications for two of the world's largest law firms and prior to that, she worked in Presidential and state politics in the US. Her ancestral roots are in the English countryside of Derbyshire, where Shallcross Manor was located, and Susan has been studying the history and culture of Great Britain since childhood. She holds a BA in English/History and an MBA in Marketing Management.

Susan now lives outside of Washington, DC, with her husband Michael, stepson Bill, Scottish Terrier Morgan and West Highland White Terrier Marin.

Books by Susan Leigh Shallcross

LADY MADISON ABBOTT MYSTERY SERIES

Penalty Stroke

Tea at Whiddenhurst Hall

Altitude Sickness (Summer 2013)

BOOKS FOR READERS OF ALL AGES

But Where Does That Leave Me? A baby brother comes home

susanleighshallcross.com

COMING IN SUMMER 2013
Altitude Sickness

Klosters is a renowned mountain resort nestled between the sophisticated cities of Zurich and Davos in Switzerland. A well-known playground of the jet set, film stars and royalty, the romantic, friendly Swiss village is rife with picturesque chalets, horse-drawn sleighs, fantastic skiing—and murder.

Lady Madison Abbott's vacation is cut short in *Altitude Sickness* when an esteemed colleague is murdered. In this exciting follow-up to Penalty Stroke, Madison and Scotland Yard detective Kyle Ward race down the slopes of the posh ski resort find a killer before she and her friends become the next victim.